# LOYAL
## to
# YOU

*A HEARTHSTONE NOVEL*

# SARAH KADES

STARK

PUBLISHING

**Stark Publishing**
**Waterloo, ON**
**www.starkpublishing.ca**

Publisher's Note: This is a work of fiction, and a product of the author's imagination. Real locales and names may sometimes be used for atmospheric purposes. Any resemblance to actual people, living or dead, or to businesses, companies, events, institutions, or locales is either completely coincidental or is used in a completely fictional manner.

Canada Council   Conseil des arts
for the Arts      du Canada

*We acknowledge the support of the Canada Council for the Arts*

The Canada Council for the Arts contributes to the vibrancy of a creative and diverse arts and literary scene and supports its presence across Canada and around the world. The Council is Canada's public arts funder, with a mandate to "foster and promote the study and enjoyment of, and the production of works in, the arts." The Council's grants, services, initiatives, prizes, and payments support Canadian artists, authors, and arts groups and organizations. This support allows them to pursue artistic expression, create works of art, and promote and disseminate the arts and literature. Through its arts funding, communications, research, and promotion activities, the Council fosters ever-growing engagement of Canadians and international audiences in the arts. The Council's Public Lending Right (PLR) program makes annual payments to creators whose works are held in Canadian public libraries. The Council's Art Bank operates art rental programs and helps further public engagement with contemporary arts through exhibition and outreach activities. The Council is responsible for the Canadian Commission for UNESCO, which promotes the values and programs of UNESCO to contribute to a future of peace, reconciliation, equity, and sustainable development.

**Loyal to You / Sarah Kades** – 1st ed.

Trade Paperback ISBN: 978-1-989351-80-2
eBook ISBN: 978-1-989351-81-9

# Dedication

*To James.*

# Prologue

Bruce pushed the plunger of the needle in. Relief would soon return. He let out a breath. He'd had this studio apartment for years with no one the wiser. He had actually committed his first murder in the apartment. He was safe here. He just had to figure out what he was going to do next.

Bruce had torched Becca's barn, but the little bitch had lived. So had Meredith. And that piece of trash, Chasseur. It had been a disaster, but he'd correct everything. He would find a way to cash in on the land and the Fischers' patent. Bruce Tanner always landed on his feet.

The door at the far end opened, and he spun around. Bruce pulled the needle out and tossed it to the side. A man he had never met stood just inside the studio apartment. The door closed behind him, echoing in the sparse open space.

He watched Bruce a moment. "Hello, Bruce."

"What? Who are you?" Bruce's heart had kicked up, and it was hard to hear anything above its pounding.

The man laughed. "Cute." He walked across the room, hands in his pockets and looking around. "Don't stop what you're doing on my account. Take your time."

Bruce eyed the man. "Are you looking for money? I don't have money if that's what you're looking for." He did, loads of it, not that he'd give a dime to this clown.

"I don't want your money," the man said, continuing to circle the room.

"What do you want?" Bruce pulled at the collar of his shirt, needing to get more air in his lungs.

The man's lips moved, but Bruce didn't hear his response. He popped his ears, and sound flowed in again. "What did you say?"

The man ignored him. "You know, I'm surprised. I was expecting your lair to be, I don't know, bigger? You have extravagant tastes."

"How do you know what I like?" Bruce could feel his heartbeat in his lungs. It was a good high.

"I know a lot about you. I know you tried to kill my sister and that you would have killed my brothers, too."

Bruce's buzz dipped before racing back. The room shifted. He pulled his collar again. "You're not making sense, and I'm not giving you any fucking money. Get out of here." He stumbled, trying to herd the man out the door.

The man watched him. "Disoriented, loss of motor skills. Right on track."

Bruce was on the ground. How did he get here? He crawled, trying to form words. Sounds gurgled up. Finally, he managed, "How … find … me."

"I always know where to find you, Dad."

A wave of clarity rolled over Bruce. "Who is dad?"

The man was now in front of Bruce. He crouched down. "Aw, that hurts, *Dad*." He held something in his hand.

"That … what." Bruce forgot what he was trying to say, his throat felt like it was missing.

"This? It's a Naloxone kit. You're going to need it soon."

Bruce watched the man smile. It was as cold as fuck. "Tanner?"

"What, are there more of us?"

Bruce shook his head. Foam flew from his mouth. He tried to work his mouth. "Good boy."

His son didn't like that. His eyes darkened. "You haven't been a very good boy, have you, Dad?"

Bruce couldn't speak. He clawed for the kit.

Tanner held it out of reach. "You tried to kill my siblings." He shook his head. "You shouldn't have done that."

Bruce's whole body spasmed. He tried to make his limbs work, but they wouldn't. He flailed, helpless. Bruce tried to blink, to make the image of his son clearer. Doris had always said Tanner was such a good boy, his son would help him.

Tanner whispered, "Dad?"

Bruce was beyond speech and could only grunt, willing his son to understand, to use the kit. He tried to nod.

Tanner crouched lower before whispering, "Go to Hell."

# Chapter One

Grace was almost out of time.

Dark clouds scuttled low, and the salted wintry air blew in from the North Sea as she darted, such as she could in the heeled winter boots, across the slushy street, her couture shearling long coat billowing behind her. She dodged stunned commuters as their country's heir apparent sprinted across several lanes of traffic.

Grace kept her left arm tucked tightly against her body, holding the precious file securely in place. She vaulted a low snowbank, landing with the barest of wobbles on the cleared and sanded sidewalk. Still moving, she eyed the low wrought iron fence of the federal building, festively decorated with bright red ribbons and aromatic pine boughs. She could shave at least a minute or two off her time if she cut across the yard.

She stutter-stepped into position before leaping, then held her breath, her coat flapping like wings behind her.

She cleared the fence and smiled.

"*Oof.*"

She didn't make the landing.

Her feet slid out from under her, and she landed in an unceremonious heap on the slushy snow.

Undeterred, she swallowed her embarrassment and scrambled up, slipping twice on the slick lawn. Snow had drifted in spots, and she trudged, more than ran, across the yard of the federal building.

Once clear of the yard, Grace carefully two-stepped up the stone stairs and heaved open the enormous door. The wind gusted, sending the oversized wreath vibrating hard against the door and Grace's now-wet hair flying in her face.

Inside, Grace kept her left arm tight against her body, holding the file safe, before self-consciously tucking a mass of wet hair behind her ear as the throng of business elite gaped in surprise.

She had interrupted what looked like a large Christmas gathering in the main lobby of the ancient federal building. A massive tree, nearly two stories high, stood like a sentinel in the middle of the old stone and new glass-featured room. Where other buildings around the world had managed to pull off the effect, here, old and new were trapped in an awkward holding pattern, thrown together to tick boxes rather than work to each other's strengths. The tree was decorated with white lights and traditional red and green glass ball ornaments. It was ringed by oversized boxes wrapped in silver and gold paper.

Grace angled her right arm through the crowd like an arctic icebreaker. "Excuse me … pardon me."

She wove around only a handful of women in their tailored power suits and scores of men smelling of money and power.

Her father and grandfather smelled like that, though she had never been able to put her finger on what it was precisely.

Hurrying, she said, "Sorry, excuse me, I just need to squeeze past..."

Grace tried not to wince as whispers followed in her wake.

*Is that the princess?*

*No style, no grace.*

*She always was an embarrassment to the royal family.*

Automatically, Grace ducked her head, embarrassed and angry. She broke for the stairs and barreled up them like the hounds of hell were after her.

They weren't. They were after a different woman. A happily married mother of two who had the audacity to be born somewhere else.

With renewed speed, Grace careened into an open office door. "Stop! I have them. I have her papers."

An older woman in a severe business suit turned. She wasn't smiling.

The middle-aged man standing next to her broke into a satisfied smile. "As you were saying, Counselor Olsen?"

The woman made a disapproving face. "Don't be smug, Andrew. It doesn't suit." To Grace, she said, "Your grandfather won't be pleased. You're supposed to be at the school opening."

Panting from her sprint, Grace nodded. "I know. And I was." She pulled out the sheaf of papers and handed them to Andrew. "This secures Mrs. Fontaire's release."

The man accepted them with a wide smile and dashed into the adjacent glass office. While waiting on the phone, Grace saw him give a reassuring smile to the small family huddled on the single couch in the glass room.

The family looked terrified. Their tense faces were in stark relief to the trio of dancing snowmen on the desk.

Counselor Olsen crossed her arms. "You're supposed to be at the school opening."

Grace finished counting to ten. It didn't work. She still wished bodily harm to the cruel women in front of her.

"I was," Grace repeated before a disturbing thought surfaced. Her grandfather, the grand duke, had wanted her busy when Mrs. Fontaire was deported.

Counselor Olsen looked at Grace with blatant hostility, and Grace fought the urge to run a hand through her hair and re-button her jacket. A meticulous presentation was required armor for anyone in the public eye, and she knew she disheveled.

Counselor Olsen's voice was snide when she spoke. "Your side won't win, you know, the grand duke won't allow it."

Grace rubbed her temple and tried not to sigh. "Helping people shouldn't be a side. What did you hope to gain, anyway?"

The woman sneered. "Your grandfather is right. You're not fit to wear the crown. You're too busy stirring up anti-tradition demonstrations and following ridiculous causes to see the damage you're doing. You're nothing more than a serpent, ruining this country for the rest of us."

Anger sparked. "Did you miss science class? Serpents are incredibly intelligent and well-adapted."

"Serpents are the devil," Counselor Olsen spat. "You should be setting a proper example. Women are supposed to be lambs. Lambs are … well, they're …"

"Mutton?" Grace supplied helpfully.

The councilor's mouth pinched into a severe frown. "A husband would keep you in line. Your younger sisters know their place. They are already supremely matched."

Grace swallowed the swift correction that screamed to be voiced. Her brothers-in-law were misogynistic assholes. Grace had begged her sisters to consider the ramifications of their spousal choices, but the twins were nothing if not preprogrammed and obedient. They not only toed the line, but they also celebrated it.

Grace felt like a fiery torch in a family of practical flashlights, constantly burning herself with her own fire.

She squelched the tidal wave of objections and instead inclined her head like she had seen her mom, the queen, do. "I regret my marital status is so displeasing to you, Ms—I mean Counselor Olsen."

The slip wasn't intentional. Grace silently berated herself, but the damage had been done.

The older woman gasped, her hand flying to her throat. "*Well, I never.*"

The aging counselor considered anything less than *Mrs.* derogatory. That someone would point out her unmarried status at her advanced age would be regarded as poor quality.

Grace hadn't meant the slight, nor did she consider an unmarried or childless woman somehow less than.

Stupid patriarchal bullshit.

The counselor's voice shook with anger when she said, "Our situations are completely different."

Ingrid Olsen was rumored to be one of the illegitimate children of the grand duke himself. If true, she was Grace's biological aunt, though the grand duke had never publicly claimed her.

"Of course," Grace said gently.

"The grand duke will hear about this."

Grace nodded. "You are one of his most loyal followers." She winced. That had come out wrong, too.

The woman's eyes flashed. "How dare you. It is an honor to serve the grand duke."

"Just not the princess," Grace muttered. "I have to go."

The counselor pointed angrily at the young family in the other room. "It's lowlifes like that who are destroying this country. Scripture says so."

Grace was fairly certain it didn't. As part of the royal family, she was obliged to endure the prescribed religious worship. "And here I thought it was the exploding climate crisis, energy insecurities, and rolled back social programs—" Grace turned her head at the movement at the door.

Thorsen, the head of royal security, had walked in. Before he gave her a pointed look, his eyes took in everything, including the family huddled in the adjacent glass-walled office.

Grace dipped her head. She had broken protocol when she had dashed off without a security detail. "Can I have a sec?"

He nodded once like she knew he would, looking both intimidating and protective.

Relieved, she crossed to the glassed room. Her smile was forced, unsure of the welcome she would receive. "Hi, may I come in?"

Andrew, still on the phone, waved her in.

Thorsen moved when she stepped into the room, parking himself inside the door.

Both parents immediately stood. Self-consciously she waved off their reverent nods. "Please, don't." She shook both of their hands. "Everything should be sorted now. Andrew will help with anything you need." Grace cleared her throat, unsure what more to say.

The older child, though still quite young, spoke up. "Does our mom have to go away?" The brave little guy's lower lip quivered. "I don't want her to go."

The mother blinked quickly, fighting tears, as the father squeezed the little man's shoulder.

Grace knelt next to the boy. "No, she doesn't. That was kind of scary, wasn't it?"

The boy nodded.

Grace whispered, "It was for me, too."

This kept her up at night, that she wouldn't parry her grandfather's machinations in time, and innocent people would get caught in his crosshairs.

His younger sister tugged on Grace's jacket.

"Yes, sweetie?" Grace hoped her voice didn't crack.

"You're pretty." She pointed. "Like my mom."

The mother smiled through fresh tears and kissed the tops of her children's heads, and Grace wondered if her mom had ever done the same with such obvious care and love.

She blinked quickly. "Thank you. So are you."

The girl squealed in delight.

Grace abruptly stood, desperate to hide the complicated emotions churning within her. "Please let Andrew know if you have questions or need anything at all."

Andrew, still holding the phone, nodded and gave a thumbs-up.

Grace waved to the family before following Thorsen out of the room.

Counselor Olsen looked at her coldly. "I will remember your meddling."

Anger flashed, chasing away the tears that had pooled behind her eyelids. "And I will remember your bigotry."

"*Heathen child.*"

The counselor had said it low, but Grace heard and had enough.

With a snap, she commanded, "Bow."

The counselor's eyes widened, and her lips pinched together.

Grace waited, eyes locked on the angry old woman. Refusing royal protocol simply wasn't done.

The older woman gave a wooden curtsy. "You're not fit to be queen."

This time Grace's smile was cold. "We both know, neither are you." She turned to Thorsen. "Let's go."

Thorsen waited until they were in his vehicle before he looked in the rearview mirror at her. "Ingrid Olsen is an enemy you don't want. You're taking too many risks."

Grace turned to stare out the window. "I'm trying to right wrongs, and that one was cutting it entirely too close. I should have realized sooner—"

"No, you need to pull back. The grand duke is acting more erratic than usual, and the upcoming election only makes things worse."

Grace stared at him. "That family needed my help. I couldn't just abandon them to a broken system. I still can't believe taxpayer money pays for monsters like that to terrorize innocent people. It's not right."

Thorsen glanced at the mirror as he drove.

"Yes, but did you really have to make her bow?"

"She's an elitist ass. Fuck her."

"She thinks she's doing right by the country and will aggressively pursue her idea of justice. Try and see it from her point of view."

"You mean the crushing self-loathing she must feel to do such awful things?"

"Not exactly what I was going for. The grand duke is positioning his people. If they don't win—" Thorsen broke off.

"What were you going for?"

Thorsen's sigh was heavy. It alarmed Grace. "What's wrong?"

He hesitated. "I think some of my staff and military personnel are loyal to the grand duke."

"Shit, are you serious?" What Thorsen spoke of was sedition or treason, two of the few charges in their small country that still carried the death penalty.

"The queen has forbidden an investigation. It's too close to the election. She doesn't want an investigation to favor either side or disgrace the palace."

Ice crept through Grace. "Because she thinks you're right, that there is something to uncover?"

"That would be my guess."

Grace contemplated what Thorsen had said as much as what he hadn't.

If he thought there was something to investigate, there was.

Her stomach rolled. It was terrifying to consider that the grand duke and his fanatics could be building a private army. It was too easy for the powerful to set up innocent people as collateral damage in their political and cultural wars. Oh, shit—or silence the wayward heir to the throne.

"I'll be more careful and less reactive. I promise."

In a healthy political ecosystem, political parties kept each other honest while still moving the country forward.

The rift in the royal family mimicked the increasing polarization of their small country huddled in the North Sea. Her grandfather, the grand duke, vocally opposed Grace's left-wing sensibilities and the environmental and social policies she supported.

His brand of conservatism rallied for extreme prejudice and actioning hatred. The grand duke's extreme views had torn their conservative party apart while emboldening the country's left-wing fanatics in violent rebuttal.

This worried her, as she could feel what Thorsen was talking about. Increasingly agitated citizens, politicians maneuvering with an increasingly powerful church, and a royal family at significant odds, matched with the climate and energy crises, high inflation, and unemployment—it was a perfect storm of epic proportions.

No one knew what would crack first.

# Chapter Two

Detective Tucker Tanner rechecked his map app before looking through the windshield of his truck. The snow was falling harder, and he had to turn his wipers on to see anything. Oversized clusters of snowflakes filled the night sky, giving the light from the streetlight an exaggerated boost. Everything glowed in the snow, and nearby skyscrapers and condo towers blinked with holiday and Christmas lights.

The downtown apartment building he was parked a half block away from had been a dilapidated, pint-sized factory that had gotten a series of ever-trendier facelifts over the years.

Still, it had never gentrified, not even close.

Tucker watched three drug deals go down, a sex trade worker working, and deeper in the shadows, the tell-tale flickers of crack or meth pipes.

Several stints undercover had taught him just how dangerous the shadows were in the community he lived in.

Tucker should be back at work instead of chasing a ghost. A double homicide had come in overnight. His colleagues would be working around the clock while Tucker was off active duty and instead hunting down his murderous missing father.

Daddy dearest.

Bruce Tanner had never won any father-of-the-year awards, but in the last few months, his cruel calculations and overt lies had become deadly. Tucker couldn't change the past; half of his family had nearly lost their lives because he didn't see the signs. But he could hunt down his father before the lunatic hurt anyone else.

Tucker squinted through the windshield. Parking Authority records showed Bruce Tanner's Jag had been towed weeks ago from this location. That single clue had been a toehold, and Tucker discovered his father had owned an apartment in the building. Secretly. For years.

Fucking lying, cheating bastard.

Tucker's hand moved to his chest, though he couldn't feel the trio of fresh, puckered scars through his jacket. His body had caught bullets meant for another man. His father hadn't pulled the trigger. His associate had. Tucker had simply beat Bruce Tanner to it, getting himself shot up in the line of duty before his father took aim.

Tucker squashed down uncomfortable emotions and eyed the surrounding buildings. It was hard to tell through the snow, but cameras could be seen from many buildings, and several businesses were on the ground floors.

A set of headlights cut through the snow, and an SUV stopped in front of the apartment building.

His phone pinged.

It was the real estate agent.

He got out of his truck and walked up to the SUV, giving a short, friendly wave. He recognized the woman in the driver's seat from her ads. A second woman sat in the passenger seat. The first woman said something, and the other nodded.

Tucker looked around and could have kicked himself. When he had booked the viewing, he hadn't cared one way or another about the gender of the agent. Now he wished he would have considered the neighborhood and at least booked the viewing during daylight. Women had to put up with enough shit in the workplace. They shouldn't have to bring a safety buddy just to show a listing.

He eyed the side of the building. None of the earlier characters he had noticed were afoot.

Tucker let both women make eye contact with him. He kept several paces from the SUV with his hands loose at his sides as they both got out.

"Mr. Tanner?"

"Hi, yes." Tucker gave another small wave. "Ms. Ruckers, thanks for agreeing to see me on such short notice."

She smiled cordially and stepped forward, holding out her hand. "Of course. This is my assistant, Mia."

"Hi, Mia." Tucker nodded in greeting.

Ms. Ruckers glanced around as she led them to the front door. Her careful eyes were wary. "So, is there just the one apartment you're interested in? I have several listings downtown."

She unlocked the door and let them in.

"An acquaintance mentioned this is an up-and-coming building." Tucker stepped into the foyer after the two women. The smell of urine immediately assailed his nostrils. Three discarded needles perched on the small ledge above the rows of mailbox doors. "Though, I'm realizing we have different ideas of what that looks like."

Mia dipped her head but not before Tucker saw her smile.

"Yes, well, some areas turn." Ms. Ruckers frowned as she looked around. "And some never do."

Tucker followed the women up the narrow stairs.

The women had cleared the third-floor landing, but Tucker was still on the stairs when two men, dressed in shabby clothes and reeking of alcohol, pin-balled against the stairwell's walls as they made their staggering descent. The first man bumped into Tucker, apologizing with volume and verbosity. The stairwell was too narrow for Tucker to pass the man as he windmilled his arms in his less-than-sober illustrations. Tucker patiently waited for the long-winded apology. Tucker could barely see the second man behind the first, but from the tilt of his head, Tucker guessed he was on his phone.

Tucker's patience had run out, when after a heavy sigh, the second man finally tapped his friend on the shoulder. "You're sorry, he knows. Let the man pass."

With a flourish, the first man bowed unsteadily. Tucker grabbed him before the guy could take a header down the stairs.

The second man, less lit than the first, had also moved, grabbing his friend from behind.

When they had him righted, the first man finally squeezed past Tucker. The second briefly patted Tucker's side. "Thanks, bro, my friend meant no harm."

"No worries," Tucker said, then joined the two women on the landing above.

"That was weird." Mia eyed the men making their way down the next flight of stairs. "You okay?"

"I'm fine, thanks." Tucker hated that he had to pad his pockets to check he still possessed his phone, keys, and wallet. "Would have been different if they were violent. Happy drunks I can deal with."

Ms. Ruckers shook her head. "I couldn't deal with that every day. Follow me, please."

She hastened her way down the hall.

Tucker asked, "Do those security cameras work?"

"That's what the listing says." Ms. Ruckers's tone held undisguised censure as they walked past one with wires clearly cut from behind.

Tucker eyed the camera angles, nearly bumping into Ms. Ruckers when she stopped.

"Here we are." She unlocked the door, and he stepped in, finding the light switch.

Tucker took in the studio layout. "Are all of these units the same layout?"

The space was open, unexpectedly airy, and probably five hundred square feet, give or take. Large wooden beams were evenly spaced, and the windows were all on the top quarter of the over-tall walls, keeping the apartment's factory roots visible. The floor consisted of wide, knotty boards. It would have been a pretty cool space if it wasn't a hotbed of criminal activity.

"Yes, I believe so." She sniffed. "I do have other listings that you may find more—"

"Safer?" Tucker supplied.

Ms. Ruckers smiled for the first time. "I was going to say *amenable*."

"Mind if I take pictures?"

She waved her hand. "Of course."

Tucker pulled out his phone, getting a visual record of the space.

From what Tucker had found out, his father's apartment was adjacent to the listing and currently held a tenant.

He pointed at the wall. "Is that load bearing? You could really open this up if you bought the next apartment, too. Think they'd be interested in selling?"

Ms. Ruckers sniffed. "A shell corporation owes it. Absentee landlords are a bit of a wild card. Would you like me to inquire?"

Tucker smiled. "No, thank you, Ms. Ruckers. I think I've seen enough."

She smiled, clearly relieved to be gone from the shady building.

"One more question. Wasn't this building in the news recently?"

Ms. Ruckers blanched, and Mia stepped forward, motioning for Tucker to exit the door.

"Yes, I do believe it was, Mr. Tanner, though I can't recall for what," Mia said.

Smart woman.

They filed down the stairs and out the front door.

"Thank you both. I'll be in touch."

"Are you parked close?" Mia asked, assessing their surroundings.

"Yes," Tucker nodded to his truck a half block away. As an afterthought, he added, "Thanks," and meant it.

Tucker waited until both women were in the SUV, and he heard the locks click and the engine growl to life before he headed to his truck.

Their SUV didn't pull away until he got into his vehicle. After the darkness of the last several months, it was an unexpected pleasure to have total strangers looking out for him.

Another set of headlights flashed, and a patrol car slowed as it drove past him. He didn't recognize the uniform driving it, but Detective Jones was in the passenger seat and staring right at him.

Tucker ducked his head like he was checking his phone.

It was reasonable that the truck's interior was dark enough to keep him hidden. Tucker's truck, however, was electric, and Jones was a grease monkey—he could identify most makes and models by headlight.

Tucker was on medical leave until further notice. He most certainly was not supposed to be tracking down his father.

The cruiser did a U-turn behind him.

*Shit. Shit. Shit.*

It stopped next to him. Detective Jones rolled down his window, and Tucker did the same.

"Hey, Tanner."

Tucker gave his best grin. "Jones, it's been a while."

The detective assessed the street with a critical eye. "What are you doing here?"

"Apartment hunting," Tucker answered smoothly.

Jones raised his eyebrows. "Here?"

"That's the same look my real estate agent gave me."

"I thought you lived in one of those fancy condos in East Village."

Tucker shrugged. "I got a lead."

"I bet you did." Jones did not look happy. "You're good?"

"Good enough." Tucker didn't want to lie, especially to Jones. The senior detective had been the first of Tucker's colleagues to come to the hospital after Tucker had been shot.

Jones gave him a long look. "I'm here if you need me."

"Thanks, man. I appreciate that."

Jones nodded, waiting.

Tucker smiled and slung his wrist over the steering wheel like he had all the time in the world.

Finally, Jones nodded, and the cruiser drove off.

Tucker followed. Damn. Jones was suspicious. Tucker would have to come back and canvas the nearby businesses. If someone had video surveillance of Bruce Tanner, Tucker would find it before his father could hurt anyone else.

# Chapter Three

"Ohmygod, we stink." British Special Forces Agent Omran Forest slid into the front passenger seat of the large black SUV.

Agent Tanner Stone scrunched up his nose. They reeked of alcohol.

He started the vehicle and cracked his window to the freezing night.

Agent Forest shot him a sideways look. "What if he hadn't caught you? Taking that header was an unnecessary risk."

Stone pulled away from the curb several blocks from the apartment building. "What was I supposed to do? You were taking your sweet ass time getting the bug into his phone."

"Are all Commonwealth countries so sensitive?"

Stone cracked a smile. "No idea. I've only worked for three of them."

"So that's how you guys fill your rosters."

"Something like that." Stone turned on the windshield wipers before merging onto the deserted downtown street. "A copper wouldn't let a hapless drunk fall down the stairs."

Agent Forest cackled. "Right. Because a law enforcement officer would never let a couple of street bums fall."

"You said he was good people," Stone reminded him. The fresh blanket of snow had turned downtown into a clean blank canvas, making everything glow primly. It was an illusion. The snow hid layers of filth and grime, the years of hard use and neglect. Within hours the fresh scene would be dingy and gray, just like reality.

"He is good people. You were the one who said you didn't trust him."

Stone didn't, not yet, anyway. In an explosive confrontation with a former MI6 courier, his half-siblings had recently discovered he existed. They had no idea about his clandestine work or that he had been assigned to track their father, Bruce Tanner.

Stone gripped the steering wheel tighter. "Just turn the bug on."

Agent Forest pulled out the receiver, tapping instructions onto the screen until the sound of Detective Tucker Tanner speaking with his realtors could be heard.

Nothing was said that Stone and Agent Forest didn't know.

"See if he texts anyone," Stone said.

"Wait, who is he talking to now?" Agent Forest turned up the volume.

*"Jones, it's been a while."*

*"What are you doing here?"*

*"Apartment hunting."*

*"Here?"*

Stone glanced at Agent Forest before looping around and heading back toward the shaggy apartment.

A police cruiser was idling next to Tucker's truck.

Agent Forest's voice was reasonable when he said, "That's not unusual. He is a copper."

Stone leveled a look at the British special forces agent.

"Unless his service has reason to follow him."

# Chapter Four

"*Oof.*" The blow nearly knocked the wind out of Grace. On instinct, she stepped forward, pivoting hard and fast to land a tight, sharp hook. The kidney shot connected with painful accuracy, and the large man winced. Grace didn't wait, she followed the hook with an explosive jab-cross double-tap, taking care to drive her fist through the space her opponent's face was taking up.

His head gave a respectable bobble, but to her dismay, he stayed upright.

"*Godamnit*, you guys are fucking rocks," Grace complained, dodging to avoid the expected rebuttal.

The well-built black man in front of her had the audacity to grin. "You're doing good. You're small, but you've got speed."

Grace circled the large man, arms at the ready. "I'm not small, you're freakishly large. What did you say your name was again?"

He grinned. "Charles."

"Well, Chuck, nice to meet you." Grace waited for a beat. The man almost managed to hide his irritation.

She took pity. "I'm totally kidding, Charles. You should see your face right now."

He stopped, his brow furrowed. "Your Highness—"

She circled cautiously. "Please, no, I look for my mother or grandfather when I hear that. You can call me Princess Grace of Awesomeness."

After the barest of pauses, he said, "As you wish."

Grace jabbed, catching the side of his torso before he deflected.

She circled the large man again, arms back up at the ready. "I'm kidding. Grace is fine. How long have you been with the Royal Guard?"

The sound of a throat clearing interrupted her. "Gracie, quit harassing the new guy."

Grace grinned as Thorsen walked onto the sparring mat. He held a large envelope. She said, "I thought you would have warned him. Don't you guys have an SOP for that sort of thing?"

"Royal security wouldn't dream of anything so vulgar as preparing a document naming our royals and their idiosyncrasies."

"Too long?" Grace asked innocently, keeping her gaze carefully divided between both men. Thorsen had a tendency to join training sessions, wanting her to be prepared for shifting scenarios, including ambush.

He crossed his arms, still holding the envelope, and cracked a smile. "Something like that."

Charles was watching their exchange. "Sir?"

"At ease, Agent Lawson. Gracie is a royal p—"

Grace had circled close enough and fired a lightning-fast jab at Thorsen. "Pleasure. That's what you were going to say, right?"

Thorsen rubbed his shoulder. "Of course, I was. Nice speed, by the way." Still rubbing his shoulder, he held out the file he was holding in his other hand. "Here."

"Nope." She danced out of reach. "Chuck and I still need to do arms combat."

"Beg your pardon?" Agent Lawson looked to Thorsen. "That wasn't in my brief, I'm not sure I should—"

"Have you had training?"

"Yes, sir."

"Then you're fine."

Relief filled Grace. Aggressive training helped her maintain a sense of personal autonomy and gave her a taste of beautiful chaos in her overly structured and proper life. Being thwarted by paperwork was an uncomfortable reminder that no matter her rank or title, she had a place. It might be a prestigious, gilded cubbyhole, but it was still a box meant to contain.

Before either Thorsen or Charles could change their mind, she trotted over to the side of the sparring area and selected one of the prop handguns, and frowned. Their heft and realness always made her feel uneasy.

She shook off her unease and passed it to the new guard. "Here. I'm supposed to disarm you as you pretend to shoot me."

Agent Lawson again looked to his boss. Thorsen nodded and tucked the envelope under his arm, watching.

Lawson aimed.

Grace went for the gun.

Their scuffle became a tumble.

*Pop.*

Grace had to catch herself before she fell on Lawson. He was on the ground, gripping his left leg.

"She shot me." Lawson stared incredulously at the blood that oozed between his fingers.

Thorsen leaped forward. "What the hell?"

Grace realized the gun in her hand wasn't a prop and gagged.

She swallowed hard and, with shaking hands, set the gun on the mat as Thorsen assessed Charles's bleeding leg.

Tears streamed down Grace's face. She dropped to her knees next to the two men. "I'm so sorry, Charles."

Lawson's face was ashen when he looked at her. "No. If you weren't so fast, I would have killed you."

# Chapter Five

Tucker stood alone in his darkened high-rise condo living room. To his right, a fist-sized hole, shoulder height, punctured the drywall. In front of him, floor-to-ceiling windows revealed the downtown skyline cloaked in snow flurries. The large flakes had transformed the harsh city night into a soft glow. Christmas lights blinked on nearby balconies, and one of the downtown bridges was lit with green and red spotlights.

The apartment building had been a bust. Tucker knew it had been a long shot. So had police impound. It had been closed due to security updates when he went to pick up his father's car. He'd try again. He could also recheck his sister's surveillance footage from the night of the fire to see if they missed something.

Tucker strode across the open space to his kitchen, usually a place of warmth. He rested his hands on the long, narrow island counter. He'd learned his way around a kitchen to impress girls. It wasn't hard to get a woman to sleep with him. Getting the ones he liked to keep choosing him, without commitment, was oddly easier when he cooked or baked for them. Sex had led him to his one true love—the culinary arts. His kitchen, so sleek and tidy, used to be his happy place, his sanctuary. A place to reboot after a shitty day at work.

Since he found out his father had tried to murder half of their family, the pain had spread everywhere, filling the cracks and crevices of his life, the toeholds where happy had once reigned.

Tucker glanced at the hole in his living room wall. Anger wasn't helping. Hesitating, he finally moved to his oven and tapped in a preheat temperature. Then he pulled out ingredients, added a large mixing bowl, along with measuring and mixing utensils. He turned on an alternative rock radio station instead of a streaming service, wanting to hear the banter of normal people complaining about mundane problems.

Tucker went through the grueling process of measuring ingredients, though he didn't need to. He had made this recipe a hundred times.

He stopped abruptly, pulled out his phone, and punched in a familiar number. When she answered, he asked without preamble, "Do you really put coffee in your brownies?"

"Damn it, Tucker, you'll give me a heart attack yet."

Shit, he shouldn't have called so late. "Sorry, Rose, sorry!"

"Stop fretting. I already have a son who constantly frets over me."

Tucker cracked a smile. Rose's son was Tucker's soon-to-be brother-in-law. Jason Chasseur was a dedicated lawman and rather imposing when he wanted to be. Only the women in his life—his mom and Becca, his fiancée—would ever accuse that man of fretting.

"You calling for a rematch?" Rose teased.

"Maybe." Rose had been the one to pull Tucker out of the dark head space he had slipped into after the shooting and fire. She had done it with regular bakeoffs.

"What kind of coffee? How much?"

"Tuck, the best recipes, like life, use what we got. Did you clean out your fancy French press yet?"

Tucker eyed the cylinder still filled with used grounds from the afternoon. "No."

"Good. Splash whatever is left in. Not too much, mind you, a big spoonful is all you need."

A smile tugged at the corners of his mouth. It was rusty but real. "Thanks, Rose."

"Thank me by stopping by and giving your sister some of those brownies. She worries about you."

Tucker worried about her, too, though less now that she and Jason had each other. Those two took care of each other. Dropping off brownies would be a good excuse to pop in, and he could check Becca's surveillance footage then, too. "Good idea. Thanks, Rose."

"Anytime, kiddo, anytime."

"I'm a grown man," he muttered.

"Would you rather I ask if any nice woman has caught your attention?"

"I'm good," Tucker rushed.

Rose laughed. "Yes, you are. Goodnight, Tuck. Call anytime."

"Goodnight, Rose." Tucker smiled as he pocketed his phone. He added the last splash of coffee to the brownie batter and stirred, looking forward to visiting his sister. When he got all caught up in his head, which was constantly lately, Becca would make some uncanny offhand comment that immediately snapped Tucker back down to earth.

Tucker's smiled wider. He would bring the pan of his sister's favorite treats—literal brownie points.

He had just closed the oven door and set the timer when his phone rang.

Frowning, Tucker answered. "Meredith, is everything okay?"

Why was his stepmom calling?

"Yes, yes, I'm fine, dear, I didn't mean to worry you. I wanted to thank you for picking up Bruce's car from the impound lot." She cleared her throat. "This all has been very upsetting."

Tucker had never warmed to his stepmom. She had been the *other woman*, the last straw that finally broke his parents' marriage beyond repair. In hindsight, Meredith may have well have saved his mom's life.

"I didn't pick up the car, Meredith. I tried to, but it was closed for a routine security upgrade." Tucker had thought that was weird, but he was hardly privy to the inner workings of each city department or service.

"That's odd. My insurance company called earlier today and said it had been picked up by a man." She hesitated. "Who else could it have been?"

"Didn't they give you a name?"

"No," she said carefully. "They said there was some sort of a computer glitch, and the record was no longer available. But Gabe is back in Toronto with Savannah, and Colt is neck-deep preparing for the baby and wedding with Lillian. Do you think it could have been Officer Chasseur?"

"Jason would have told us if he picked it up. Cancel the insurance and report it stolen."

Her voice shook when she said, "It's Bruce, isn't it? He's back."

Tucker rubbed the bridge of his nose. "We don't know that, Meredith." He checked his watch. "I can pick you up. You can stay here until we sort it out, or I can stay with you—actually, where are you? Sorry, I have no idea where you live now." Meredith hadn't gone home after her husband had tried to murder her. She was terrorized, jumping at shadows and waiting for his next attack.

"That is kind of you, Tucker, but I fly out tonight. I'm staying with friends out east."

"Are you sure?" Tucker couldn't just leave her. "It's no trouble."

"Thank you, that means a lot, but I'll be fine. My friends have a bit of a compound. I'll be safe."

"Excuse me?" Tucker couldn't have heard her correctly.

Meredith laughed, it was a bright, lovely sound. "I surprised you, didn't I?"

"You did." Tucker added carefully, "I didn't realize you hang out with compound types." The Tanner siblings had assumed Meredith to be a frivolous socialite type. In the last few months, they had realized she had more gumption and integrity than they had given her credit for. She was a kind, generous woman who had fallen for the wrong man.

"I'll be safe," she promised. "Call if you need anything, and I mean anything."

"We will," he answered automatically. "You, too."

"Tucker, I mean it. You need anything, you call me. Whether you kids like it or not, I consider you family."

"Thank you, Meredith. We do, too," Tucker said quietly. Trauma created a weird sort of glue.

His phone beeped, indicating another call was coming in.

"What was that?" Meredith's voice was thick with worry.

"It's just my boss calling. I can call him back."

"No, no. You kids stay safe. I'll call soon." She hung up.

Tucker blew out a breath, trying to switch mental gears.

He answered the incoming call. "Good evening, boss."

"You canceled our meeting."

No preamble or kid gloves with his sergeant.

"Yes, sir."

"Why? And don't bullshit me. I want the truth."

Tucker walked into his living room and stared out the bank of windows. The snow was falling harder. He glanced at the fist-sized hole in his wall again. There was another one in his bedroom.

"I'm a liability to the team like this, sir." There, he had said it. Tucker was a ticking time bomb. Overwhelming guilt. Consuming anger. Short temper. He was barely sleeping, and what little he got was punctuated by violent nightmares of his father coming and murdering everyone he cared about.

"What does that mean?"

"I'm angry, sir."

He had recently made detective. Tucker should have detected his father was psycho before the bastard had a chance to hurt anyone.

"That's understandable."

Tucker swallowed the automatic flippant retort. "I've followed the handbook. I've done my required physio and, as suggested, spoke with the head doctor."

"Yes, yes, I know that," his boss said.

"Then what do you want?" Tucker snapped.

His boss blew out a breath. "Forget the damn play-book. What do you need?"

He needed to find his damn father before the bastard murdered anyone. "No idea, sir."

Tucker realized his hand was in a fist and made himself release it. He heard keyboard clicks. "Take through New Years. We'll re-evaluate then. You need anything, and I mean anything, you call. Understand?"

"Sir?" Tucker knew he wasn't fit for duty, he was barely fit to order a pizza. But that was six weeks away.

"It's the holidays. I don't know, cook something—shit, Gloria asked me to get your recipe from last year's Christmas party."

Tucker wracked his brain. "The crab cakes or butter tarts?"

"I don't know, both?"

"Yes, sir," Tucker answered.

"Thank you, saves my ass from getting an earful. And Tuck, I'm not kidding, you need anything, say the word."

"Yes, sir," Tucker repeated, amused at his tough-as-nails sergeant getting scolded by his wife.

"And stay out of trouble." The sergeant sighed. "I know it's hard, but let the team find your father."

"I will, sir." Tucker had never lied to his sergeant before and felt a shiver of unease. The sergeant had reason to be concerned, Tucker had no idea what he'd do when he found his father.

He couldn't change the past, but he would hunt down the lunatic before his father could hurt anyone else.

# Chapter Six

Sergeant Leslie hung up the phone and stared at his desk. With a sick feeling churning in his gut, he popped apart his desk phone, checking for a surveillance breach.

It was clean.

Sergeant Leslie reassembled his phone. He looked up as a knock sounded at his open door. His most senior detective, Jones, stood in the doorway.

"Sir, is everything okay?"

Sergeant Leslie finished reassembling his phone. "Yes. What do you need?"

Jones eyed the phone. "Sergeant?"

"What do you need?" Leslie repeated firmly.

Jones looked down at the file in his hand. "There's a John Doe that's been in the morgue a month, an overdose. The medical examiner reached out when no one came looking for the body."

"That's not unusual." Unfortunate, but not unusual.

Jones tapped the file against his palm. "We suspect the John Doe is Bruce Tanner, sir. The body was in rough shape a month ago and likely deceased a while before being discovered. There was no ID on the body, nor in the apartment."

"Why do you think it's Bruce Tanner?"

"Detective Tanner pulled the Parking Authority records last week, and I looked into it. Five weeks ago, a vehicle registered to Bruce Tanner was towed from the street in front of the building."

"That's a bit of a stretch."

"That's why we secured three known DNA samples from his primary residence, his toothbrush, a pair of shoes, and one of his shirts. Those are being run against the John Doe's sample."

Sergeant Leslie's mind pinged with possibilities. "Anything else?"

"The vehicle was released from impound yesterday. The guy showed ID, but there was a system glitch. The record is no longer available to check who recovered it."

Leslie asked, "Cameras?"

"All we know is that a man picked it up and he was over six feet tall."

Relief uncurled within Leslie. Detective Tanner was five-eleven tops. He asked, "Think it was an opportunist?"

"Maybe," Jones answered slowly. "That would be the easiest answer."

Sometimes the easiest possibility was the correct one. "What did the scene look like?"

Jones shuffled papers.

"According to the file, drug paraphernalia was found near the body. Nothing to indicate it wasn't an overdose, and the ME confirmed it. No identification was found."

"Check it out yourself. Maybe the initial crew missed something."

"Can't. The apartment was cleaned out, and there's been a new tenant there for the last three weeks."

"Christ, seriously?"

"Yes, sir. And some of the cameras in the building have been tampered with. Specifically, the ones that led to and from the apartment the body was found in. Not unusual if there was drug activity."

Sergeant Leslie rubbed his temple. "Anything else?"

"Detective Tanner was there last week."

Sergeant Leslie did not want to help his rookie detective to do something stupid. "Does he know anything about the John Doe?"

"No, sir, not that we know of."

It would be unusually tidy if Bruce Tanner overdosed. Sergeant Leslie didn't trust tidy, not when it came to death. "Good. Keep me updated."

Jones nodded before walking away.

Sergeant Leslie was alone again. He steepled his hands, staring at his phone as the years of darkness closed in, taunting and haunting him.

Every man had a breaking point.

Sergeant Leslie just hoped Bruce Tanner wouldn't be Tucker's.

# Chapter Seven

"I swear I didn't know it was a real gun."

Agent Lawson sat on the edge of a physiotherapy table. The large, affable man looked defeated.

Grace tried to reassure him. "I didn't either."

Thorsen's jaw flexed as he finished bandaging Lawson's wound. "He should have."

"Yes, sir."

Thorsen nodded at the man's leg. "That'll do?"

Agent Lawson stood, testing his bandaged leg. "Yes, sir. It was just a graze."

Grace felt awful.

"Sorry, Charles." She crossed her arms, unsure what to do with them.

"I almost killed you. I will hand in my resignation—"

"No."

"No?" Thorsen and Lawson echoed in unison.

Grace uncrossed her arms. "Who uses this gym?"

Thorsen answered, "You."

"Exactly. You guys have your own gym to train in. This one is for the royal family only, and I'm the only one who uses it."

"Are you saying someone set Agent Lawson up?"

Grace shrugged. "I'm saying if I wanted someone dead, I wouldn't offer to resign if I botched the first attempt."

Lawson's eyes widened.

Thorsen swore. "Jesus, Gracie, that's dark."

Point blank, Grace asked Agent Lawson, "Did you just try to murder me?"

His eyes bugged out. "No, ma'am."

"Good. Didn't think so."

She turned to Thorsen. "There may be a completely reasonable explanation, but if someone just tried to set up Charles to *accidentally* shoot me, I want to know who. If it was an accident, I want to know that, too. Agent Lawson resigning just makes that harder for us to figure out under the radar, don't you think?"

Thorsen swung his gaze between Grace and Agent Lawson. Finally, he said, "Lawson, keep this quiet. I'll brief you in two hours on your new orders."

"Yes, sir," Lawson said. He mouthed *thank you* to Grace before excusing himself.

He walked with the slightest limp, the door clicking shut behind him.

"Think he's telling the truth?" Grace asked.

"I don't know."

Thorsen had grabbed the leftover bandaging material, and Grace thought he would throw it across the room. "How in the *hell* did a real firearm get in here?"

The outburst was as unexpected as it was gratifying.

He cared.

She gently took the wadded-up fabric out of his clenched fist. "We'll figure it out. There might be a reasonable explanation." She hoped.

Thorsen shook his head. "I don't know what I'd do if anything ever happened to you."

"I'm safe," Grace said, wanting to reassure him.

"I didn't protect you."

Grace leaned into Thorsen, speaking without words. She saw the file he had brought for her on the counter. "What's this?" She picked it up, wanting to change the subject, and peered inside.

"Gracie—"

She tried to give them back. "The grand duke can Foxtrot Oscar."

"He's your grandfather."

"Who has never acted like it."

They stared at each other. It was an old fight.

"Is that your final message? He'll ask."

"No," Grace said mulishly and pressed her palms against her eyes. "I hate this."

"I know you do." He leaned close. "The queen and the grand duke wish you to be settled." He hesitated. "So do I."

His comment stung.

She shook her head. "Don't."

"I want … I need you to be happy, Gracie."

Thorsen's voice was quiet, soft even, for such a hard, unyielding man. That hurt even more.

"How can you take their side? My entire life, I was strictly forbidden from falling in love. It wasn't proper, it wasn't appropriate. And now they wish me settled and married? With whom? You're the only man I've ever been with, and we both know the shit storm if *that* ever got out."

She fired the balled-up bandage she still had in her hand into the bin.

He waited a half beat. "Do you regret it?"

She turned. "Us?"

He nodded once, his jaw ticking.

Grace shrugged but couldn't keep her voice steady when she said, "We didn't work as a couple. It happens."

Thorsen had always been her rock and safe haven when the weight of the crown and a church she didn't believe in was just too damn much.

She crossed her arms and walked out onto the sparring mat.

When Thorsen followed her, she stopped.

He had grown up in the palace with her, though it was in service. His father, Randolph, had been their royal head of security. Now Thorsen was. Their off and on again relationship had lasted for eight years. Grace finally broke it off for good last spring when she realized she could never be his person, not with the crown and duty hanging over both of their heads.

Her heart had almost healed.

"You deserve to be happy, Gracie, married and settled."

She laughed. It sounded as hollow as she felt. "Happiness has nothing to do with it. They want me to announce an engagement before the vote. Sway the vote."

Early polls suggested the vote next week would be a historical one, crumbling the old regime's stranglehold. It would be a death knell to the grand duke's power base.

She continued, "My grandfather would have me pledge my loyalty to a politician of his choosing. I am not a pawn, I am to be queen."

Sharing her body with another was sacred to her. Any political ambitions, family expectations, or the church's abusive dogma had no place in that conversation.

Thorsen brushed a strand of her hair from her forehead. "I'm sorry."

"Stop." She pushed away from him.

"Gracie—" When he hesitated, her heart leaped. But he simply said placidly, "I'm sure it'll all work out."

Her eyes widened in disbelief. She wasn't sure what she had hoped he would say, but it sure as shit wasn't that. "Right, of course. Who knows, maybe I'll get laid for Christmas by someone other than you."

He gave her a charged look. "Do you mean that?"

She didn't. Not even close. She couldn't imagine trusting someone that much anytime soon, let alone before Christmas.

Instead of telling him the truth, she elbowed him.

He didn't take the bait.

She elbowed him again. "Come on, then. I still have fifteen minutes of training to finish." She reached for his arm in one of their training assault positions.

Thorsen countered and locked her in a tactical hold. "Nice evasion."

"Thanks," she quipped.

"Want to talk about whatever this is?"

"Nope."

She didn't want to talk. Sparring demanded she be present, not think about her family trying to marry her off or Thorsen lining up to help them.

Or that someone might want her dead.

They grappled for several moments.

"Do you really want a fella for Christmas?"

Grace shifted her position. "Maybe. What's it to you?"

"Absolutely nothing."

She fought the urge to hammer her fist into his junk.

"Maybe I should ask Santa," she said over her shoulder, trying to counter the lock he had her in.

He adjusted his hold. "You seriously want to fall in love for Christmas?"

"Who said anything about love?"

Men saw her title, not her. Her family had made sure of it. Thorsen had seen her. It had been an irresistible turn-on. Like his rock-hard body wrapped around her once had been.

"How is it that I'm the romantic one?" Thorsen asked, maneuvering for a better hold.

"I'm a realist," Grace said between breaths, counter-ing. If he had ever loved her, she'd never known. It was always acutely painful loving someone who didn't love you back. Thorsen had taught her as much as her con-tained, duty-bound family ever had. He was loyal to the country, the crown, and then her, in that order. Thorsen neatly avoided entangling himself with church politics, though not for their lack of trying.

Finally, Grace slipped out of his tactical embrace and spun.

He was ready for her offense. She clipped him but didn't properly land the punch.

"Do you have any gear besides kick-ass?"

She smiled sweetly and fired a kick at him. "Nope. You taught me well."

He dodged the assault, dancing out of the way. "An-other man might have other ideas of foreplay."

"He'd have to exist first."

Thorsen had been the only man in the country who hadn't been afraid to touch her.

It wasn't enough.

She needed someone as loyal to her as she was to him. Anything less only lead to heartache.

# Chapter Eight

Tucker had almost turned around a half dozen times between town and his sister's place nestled in the foothills of the Rocky Mountains. He hadn't slept worth a crap last night and felt like an ornery bear, ready to snap.

Now he sat in his truck in the ranch yard of his little sister's eco-inn, a fresh pan of brownies on the passenger seat, hesitating.

But it was too late. Becca was trotting down her front porch steps, heading toward him.

Resigned, he grabbed the pan of brownies and climbed out of his truck.

She had dashed out without a jacket and wrapped her arms tight around herself.

"Whatcha doing? It's freezing out here—woah, are those your peppermint brownies?"

Tucker made himself smile, trying to hide his malaise. "Who's your favorite person on the planet?"

Becca reached for the pan. When it was safely nestled in her arms, she said, "That's a trick question. Your brownies, especially your Christmas ones, are heaven, but Jason does these incredible things with his—"

Tucker clapped his hand over his sister's mouth. "Nope." He did not want to hear what his sister and her fiancé did to each other.

She was laughing so hard that she almost dropped the pan. Righting it, she said, "Come on, let's get inside."

They scaled the front porch stairs and headed inside. Blowing snow followed them into the eco-inn's foyer.

Tucker hung his parka on a free peg and unlaced his boots. "I would've called, but my phone was dead, and I forgot to bring my charger."

Becca's fiancé, Jason, appeared around the corner in his RCMP uniform.

"Hey, Tuck, good to see you." He held out his hand, and Tucker shook it.

"Jason, likewise."

After years of being each other's nemesis, Becca and Jason were now blissfully engaged.

Jason quickly laced up his work boots. "What brings you out?"

"Becca said she wanted real Christmas cookies," Tucker answered smoothly. "And last year, she put in a standing order for peppermint brownies."

Becca clapped her hands together. "I did, didn't I?" She threw Jason a smug look. "You're welcome."

Her fiancé grinned and shrugged into his jacket. "Yes, dear."

Becca opened the lid of the pan and peeked inside. "Ooh, this is a big batch."

Jason sniffed. "They smell fantastic. I've gotta run." He turned to Becca and dipped his head. She tucked the pan under her arm like a football and cupped his face with her free hand, immediately locking her lips to his.

Tucker waited. It was not a quick kiss.

He cleared his throat.

Nothing. They just kept making out right in front of him.

"I'm just going to squeeze past—" Tucker awkwardly darted between the embraced couple and the wall.

His little sister and Jason finally broke apart, grinning like idiots.

Jason had a blissed-out look in his eyes.

Becca tucked a strand of hair behind her ear. "Sorry."

Tucker snickered. "No, you're not. Not that I'm complaining, it's good to see you happy."

It was. Becca had a rocky go this last bit.

"Good to see you, Tuck," Jason said before he leaned in, giving Becca a quick kiss on the cheek. "See you tonight, honey."

"Be safe." She let her hand trail down his body.

"Always." Jason winked at her before heading out. The door shut behind him with another swirl of snow.

She clicked the lock shut.

Tucker stepped farther into the eco-inn, glancing around the sprawling ranch front room. Pine boughs and soft red plaid ribbons were wrapped around the railing leading up to the second-story rooms, and fresh wreaths hung on all the doors. A live Christmas tree—undecorated—stood against the large far wall. "Looks great."

"Why are you really here?"

Tucker turned swiftly. "What do you mean?"

Becca's arms were crossed, and she gave him her best because-I-know-you-stupid looks.

"Mind if I check on the security cameras Colt and I set up."

Sarah Kades

Becca leveled a look at him. "Jason routinely inspects them. And I'm pretty sure Lillian's secret agent types still rotate through on a regular basis."

Tucker hesitated. "I was thinking of putting some cameras up in my condo."

Becca stilled. "Has something happened, I mean, more than has already?"

"No, no, nothing like that."

Tucker didn't want to worry his sister, but he did want to see her surveillance footage.

"No, um, my doctor thought it would help me feel better, is all." Wow, he was digging this hole deeper and deeper.

Becca smiled and nodded, her arms still crossed. "You're going to a doctor, now?"

"Yup."

"That's wonderful news. Is it helping?"

He didn't need a head doctor, he needed to check Becca's surveillance footage.

"Yup."

"Tucker?"

"Yeah?"

"You suck at lying."

It took a moment for Tucker to recover his surprise.

"Nu-huh. The chief called my undercover work brilliant."

"No, he didn't, his content writers did."

"He did. It's on the video. I replay it sometimes."

"Dork." She laughed. "For real, what's up? I can take it."

"Nothing, I'm fine."

She abruptly shushed him. "No more keeping secrets *for our own good* bull crap. Spill."

Tucker jammed his hands through his hair. "Fine. I'm trying to find Dad."

Becca stilled. "What do you mean?"

"I'm trying to find Dad before that lunatic hurts anyone else."

She blinked.

Fuck. He *knew* he shouldn't have said anything. "This is why I didn't want to tell you. I didn't want you to worry. I'm just hoping to see anything we might have missed on the video footage."

"Good … yes. I think that's a good idea." She headed into her front room and dropped into a chair. She set the pan of brownies on the coffee table.

Tucker followed her. "You do?"

Not in a million years.

"If hunting Dad means I get my brother back, yeah, go for it. Safely and all."

Tucker wasn't convinced. "You're not worried?" He dropped into the chair opposite her.

"Of course, I am. He's a loose fucking cannon. But you're more important. I need you back to you." She paused. "Whoever that is now."

He knew what she meant, trauma changed people.

Tucker let out a breath. "I punched two holes in the wall at my condo."

Becca's face lit into a huge smile, and she blurted, "I cut Dad out of every family photo I have and erased him from all the digital ones. If you were wondering, scissors are, by far, more therapeutic."

He blew out a breath. "I thought you'd be freaked out."

"So you punched a hole through your drywall. I'm assuming you were alone."

His eyes widened. "Um, yeah. Rage is hardly a turn-on." Not that he'd tell his sister, but Tucker hadn't been with anyone since everything had gone down.

"Just checking." Becca sat forward. "I should call Meredith. It's been a few days."

"She's out east. Someone picked up Dad's car from the impound."

"So?" Becca rested her elbows on her knees, folding her hands in front of her.

"It wasn't one of us."

"Who was it?" Becca's voice pitched higher.

"Not Bruce, if that's what you're worried about. The video surveillance is inconclusive, but it was a man over six feet. That rules out Dad."

Becca frowned. "Shouldn't there be a record or something?"

"There was a computer glitch, and the record was erased."

"Of course, there was." Becca sat back. "Who do you think it was?"

"That's what I'm trying to find out." His hands had clenched into fists. He forced them open and wiped them against the tops of his legs.

She watched him. "You could stay here, chop wood, clean."

He raised an eyebrow. "Channel my anger into your menial tasks? Ha ha."

She winked. "Something like that."

He cleared his throat. "Um … thanks for understanding."

"Anytime, bro." She waggled her fingers at him. "Now that you're here, I can mother hen you more."

Tucker swatted his sister's hands away. "Save your mother-henning for Jason."

Becca pushed herself out of the plush chair. "I do many things to that man, none of which I could reasonably call *mother hen*."

Tucker jammed his fingers in his ears. "La la la la."

She laughed, hooking her arm through his elbow and pulled hard, dislodging one of the fingers he had jammed in his ear while pulling him out of the chair.

He dodged his head out of her reach as she launched for the other one. "Stop that. I do not want to know what my grown sister does with her fiancé. I'll be scrubbing my eyeballs for days trying to get the image of you two this morning out of my head."

Becca dropped her hands, grinning. "You started it."

Tucker tugged his sweatshirt back in place. "Your tree's empty."

"Are you offering to decorate it?"

He had walked into that one.

"Sure, let me decorate your tree," Tucker paused. "I dare you."

Becca elbowed him. "Brothers."

Her smile slipped, then, and she wrapped her arms around herself.

"Tanner still hasn't called back?" Tucker gently asked. She shook her head.

A few months ago, they had found out in an explosive confrontation with their brother Colt's MI6-connected fiancé that they had a half-sibling, Tanner Stone. Gabe had stumbled into the secret as a child, and their father had terrorized Gabe into keeping the secret all this time.

Becca had been trying to reach out to Tanner since, to no avail.

"Give him time. It's all a bit much to process. How are you doing?"

Becca shrugged. "Have I fallen to pieces with being nearly murdered by our father? Not yet, but the day is young."

"Dark humor." Tucker nodded sagely. "A solid coping mechanism."

"I don't know how you and Jason deal with this kind of thing, day in and day out. And Gabe, what he must have seen with CSIS or Colt when he was kidnapped."

Their oldest brother had joined Canada's Security Information Service to pay for his archaeology grad degree. He retired from CSIS after getting shot in the head. A couple of months ago, they discovered their father was suspected of having a role in Gabe's ambush, and Colt had been kidnapped by a double agent selling state secrets, who happened to be his girlfriend's ex. All of that besides their father trying to murder Becca, Jason, and Meredith a couple of months ago.

It had been a hell of a year.

Becca eyed him with one of her eerily knowing looks. "The kitchen is stocked."

Her words hung in the air, daring him to grab the lifeline.

Tucker glanced at the hallway that led to the large kitchen. "What about your chef? I don't want to step on toes."

Becca laughed, breaking the suddenly-charged moment. "Are you kidding? You're the only one Roman willingly allows in there. And we've been getting steady restaurant bookings. We're stretched tight, but I can't turn them down, I'm still playing catch-up from the fire—" She broke off, chest heaving.

Tucker tried to reach out to her, but she held up her index finger. "I'll be fine in a sec."

He had been so busy grappling with his anger that Tucker hadn't realized how tormented his sister was and felt like an ass. "I should have come sooner—"

"What?" She looked confused. "That? Oh, that's just processing. Yeah, I'm angry, I'm fucking pissed, actually. But when the anger bubbles up, I ride the wave and try to let it flow out. If I don't, it feels like I can't breathe … like the fire."

Tucker stepped forward. "Becca?"

She blinked. "I'm fine, I'm fine. And like I said, fuck him. The only air time I let that monster get in my head is to let that dark shit go."

Tucker looked at his little sister with more than a little awe. She was a hell of a lot stronger than he realized. "Don't take this the wrong way, I love you, sis."

Becca cackled. "I *have* brought you to the dark side. You're sharing your feelings. Soon you will be menstruating—"

Tucker winced. "You can't say shit like that to a guy."

"Quit whining. Come on. Cook me something. Then I want your peppermint brownies. And Christmas cookies. Like *good* ones. French macaroons or something with coconut and chocolate. I'm sure Roman will be ecstatic if you help out in the kitchen tonight."

He followed her down the hall to the kitchen. When they were almost there, they could hear loud, angry voices, and they sprinted the last few steps.

Both of them froze for a half second at the sight before them.

Christopher Fischer, one of the former arms and drug dealing brothers that Tucker had taken the bullets meant for, stood in Becca's kitchen. He had her chef, Roman, in a headlock.

Tucker leaped to intercept the fighting men. "*Jesus Christ*, Christopher, what the hell are you doing?"

"My job," Christopher retorted.

"*Stop.*"

The three grown men froze at Becca's fierce command. Christopher let Roman out of the headlock.

She held up the drug paraphernalia she had picked up from the large island counter.

"Whose is this?" Her voice was sharp. Tucker had never heard her use such a tone.

When had his little sister grown up?

"Mine," Roman said, his voice defeated. "Christopher wasn't hurting me, he was trying to stop me from doing something stupid."

Tucker let go of the hold he had on Christopher's sweater. "Sorry, man. Wait, what are you doing here?"

Becca stepped forward. "He's my sommelier."

Tucker stared in disbelief. "What the fuck, Becca?"

"Hey, I'd be dead now if it wasn't for him. So would Jason and Meredith. I know this is messed up, but he more than proved himself."

Tucker glared at the man in question. Christopher glared right back. Becca had a point, but trust wasn't something Tucker felt a lot of lately.

Roman held up his hands and took a couple of steps back. "I can't do this."

"Do what?" Becca asked.

"Christmas is always hard." He was backing up more. "I thought I could handle it. I was wrong."

Becca's eyes widened. "About what?"

"Just through the holidays. I can't … you're taking a chance on me. If Christopher hadn't been here just now —" He broke off.

Becca scrubbed her face with her hands. "What exactly are you telling me?"

"I need help. I'll check myself in over the holidays."

Becca's mouth opened, but no sound came out.

Christopher's voice was hard when he said, "Think about what you're saying, man." He pointed at Becca. "You promised her."

"I can't." Roman turned to Tucker. "He can fill in for me."

Tucker held up his hands. "Woah, I'm a police officer. I'm nowhere near the chef you are."

"You're better. You're sober."

It was like the air was sucked out of the room at the painful admission.

"*Roman.*"

"I'm so sorry, Becca. You were the only one who took a chance on me. I'll understand if I can't come back."

Becca swore under her breath before standing tall. "We'll talk about it later. Do you need a ride?"

Christopher stepped forward and said quietly, "I can take him."

Becca nodded, and the two men exited the kitchen.

She eyed Tucker. "Do you want it?"

Tucker felt an unsettling flicker of hope. Most chefs had to pay a hell of a lot of dues before ever getting the opportunity his sister was waving in front of him.

"There must be a thousand more qualified you could hire. You can't want me."

"And yet, here I am, offering it to you."

"I'm an unpolished police detective with anger issues. Your clientele is," he waved his hands in the air, "fancy."

His sister's smile didn't reach her eyes. "You'll fit right in. The news articles about our fucked-up family haven't been kind. Word has gotten out, and my brand new eco-inn has an edgy reputation."

Still, Tucker hesitated.

Becca crossed her arms. "Pretend you're undercover."

"What?"

"When you were undercover, how'd you pull it off? We both know you lie like shit."

"Balls." He could have said confidence.
Becca rolled her eyes but added, "You made my point." She motioned around them. "The kitchen is yours over the holidays if you want it. Are you in?"

# Chapter Nine

The hallway was centuries old, the plush carpet a recent upgrade that muted Grace's brisk footsteps. Since she was a child, this length of the great hallway, the backbone of the palace, had always made her uncomfortable. Row after row of oversized oil paintings in gold and gilded frames stared down at her. Some were from the last century, most were earlier. A few were ancient. Her ancestors looked either formidable, dour, or both. None appeared happy.

As a child, Grace had felt the heavy weight of those stares, terrified at the gazes that seemed to follow her as she passed and wondering what would make them embody, leap off the canvas to scold her, or worse. Weapons featured prominently in more than she would have preferred, and a few included slain foes for effect. As an adult, she knew to avoid looking at the unsettling ones.

When the carpet had been installed, it had changed the smell of the space, dulling the curiously earthy blend of stone walls, old canvas, and fading paint. Now it was an unsettling mix of earthy old and discordant new that never quite dissipated or found harmony.

It was a hallway of secrets. History was filled with much to regret, and her ancestors had their fair share of intrigue, betrayal, and nefarious business. It made her uncomfortable, knowing her likeness would hang here, though she hadn't quite sorted if it was her own insecurities or the disappointing disdain that was the cause. Families could be painfully treacherous.

Grace ducked into her study, closing the door firmly behind her on the hallway of ancestors.

She crossed the large room, her boots clicking on the enduring hardwood she had opted to keep, and closed the connecting door to her mom's private office chambers. She hesitated, eyeing the second bookshelf to the right of her desk. A hidden latch would silently swing open a narrow section of the bookshelf, revealing a small passageway that led to a chapel, though Grace didn't think of it as such. A natural spring still flowed within the crypt-like space, and, like so many sacred spaces, Grace suspected its origins of worship predated the church by millennia. The space brought her immeasurable peace and would no doubt work its magic if she let it. Dipping her fingers in the cool water always revived even her weariest melancholy.

But it was not to be, not today. As much as the accidental shooting had shaken her, she had work to do and dropped into her office chair, opening her laptop to work.

Several hours later, she was interrupted by the gravelly voice of her grandfather. "Your misguided followers are violently protesting again."

Grace glanced up from her laptop, surprised at the darkened windows. Night had fallen. Cheery holiday lights winked in the breeze, at odds with her grandfather's sour expression. He stood in the doorway of her study. His hair was formally styled, like the military dress uniform he insisted on wearing. The only action he had seen had been basic training in the palace yard. As usual, his hands were fisted at his sides, like he was perpetually mid-tantrum.

She turned back to her screen.

He raised his voice. "You are more concerned with flouting your ridiculous political anarchy than preserving the sanctity of the crown or our good church."

"Good evening to you, too, Grandfather," Grace said, not looking up.

"I told you not to call me that."

Her grandfather had not been gracious when he had been inclined by parliament to abdicate. It was a political maneuver—they would sacrifice him with a mind to save themselves from the growing secular populace unrest with outdated traditions and conservatism. What better way to demonstrate a break from tradition than successfully *inclining* the staunchly church-supportive king to abdicate?

In the coup, Grace's mom, his daughter, had been coronated.

No longer king, Grace's grandfather had demanded he be called the grand duke—by everyone.

She hadn't listened to him then, either.

Grace chose to indulge him. "Of course, Your Highness. Please be advised that I don't have followers. I have colleagues."

He gasped. "Your insolence knows no bounds. No one is equal to royalty. No one."

"Just a heads-up. It was that sort of spouting that tanked your approval rating and forced parliament to distance themselves from you."

He glared at her. "When I was your age, women did not speak so freely."

"When you were my age, women barely had the right to vote. Those were the dark ages, Gramps."

"*Silence.*"

The retort was there, on the tip of her tongue. Instead, she hit save on her laptop and discreetly closed the refugee literacy campaign she was working on. Hesitating, she closed the regenerative agricultural grant program file, as well.

She looked up. "What do you need, Your Highness?"

He tugged on the lapels of his jacket. "Have you secured a suitable fiancé, as I asked? I'd like to announce your engagement before the election."

"Did you just say 'secure'? Like a bushel of wheat or barrel of oil? Surely men would object to being likened to commodities, no? You usually only speak of women that way—oh, I see, you mean for me to marry a woman."

Her grandfather's face reddened, and he roared, "Do not speak such blasphemy. It is your duty, to the crown and the church, to marry someone suitable, which means a *man*. An appropriate man."

Grace rolled her eyes. "You forgot country."

"What?"

"Country, crown … never mind."

"A husband would keep your insolence in line." Her grandfather pointed a gnarled finger at her. "If you don't produce a respectable fiancé, I will announce my choice before the election. It's settled."

"No, far from it. As mentioned repeatedly, I do not wish to be married." Grace wished her dad was in the room. Jacques knew how to defuse the grand duke's temper tantrums better than anyone.

"I have little care for what you *wish*. You're a princess. Act like it. You are getting married to someone respectable. A man. It is your duty. I am not having a second-generation debacle."

Grace's temper ignited. "You know that's not how a constitutional monarchy works, right? No one, not you or some draconian church, can order me to get married. And what do you mean, second generation?"

Grace's parents' marriage was too sedate to be described as anything close to a debacle. They respected each other and shared a companionable warmth of sorts. But it was not love.

"Enough of this nonsense. You're just like the queen."

"In what universe?" Her mom had married the man the grand duke had picked out for her, like a pliable good girl. Grace hated that phrase, *good girl*. Why didn't you just say subservient denier of self?

Her grandfather pointed at her, the look in his eyes giving her pause. "Mark my words. You are just like the queen."

"Who is just like me, Papa?"

Grace's parents walked in through the connecting door.

"Grandpa insists I marry. Just like you did."

Her mom's face fell so briefly that Grace wondered if she had imagined it.

The queen gripped the back of one of the settees. "He just wants what's best for you. So do I. And your father, of course," she added hastily.

Though Grace's dad, Jacques, smiled at her, it didn't quite reach his eyes. "It's the way of things, kiddo."

Feeling ambushed, Grace stood, pushing her chair back. "I don't wish to marry right now. I'm not saying never, just not now." She looked to her dad for support. "Why is that so bad?"

"We can give her more time, ja? Maybe she has a point? What's the rush?"

Her grandfather pointed an accusing finger at her. "Every day we don't control this … this outrage, we risk obscene disgrace. Like her loose friend who was tried for treason for sleeping with the enemy. Shameful, it was. That is the sort you allow her to associate with."

Grace was incredulous. "You want me to marry a stranger because Lillian Kensington was targeted by a double-agent psychopath? She took down an enemy of the state. Lillian deserves our compassion and applause, not your misogynistic slut-shaming. Wake up, Grandpa, you might have gotten away with that bullshit before—"

The grand duke slammed his hand down on the sideboard, the loud clap echoing through the cavernous room.

"You ungrateful, spoiled wretch. Was I *slut-shaming* when your mother got herself knocked up by some dirt poor commoner?"

"What are you talking about?" Grace sought her dad's gaze, but he was looking at the floor. "Dad is as blue blood as they come."

"*He* is. You're not. I made your mother make an honest woman of herself," her grandfather pointed cruelly, "and you."

"*Papa,*" the queen said sharply. "You promised."

The grand duke sneered. "And you promised me she would be a dutiful heir. Look at her. Since she came of age, parliament has refused to listen to me. This country is turning into a left-wing disaster. I told you, you shouldn't have let her go to school abroad. She's a goddamn nightmare with her socialist ideas. She'd have us turn our backs on fossil fuels. Fling open the doors to immigrants. Do you know she wants to marry a woman? She's a goddamn nightmare."

Grace held up her hand. "Stop it, I am not some hippie dictator. Our elected representatives and citizens support the initiatives I've proposed. And they're working. We're pivoting our economy and shifting from energy dependency without losing jobs, all while surpassing our greenhouse gas emission reduction goals. Our workforce is adapting brilliantly. And why in the world would we shun solid workers that are increasing our numbers just because they weren't born here?"

Her grandfather threw his hands up in the air. "You're a nightmare. As uncouth as your father."

Her dad was as cultured an aristocrat as they came.

Grace looked at her parents. "What is he talking about?"

Her mother looked stricken. Her dad looked green.

"You're barely an heir. I paid Jacques to marry your mother when she was too dumb not to get herself knocked up."

The room spun. Grace grasped the edge of her desk with both hands. "I don't understand."

Her grandfather snorted. "Of course, you don't. Do you need a sharing circle to explain it? You should have gone to the Diocese University as I wanted. Everything you could possibly need to learn, they would have taught you. Your mind is filled with trash, I tell you, nothing but airy fairy trash."

Grace tried to remember how to breathe and make sense of the ridiculous things her grandfather was saying. "How? If what you said is true, I couldn't be the heir, and then you wouldn't be fussing that I marry. This doesn't make sense."

"The church will conduct *matrimonium postmortem* under the right circumstances. Your mom's indiscretion was just the sort of circumstance it was created for."

Grace's stomach lurched. That couldn't possibly mean what she thought it did?

"*Papa, you promised,*" her mom hissed.

"I've had enough of her tainted blood ruining everything. Our country deserves better. She needs a firm god-fearing husband, that's what she needs."

Grace thought she was going to be sick. She looked to her dad, the man she had always thought was her father.

He held out his arms to her. "Grace, I have always loved you. I always will."

But his eyes betrayed the truth.

She wasn't his biological kid.

# Chapter Ten

"I've got three flash drives, dirty needles, a pipe, oh shit—and a CPS wire-ringed notebook," Agent Omran Forest said from the driver's seat as he riffled through the Jag's console wearing the latest in biohazard latex-blend gloves.

Tanner Stone stopped pulling up the after-model cargo panels from the trunk and called, "What's the content?"

The two agents were in the oversized garage of their safe house, going through Bruce Tanner's car. Their preliminary analysis had identified bodily fluid stains, including some in the trunk. The more they dug, the more skeletons they found in Bruce Tanner's sizable closets. Bruce Tanner had left a dangerous door open when he died. He'd also left crumbs that loosely pointed to his son, Tucker, being a dirty cop. Part of Stone wanted his half-brother to be dirty—it would make pretending he didn't exist easier.

Omran flipped through the notebook. "Looks like your dad is old school, bro."

"Not my dad," Stone called. Not the way it counted, anyway.

"My bad," Omran corrected. "The unfortunate sperm donor is old school. Looks like an ongoing to-do list. He either didn't trust, or know, there are apps for that now."

Stone had his hand on the next cargo panel when his earpiece hummed to life. "Be advised, you've been identified by Jordemorden CSIC."

He frowned, releasing the cargo panel. Being made was not ideal. Jordemorden was an outlier in global politics. Their military was small but exceptionally well-trained. The country wasn't exactly progressive, but swinging heavily in that direction a decade ago since their heir apparent started becoming more involved in politics. Stone was still trying to confirm why Jordemorden agents had been protecting former MI6 courier Lillian Kensington a few months ago.

Stone peered around the open trunk to Omran. The agent gave no indication he had heard.

Still watching, Stone asked quietly, "Just me?"

"Affirmative."

Stone signed off with clicks.

Omran looked over at him. "Did you say something?"

"Yeah, what do you know of Jordemorden CSIC?"

"Not much. Why?"

Stone's Spidey-sense flickered. "Nothing, just remembering something in the field files."

Omran held Stone's gaze. "They're well trained. Under extraordinary circumstances, they can be for hire."

It was a nuanced answer.

As Stone pulled up the next cargo panel, he wondered what would constitute an extraordinary circumstance before swearing.

Neat rows of half kilo packages lined one side.

Stone picked one up.

It had an evidence tag on it.

# Chapter Eleven

Grace slowed her pace, eyeing the two guards posted on either side of the family room double doors with open hostility. They were not palace security, and this part of the palace was supposed to be private.

"Who are you?" Grace asked.

Both men stared at her but remained silent.

Her mom called from within the family room and waved her to enter. "They're fine."

Grace pulled out her phone and held it up, snapping several pictures.

One of the guards advanced on her.

The chill in her voice scared her. "Take another step, and I'll break your arm."

He hesitated.

She held his gaze, surprised she wanted him to instigate an altercation. She wanted to hurt him, wanted to bleed off the pain drowning her since her grandfather's outburst.

He glanced nervously at his partner, who gave his head a brief shake.

The guard stepped back, giving Grace plenty of space.

"Grace?" Her mom hadn't seen the exchange.

"Coming." Grace entered the candlelit room, closing the leaded glass double doors behind her.

Dozens of fresh white candles of numerous sizes were artfully arranged throughout the space, including several wall sconces. Tree trimming decorations had been laid out. The family's Christmas stockings already hung from the large stone mantle over the fireplace, fresh evergreen boughs draped across the tops of the window boxes, and the dark blue curtains had been replaced with festive red plaid ones, as was tradition. Everything was lovely.

The queen held up two different boxes. "What do you think? Should we use the blue and silver or red and green color palette this year?"

Grace picked up a throw pillow and traced her fingers along the artfully embroidered snowflake. Decorating for Christmas with her family was exactly what she needed. She hugged the pillow to her chest. "Shouldn't we wait for Hope, Faith, and Dad?"

"Your sisters won't be coming."

"But we always trim the tree together."

The queen didn't meet her gaze. "The twins won't be arriving until just before Christmas Mass."

"Oh." Grace's stomach dropped. "What about Dad?"

"He's been called to the Chambers."

Grace realized she had been holding out hope that this was all a sick ruse, that her grandfather's outburst was an exaggerated tantrum.

Grace blinked back the tears that had pooled. She dropped the pillow on the settee and cleared her throat. "What's with the guards?"

"There was a firearm incident with one of the royal guards. The grand duke ordered extra protection." The queen held the boxes in her hands higher. "Blue and silver or red and green?"

Grace stared. "By law, we're protected by the palace guards." Grace hiked her thumb behind her. "Those guys are private security, not extra protection. Mom, what's going on?"

"I'm sure that is not the case. The grand duke is upset. You know how protective he gets. My goodness, your imagination, it has always been so colorful."

Grace bristled. "Pathologically controlling is not the same as protective. What the fuck is wrong with him?"

"Grace, language!"

The candles between them flickered wildly.

Grace turned away first, her gaze taking in the boxes of decorations, and her shoulders sagged. Maybe playing something Christmasy would help rescue the disaster this was turning out to be.

She pulled out her mobile and opened her music app.

An icy awareness swept through her. Someone had accessed her phone.

The app timestamped everything. The last time it was opened was four in the morning. Grace had been up at four, working on details for the next women's reproductive rights rally. She had not been listening to music.

Grace looked at her mom. The queen was hanging ornaments on the tree.

Frowning, Grace took a screenshot to show Thorsen before finding a holiday music station. When she tried to connect it to the wireless speakers, nothing happened.

She quickly went through the usual troubleshooting methods.

Still nothing.

She tried to make a call. Nothing.

"Mom, can I borrow your mobile?"

The queen's smile was brief. "Of course, dear."

Grace accepted her mom's mobile and tried to make a call. Again, nothing.

Her mom looked over. "What is it, dear?"

Grace eyed the two guards through the leaded glass doors. She was almost certain a signal jammer had been deployed.

She opened the door, demanding, "Give me your mobile."

He stared at her.

She stared back.

His partner handed her his phone. It worked fine.

Grace handed the phone back to him. "Unjam them."

The first guard stood straighter. "Our orders—"

"Were they from the queen?"

He did not make eye contact. "No, Your Highness."

"Than we both know your orders are irrelevant. Unjam them."

"Yes, Your Highness." The guard made a brief call. Within moments, her phone was online.

"Do you know the penalty for sedition?" Grace asked.

The first guard swallowed. "I wouldn't know, Your Highness."

"We still behead for that. The left has never managed to abolish that barbaric practice."

Both guards stilled.

"Hold out your hands."

They did as she bid. She keyed in a few strokes on her mobile. Within seconds she had logged their biodata.

"What did you just do?" the first guard asked. Fear had crept into his voice.

"I took out insurance."

Four palace guards appeared. Grace nodded at them. "Get these guys the fuck out of here."

Trying not to shake, she walked back to her mom.

"The grand duke did that, didn't he?" The queen's voice was as unsteady as Grace felt.

Grace threw her hands up. "Who else? You know this crosses the line, right? Not only was that not right, but it's also not legal."

The queen glanced where the two private guards had been posted at the door.

"Mom?"

An uneasy silence fell.

Grace pressed, "Am I in any danger from grandfather?"

"I don't know," the queen answered quietly.

Fear flickered. Grace forced herself to pick up a hand-blown glass confection from its box and hang it on the tree.

Her mom did the same.

Grace tried to focus on the twinkling ornaments and flickering candlelight.

"Why haven't you told me about my biological father?"

The queen's hands shook as she hung one of the few decorations from Grace's childhood.

Grace pressed, "Whatever it is, I can handle it."

The queen picked up a clear glass ornament, a perfectly molded generic icicle, unencumbered with sentimental baggage.

"Was he a criminal?"

Grace held her breath.

"Of course not."

"Was he married, then?"

That could explain a lot.

"No. Stop this nonsense."

"This is not nonsense, not to me!" Grace lowered her voice. "I deserve to know who my biological father is."

She heard a discreet throat clearing.

The queen turned toward the door. "Yes, Geoffrey?"

The veteran servant stood in the doorway. "The prime minister and her husband are just pulling into the drive."

The queen inclined her head. "Thank you. We will join them shortly."

Geoffrey nodded before retreating.

"Darling, I know you deserve answers." The queen ran her palms down the front of her dress.

Grace watched the measured movements, the unsteady hands, and an uneasy feeling surfaced. What had her mom been through?

"Mom?" Grace reached for her, worried.

The queen stepped back, holding a staying hand to halt Grace's hug. "I am barely hanging on here."

Grace froze.

"I loved your father," the queen whispered. "Men like him you don't get over, do you understand me? Remember that. He was everything kind and good, and I didn't deserve him."

Grace's eyes widened. "You still love him."

The queen swept her hair from her face. "Settle. It hurts less than falling in love. Get married and have babies of your own."

"But I don't wish to marry," Grace whispered. She didn't want to imagine marriage without love.

"You don't wish to have children?"

Her mom looked so stricken, and Grace felt a hot pang of despair. "What I want is irrelevant, you know that."

"That's not true."

Grace picked up a delicate spun glass fairy. "When I wanted to study archaeology and physical anthropology, what did you and the grand duke decide?"

Her mom had the grace to look down. "You would study political science and shifting global economics."

Grace stared. "And?"

"Christian theology."

"When I was a kid and asked for a puppy, you bought me four horses."

The queen snapped her head up. "But our ceremonies require equine salutes, not canine."

Grace had wanted the puppy, something soft when everything around her was so damn rigid.

The queen sounded genuinely confused when she said, "I thought you liked your mounts."

"Of course I do, they're extraordinary creatures, but why four?"

The queen cleared her throat. "I wanted you to be prepared. Our ceremonies are rather intricate. I didn't want you to feel intimidated."

Grace had felt contained, duty-bound in the worst ways growing up, but never intimidated. "Mom, your loyalty is to the grand duke and the crown."

*Please, tell me I'm wrong.*

"The grand duke means well. Your grandfather—"

The spun glass ornament snapped in Grace's hand. "Has never acted like one. There's nothing paternal about him. Patriarchal, absolutely. Paternal, no way."

Her mom chided. "You don't know everything."

"Then tell me! I'm here, begging you to tell me something, anything, to make sense of the horrible things grandfather said."

Fighting tears, Grace carefully stacked the sharp pieces of the broken fairy on the tea service.

"Grace, the less you know, the better. I'm not saying anything more about the past. You're getting married, and that's final. Pick someone appropriate, or the grand duke will. It's our tradition."

Grace whispered, "When traditions hurt us, it's time to update our traditions."

The queen folded her arms. All the fight had gone out of her mom's voice when she said, "Pick someone, don't pick someone. Either way, you're getting married. The grand duke demands it."

Grace had been desperate for her mom to understand, to take her side for once, especially with something as sacred to Grace as the person she would choose to spend the rest of her life with, the person she would represent a country with.

But the queen said no more.

Grace folded the lid on the ornament box closed and turned toward the door. "Excuse me."

"Where are you going?"

Tears burned the back of her eyes as she wrapped her arms around herself and walked quickly toward the door.

Her mom called after her, "We have dinner with the prime minister and his wife. Our guests are already arriving. Your father," her mom paused, "Jacques will be back any moment."

Grace called over her shoulder, "Yup, got it, crown first."

She glanced down one side of the hall, then the other, the portraits of her ancestors mocking her indecision.

Grace couldn't stay here.

But where would it be safe?

# Chapter Twelve

Tucker stared at the offending bowl of frosting. The organic food coloring his sister sourced wasn't doing what he wanted it to. Before, he would have considered the mild hiccup a confectionary puzzle. Right now, he was unreasonably cranky, and he knew it.

The doorbell rang.

Tucker waited for someone to get the door as he added more drops of food coloring and kept stirring.

Nothing. Not the green he wanted, and no one was answering the damn door.

"Becca, kind of busy here!"

The doorbell rang again.

Swearing, Tucker wiped his hands on a tea towel and stomped through the inn. He flung open the door. Rose Chasseur, Becca's soon-to-be mother-in-law, stood before him, a large craft bag slung over her shoulder.

"You forgot about our baking day, didn't you?"

"Of course not." Tucker swung the door wider. He had totally forgotten. "Come in, come in."

He reached for the large bag she carried. "Here, let me take that."

"You don't lie worth a darn, but I like your style." Rose handed him the bag. "Thank you, that's a nice young man."

"I was just—"

Rose assessed him, her eyes missed nothing. "If I were to guess, not sleeping worth a crap. Are you eating okay? Come on, I'll fix you a sandwich."

Rose took off her snow boots and hung her coat on one of the hooks before Tucker could offer. He trailed after her as she made her way to the back kitchen. "I'm fine, you know."

She waved off his protests and kept walking down the long hall.

"You don't have to make me a sandwich. I ate."

Had he? Tucker put a hand on his stomach. When was the last time he ate anything?

Once in the kitchen, Rose washed and dried her hands before putting on the kettle.

"Let's see what your sister has." Rose headed to the large walk-in pantry. She came out with a couple of cans of tuna. "One sandwich or two?"

"Two, please. Thanks," he mumbled. Tucker felt like a little kid.

Rose smiled, making sandwiches and tea.

"I'm supposed to be doing that." It was barely a protest. Tucker's mom, Samantha, wasn't particularly maternal.

Rose's nurturing, soft energy felt like the neglected parts of him were finally being tucked in with a warm blanket and bedtime story.

It was as unnerving as it was captivating.

"Yes, I heard you're helping while Roman sorts himself out. That was nice of you, dear."

Tucker crossed his arms, uncomfortable with her praise. "Anyone would have. Seriously, you don't have to do that."

Rose just smiled. "Do sit down and let an old woman make you a sandwich. That's how you kids still let us take care of you."

Tucker sat at one of the stools at the large kitchen island, touched he had somehow made it on the list of people this mom wanted to nurture.

She hummed as she added dill, lemon, and mayo to the tuna. Rose spread the mixture between slices of fresh bread before cutting diagonal. She stacked his sandwiches on a plate and slid them over to him.

"Aren't you eating?"

"I've got mine right here."

Tucker jumped up. "I'll get the tea."

Rose indulged him. "That would be lovely, thank you."

They drank tea and ate their sandwiches.

"Have you met a nice girl yet?"

Tucker almost choked on his tuna sandwich. He coughed several times before he could take a sip of tea.

"So, that's a no, then?" Rose asked.

Tucker wiped his mouth and cleared his throat. "That's a no."

Rose smiled and waved to the abandoned bowls of frosting. "What is all this?"

"A disaster. I couldn't get the greens right."

Rose brushed the crumbs off her hands onto her plate and stood. She rummaged in the craft bag she had left on the counter, pulling out a festive apron and putting it on. "I bet you I can make the shade of green you want."

Tucker stood. "Oh, you're on."

"Same stakes?"

Tucker hesitated. "Dishes?" Rose baked like an angel. She left a trail of chaos to get there. "You get pans dirty you don't even use when you bake."

"*I know,*" Rose cackled, her eyes twinkling. "You've never seen the mess I make with Christmas cookies."

It sounded like a threat.

Tucker rounded the island and pulled an apron out of the bottom drawer. He snapped it open before tying it in place. "You're on."

Five hours later, Becca walked into the kitchen. Her eyes bugged when she took in her previously immaculate kitchen. Pots and pans were stacked throughout the kitchen, punctuated by metal cooling racks and tea towels laden with freshly baked Christmas cookies, bars, and cakes.

"Were we robbed?" Becca walked through her kitchen, pausing to pick up a bowl with a ring of batter left inside. "Ransacked?"

Tucker finished tubing the snowflake design he was working on for the coconut macaroons. "It'll be cleaned before the dinner crowd. Promise."

Becca glanced at Rose. "He lost the bet, didn't he?"

Her mother-in-law nodded. "Yup." She picked up a cutting board with a large Kringle on it. "Ta-da!"

Becca's face lighted. "You made Kringle? Thank you!"

"Thank your brother. He mentioned it was one of your favorites."

Tucker ducked at the praise and the look of delight on his sister's face.

Rose set the Kringle down, nudging a cupcake tray out of the way.

Becca scanned the kitchen. "Everything looks so good, I mean, besides the mess." She looked up, her eyes watery. "Thank you both."

Rose pulled her into a hug. "You need to get used to having help, my dear." Rose pulled back. "You both do."

Tucker felt a lump in the back of his throat but kept piping frosting.

"Come on now, let's get these packaged up so Tucker can get to these dishes." Rose winked. "Nice girls like a man who can clean up after himself."

Becca laughed.

Tucker shook his head. "No nice girl will have me."

Rose swatted him with a tea towel. "Not if your kitchen looks like this, they won't. Want me to leave the green frosting, you know, for an example?"

Any ego Tucker had left shredded. "Sure, why not."

All three of them started packaging the treats.

The lump was back in his throat. How did you thank people for fishing you out of the abyss?

"Thanks, guys," Tucker mumbled as he packed the Christmas treats.

Rose and Becca glanced quickly at each other.

"You're welcome, dear," Rose said.

Becca chimed in, "Yeah, any time, bro."

Everyone kept packing treats, completely ignoring him when he swiped a hand across his damp eyes.

# Chapter Thirteen

"Going somewhere?"

Grace looked up. Thorsen stood at her door, eyeing the small suitcase she was packing.

She resumed folding the short sleeve technical shirt in her hand. "Cape Town."

"You're spending Christmas with Claire? What about your family?"

"What about them?" Tears stung the back of her eyes. "My entire life has been a lie."

Thorsen moved into the room and closed the door. "I'm not following."

Grace slammed the shirt onto the growing stack on her bed. She couldn't stop the shudder that rose the length of her body. "My dad isn't my biological father."

"What are you talking about?"

Grace filled him in on her grandfather's outburst.

"Are you okay?"

"No." Grace pressed her palms against her eyes. "You're supposed to be able to trust family. I'm—" Grace swallowed hard, dropping her hands. "Never mind."

Thorsen closed the distance between them. "Gracie, what is it?"

"I can't do this now." She picked up another shirt to fold. "The armed spies the grand duke posted inside the palace didn't help, that's for sure."

"I didn't approve any non-royal guards."

"I know. My grandfather assigned his rent-an-army, and my mom approved their access. They jammed our specific mobiles."

Thorsen's jaw ticked. "About that, what happened?"

Grace briefed him on the exchange, including how she mentioned the penalty of sedition.

"Excuse me a moment." Thorsen paced to the far side of the room and spoke quietly on his mobile.

Grace kept packing.

Thorsen returned. "Is there anything I can do?"

Grace looked at the only man she still trusted. "Why'd he do it? I mean, my grandfather could have told me in a thousand kinder ways. Why was he so cruel?"

Thorsen cupped her shoulders with his warm hands. "*Gracie.*"

She leaned forward, her forehead resting on his chest. "I mean, it's no secret my mom and dad were never a love match, but I never considered Jacques wasn't my biological father."

He held her for long moments. "Does this mean you're not in line for the crown?"

Grace stepped away from him, wringing the shirt she was still holding. "My mom married my biological father *matrimonium postmortem.*"

"Does that mean what I think it does?"

"That for a fee, the church married my mom to a dead guy, so I would be considered legitimate in the eyes of the church and state? Yeah. That's what it means."

Thorsen blew out a breath. "Damn. That's intense."

"It gets worse. Since no one would tell me who my biological father was, I tried to get a copy of my birth certificate, but it was sealed. So is their marriage certificate. It's like he's a ghost." The only ghosts she wanted were the castle ones. They didn't fuck with her head.

Grace swiped at her eyes again. "I mean, I know he's dead, but no one will even tell me his name."

"Did they tell you why?"

"No."

The look in Thorsen's eyes gave her pause.

"What? Tell me."

Thorsen hesitated. "I don't want to confuse the situation."

"*Thorsen*, tell me now, whatever it is."

"What if he's not dead? What if that's why the certificates are sealed?"

Grace felt tingles shoot through her body. Rubbing her arms, she said, "I never considered that."

Thorsen shrugged. "I could be way off base—"

"I need to see a copy of my birth certificate and their marriage certificate." That might give her some answers, at least.

Thorsen didn't miss a beat. "I'll see what I can do."

"Thank you." Grace turned to her suitcase again.

Thorsen fisted his hand, clearing his throat into it. "What about … the envelope I handed you from your grandfather?"

"What about it? Just because of some weird church ceremony thirty years ago, I'm supposed to thank my lucky stars I'm still a legitimate heir, shut up and get married already? I will not be forced into marriage. It's like they want me to be as miserable as them. Fuck that."

"They're *forcing* you?" Thorsen's voice had taken on a dangerously low quality.

Grace looked up, exasperated. "Yes, I've been telling you for weeks. I'm supposed to be an obedient, good girl, shut up, and get knocked up by the right church-going cock."

"Who do they wish you to marry?"

Something in his voice made her look up.

"Don't worry, it's not you."

There was a time she would have jumped at that possibility.

"Of course it's not, I don't qualify to marry royalty for any number of reasons."

Grace was defensive on his behalf. "Your family has defended the royal family for what, eight generations?"

"Nine. But that's hardly a qualifier, and you know it."

Grace snapped, "Disastrous pedigree. Truly sketchy."

She zipped her small suitcase closed. "You saw their short list of candidates."

It was so mortifying.

"It's not like you have to, it's not law."

Grace raised her eyebrows.

Thorsen swore. "The current parliament are puppets for the grand duke. Your right to choose is actually at stake."

Grace nodded. "At least there isn't time to push it through before the election. It would trigger the Brookefield Clause."

"He's trying to legally dictate his control of your life."

"Yes, he is. My parents are going along with it." Grace's face threatened to crumble. "How can they not see me? I've always been right in front of them, but they've never looked. If they had, they would understand how damaging this is to me. They don't even know me, how can they assume to know what's best for me?"

Thorsen stood stoic, his jaw tick the only tell of his turmoil.

Grace swiped at her eyes. "Anyway, I can't keep slamming against their fucked boundaries. I'm leaving."

Thorsen frowned at her suitcase. "We need to clear the venues you're staying at in Cape Town," he reminded her. "That typically takes a few days' notice."

She had forgotten in her haste.

She tugged her mobile out of her back pocket and pulled up a website. She held out her phone. "Is this on the cleared list?"

Thorsen took the phone. "Is that Lillian Kensington's new place?"

"Close enough. She's there all the time. It's her fiancé's sister's eco-inn in Canada."

Thorsen looked at the screen again before checking his mobile.

"Yeah, it's cleared. I can make it happen by tonight." He paused. "If you're sure?"

Grace accepted her phone back. "I'm sure."

She unzipped her suitcase and dumped the contents out on the bed.

Thorsen's eyebrows lifted.

"What? I need to pack for the northern hemisphere." Grace blew out a breath and gave a real smile. "It'll be good to see Lillian. We haven't seen each other in ages, even before those ridiculous treason charges." Quieter, Grace added, "I miss her. I can't believe they shredded her like that."

"Invite Claire," Thorsen advised.

"Sure, why?" Grace asked from her closet, coming out with an armful of cold-weather clothes.

"So when you tell your mom you're spending Christmas with Claire, it'll be the truth."

"And she'll think I'm in South Africa."

Thorsen nodded. The queen had the unfortunate habit of materializing when her daughter needed space.

Grace shoved a sweater into her suitcase, frowning. "I'd rather not fight for Christmas."

"She loves you, you know."

Grace snorted, making quick work of her packing. "She has a shitty way of showing it."

"Your family is … complicated."

So she wouldn't chicken out, Grace didn't make eye contact. "So are we. Can you assign someone else?"

"I'm always your detail." He sounded confused and maybe even a little hurt.

"Yeah. That's how we ended up sleeping together for the last eight years." She met his gaze. "I need to get over you."

His mouth opened twice before any sound came out. "Gracie, I had no idea—"

She gave him a half smile. "I know you didn't."

His brows furrowed like they always did when he was trying to figure out an unexpected pattern.

"I thought our relationship was, I don't know, comfortable."

Grace had spent her whole life comfortably playing second fiddle to duty.

"I need more than comfortable." She held up her hands. "You're a good man, the best I've ever met, actually. But you can't be *my* man, and not because of some archaic royal bullshit. I need someone as crazy about me as I am about him. That's not us."

"What do you want me to say?"

"There is nothing to say. Our relationship has never been balanced. Your dedication to the country and crown is unparalleled, and I would never ask you to change who you are. I just need someone that is dedicated to me."

"That's not fair." His voice tripped. "You have always been more than a duty."

Her heart squeezed painfully.

"Good. Because you have always been more than security. I have no regrets, I just need to move on."

He was quiet a moment. "I hope you find what you're looking for in Canada."

She sprung into his arms and pressed her lips to his one last time. He kissed her back hard.

Grace made herself break contact a moment later. Made herself pick up her suitcase. She had to go before she slid back into old patterns or, worse, jumped. Thorsen was safe and comfortable and wretchedly not in love with her.

"Let me know when I'm cleared to go." She blinked back tears.

He nodded.

"One more thing." She pulled out a small vial that held a lab swab. "Can you check this against every database you have access to?"

He accepted the vial. "Whose is it?"

"Mine. If he's alive, I'm finding my father."

She had only considered finding remnants of a family tree, maybe a distant aunt or cousin. But what if her biological father was still alive?

What if she could find him?

# Chapter Fourteen

"Where is she?" The queen blustered into the Aero Center's intelligence chambers.

Thorsen eyed the matriarch over the briefing pages he was holding. "Good afternoon, Your Highness. How can I help you?"

The queen stopped short, giving the assembled agents the barest of nods before continuing. "The princess, where is she?"

Thorsen set the file he had been reading out loud to his agents on the table, resisting looking out the enforced window. Grace should have boarded the plane idling on the tarmac a few hundred meters away.

"I was under the impression your daughter decided to spend the holidays with Claire. Didn't she speak with you?"

The queen turned to the agents in the room. "Leave us."

The men and women filed silently out of the chamber.

The queen snapped her fingers. "You there, who are you?"

The new agent stopped. "Agent Charles Lawson, mum."

She gave the man a once-over. "Your mother is Duchess Toussaint, no?"

Thorsen watched as an icy feeling spread through his chest.

"Yes, mum," his new agent answered.

"Have you met the princess? What did you think?"

Agent Lawson darted a quick glance at Thorsen before answering. "Lovely, mum?"

"She is," the queen said demurely. "You may go."

Agent Lawson looked to Thorsen, confusion plain on his face. Thorsen gave a terse nod, and the new recruit filed out of the room, hurrying after the other agents.

When the door closed and they were alone, Thorsen asked, "What was that about?"

"Agent Lawson has noble blood. I'm finding my stubborn daughter a suitable husband before the grand duke saddles her with one of his cronies. Did she like him, Agent Lawson?"

"Does it matter?"

"No, I don't suppose it does."

Thorsen fought to keep his face impassive. "Your Highness, what was it that you needed? Didn't Grace speak to you?"

The queen threw up her hands. "It's Christmas, for heaven's sakes."

"It is," Thorsen answered neutrally.

"She should be with us." The queen's voice shook. "I will do anything to keep my family together."

"Of course, mum."

She looked at him then. "You don't understand."

Thorsen remained silent. She was right. He would never understand royalty.

Through the window, the aircraft on the tarmac started to taxi down the runway.

The queen was looking at him a bit too calculating. "There's nothing for it, I'll have to go to South Africa myself. Assign Agent Lawson as my lead. I need my stubborn daughter married before she gets herself killed with her causes and protests."

Thorsen jumped to his feet. "Your Highness, if there is a threat to Princess Grace, I need to know about it *now*." Though he had found no conspiracy or specific threat to Grace's life, he couldn't shake the impending sense of dread. Something was very amiss.

"She is too headstrong by far, you know that. One of these days, she will piss off the wrong person."

Thorsen repeated, "Do you have intel on someone who wishes the princess harm?"

The queen hesitated. "No. Get Agent Lawson ready. I want to leave tonight."

The aircraft ascended, pulling away from the runway.

*Boom.*

A huge explosion rocked the building. Automatically, Thorsen launched himself at the queen, shielding her with his body.

He turned.

The plane had burst into flames on the runway.

# Chapter Fifteen

"Why do you look ready to throw that bowl of frosting across the room?"

Startled, Tucker looked up to see his brother Colt's pregnant fiancée, Lillian walk into Becca's kitchen.

The former war correspondent and MI6 courier had sized up his mood in half a second.

He pointed at the confection on the island counter. "It's all wrong. Jason's mom got it in like thirty seconds."

Lillian laughed. "Of course she did, the woman's got decades on you." She put the manilla envelope she was holding on the counter and retrieved a spoon from the drawer before dipping it in the bowl of frosting and bringing it to her lips. Her eyelids fluttered closed a second. "Tucker, you're insane. This is incredible."

He crossed his arms. "I know it *tastes* good, but it's the wrong shade of green."

"Looks green to me." She smiled at him and ate more frosting. "You should bake, like for a job."

Tucker rolled his shoulders, trying to ease the tension. "I'm actually a police officer. If anyone cares."

Not that his sergeant did at the moment.

Lillian leaned over and snagged another spoon from the drawer. She dipped it in the frosting and shoved it at his mouth. "Here."

Tucker accepted the spoon. Lillian had an uncanny ability to inspire immediate obedience from him, like a smarter older sister. She had been set up by a double agent, tried for treason, nearly murdered, yet had risen from the ashes. Tucker trusted her. He could learn a lot from his brother's world-wise fiancée.

Tucker tentatively licked some of the sugary treat. It did taste pretty good. "How are you and Colt doing with the baby prep?"

She assessed him before answering. "Wonderful. How are you doing?"

"Fine," he breezed, eating more frosting.

He wasn't. Tucker hadn't gotten a solid lead on his father's whereabouts, which was infuriating.

He dipped his spoon in the bowl of frosting.

Lillian eyed him. "Tuck, have you accepted me as part of this family?"

"What? Of course, I have." Crap, had he somehow made Lillian feel unwelcome? Not cool.

"Excellent, then as your older sister, I insist you stop being such a wanker."

Tucker nearly choked on his frosting. He dropped his spoon and reached for his water bottle, taking a big gulp.

Lillian was watching him. "I spent two years in a similar head space. I might not be able to fix it, but talking actually does help."

Tucker set his water bottle down and splayed his hands. "I don't know what you want me to say."

She took another bite of frosting. "How about you tell me what's really bothering you? Because it's not this frosting."

Whoever said Brits were reserved had never met Lillian.

Tucker crossed his arms. "My sergeant doesn't want me back at work until the new year at the earliest, and Becca's chef checked himself into rehab. She asked me to fill in."

"Do you feel guilty for the opportunity?"

His stomach twisted. "No, I already have a career."

Lillian gave a dainty shrug. "Lots of people want more than a single career provides."

"Are you joking?"

"No. Who says you have to be locked into a single career?"

Her words taunted him, daring him to imagine something bigger.

Tucker had never considered that he could be both a chef and an officer. You couldn't be top of your game if your attention was divided ... could you?

Tucker reasoned, "Your multiple careers were related. It's different for me."

"All I'm saying is you're an artist in the kitchen. Bloody hell, Becca and I can demolish your brownies—" Lillian straightened suddenly, swearing loudly. "Your sister! Bugger it, I forgot to tell her!"

At that moment, Becca blustered into the kitchen, arms loaded with Christmas decorations.

"Oh good, you're here. We can get the tree decorated. What did you forget to tell me?"

"Do you have any vacancies? A couple of my friends want to spend the holidays here."

Becca stilled. "*Your* friends?"

"Yes. Sorry about that, I meant to ask earlier, but I forgot." Lillian leaned and swiped another spoonful of frosting. "I'm telling you, baby brain is *real*."

Becca slowly set the box of holiday decorations on the counter. "Who exactly is coming and when?"

Lillian looked up from her spoonful of frosting. "Grace and Claire, why?"

Tucker scratched his jaw. "Lillian, you run in very connected circles. Compared to your friends, we're peasants."

Lillian made a face. "That's rubbish. Okay, Grace is technically a princess, but I swear she's normal."

Becca opened her mouth several times, but no words came out.

Tucker burst out laughing. It was rusty but real.

"What's so funny?" Lillian looked bewildered.

"You think princesses are normal."

"Grace is normal," Lillian said, a bit defensively.

Becca found her voice. "Your friend Grace, as in the princess of Jordemorden?"

"Yes."

Becca pressed, "The princess of Jordemorden wants to stay *here*?"

"Yes. Through New Years." Lillian looked between Tucker and his sister. "Why are you both looking at me like that?"

Tucker took pity on her. "Lillian, this is one of those cultural nuances you always talk about. Having a princess stay here is kind of a big deal."

Becca was looking a bit stunned but finally managed to add, "Lillian, a good review from one of your friends could put this place on the international map. I could recover from the fire. I still haven't recovered financially from when I had to postpone my opening weekend in the fall. I could pay Meredith back."

Lillian slid off her stool and wrapped an arm around Becca. "Stop worrying. They'll love your inn and you guys. And they *are* normal," Lillian insisted.

A soft, odd sound pinged.

"What was that?" Becca asked.

All three of them looked around and patted their pockets.

The odd noise sounded again.

Becca's voice got higher, "Please tell me my house hasn't been bugged again."

Lillian was digging in the satchel she had brought. "It's me! We're good."

Tucker eyed the device she pulled out, frowning. "Isn't that your secure phone? Why do you still have it?"

Lillian thumbed a few commands. "It's protocol. That's odd, it's Grace. She never uses this line." Lillian looked up from her phone. "I should take this."

Lillian disappeared down the hall.

Becca watched her go. "Any chance that was a butt dial?"

Tucker shook his head. "I doubt it."

Becca looked thoughtful. "Six months ago, I couldn't have imagined the shit storm we would go through, nor that we would be hanging out with secret agent types and apparently royalty. Hey, did I thank you for filling in for Roman?"

Tucker rolled his eyes. "Like a hundred times."

"Good." She pulled a note from her pocket and handed it to him. "Can I bug you to pick this stuff up when you do your shopping?"

Tucker took the list, scanning it. "No problem. And stop worrying. Everything will be fine. I'll cook and bake their socks off. I'll be fabulously charming—"

"Oh, no." Becca was shaking her head vigorously. "Do not be charming. Their clothes need to stay on. Do not sleep with either of them."

Tucker held up his hands. "Woah, that escalated fast."

"You know what I mean. You're like catnip to single women. Please, don't sleep with them. This could be a game changer for me—*oh my god, Dad's still out there.* What if he comes back and tries to hurt everyone again?"

Becca pressed a hand to her chest, and her eyes were as round as saucers. "This is it, I'm finally cracking."

Tucker snapped his fingers in front of Becca's face.

It did the trick.

She swatted his hand away, indignant. "Are you seriously snapping your fingers at me?"

He cracked a smile, straightening. "It worked, didn't it? And Lillian's covert friends made this place a citadel. Ever think that might be why their princess is spending Christmas here and not somewhere else?"

"You mean it's not because I have the coolest eco-inn worthy of the most fabulous royal guests?"

"That, too," Tucker was quick to reply.

"I can work with that." Becca paused. "Good pep talk. You're right. There is no way Dad can screw this up."

Tucker's phone pinged with a new email.

Becca picked up the box of decorations. "I'm going to go freshen up those guest rooms. Maybe I'll hold off on the tree in case Lillian's friends want to help trim it."

"Good call." Once alone, Tucker wiped his hands on a tea towel and opened his email. It was surveillance video from the take-out restaurant across from the impound lot and his first real lead.

Tucker played the video. A man could be seen driving his father's car out of the impound lot. He paused the video and zoomed in, scrutinizing the image, then took a screenshot.

Lillian walked back into the kitchen, and Tucker slid his phone into his back pocket, asking, "Everything okay?"

"I'm not sure. Grace will be coming later." Her gaze dropped to the manilla envelope on the large island counter. "Bloody hell, I forgot to give Becca the photo, too."

"What photo?"

Lillian picked up the envelope and slid a printed picture out. "This one. Becca asked me for a copy."

Tucker picked up the photo. It was a picture of Colt, Gabe, and Savannah. Gabe wasn't prone to smiling, but he was looking at Savannah in pure bliss, and she was looking just as enraptured. Colt was standing next to them, laughing.

"Is this from my dad and Meredith's wedding?"

Lillian nodded. "I was surprised Becca wanted a copy of it, you know, considering you two weren't invited."

"Becca is pragmatic and has zero tolerance for drama. A candid picture that turned out this good? She wouldn't care where it was from."

"It is a lovely photo."

Tucker studied the photogenic picture. In the background, a man could be seen.

"Do you know who this is?"

Lillian leaned forward. "No, but I wasn't there. I hadn't met Colt yet."

An uneasy feeling surfaced. Tucker pulled out his phone and the screenshot of the video he had just taken.

It was the same man.

# Chapter Sixteen

Thorsen handed Grace a small packet. "This will have everything you need. Flying commercial sucks, but you won't get dead. You and I are the only ones on the planet that know that alias. Keep it that way. And your hat on or your hood up whenever you go near CCTV."

They were sitting at the minuscule table in the cabin of a boat moored in a small, private marina. The sound of water lapping was soft, the rhythmic bobbing soothing. Beyond the breaker wall, though, Grace heard the restless North Atlantic.

She gave Thorsen a weak smile.

Grace hadn't been able to shake the insistent feeling of *wrongness* when she was set to board the plane, going so far as getting physically sick. She would be dead right now if she hadn't heeded her body's warning.

Dead like the pilots and crew.

"My family thinks I was on that plane, don't they?"

Thorsen nodded. "The queen was in the room at headquarters."

Grace's eyes rounded. "Whatever for?"

"She wanted to speak with you." He hesitated. "And marry you off before the grand duke does."

Grace stared hard at a knot in the wood paneling behind Thorsen's left shoulder, willing herself not to feel so betrayed.

Thorsen placed his hand on her arm. "The investigation will be quick. They'll know soon that you're alive."

His hand was warm, a safe harbor in her stormy life. She pulled her arm back, reluctant to lean on him any more than she had to.

"I'd be safer if everyone thought I was dead, wouldn't I?"

Thorsen nodded, solemn.

"But then palace protocols would be put in place, including succession."

He nodded again. Everyone knew her sisters were obedient to the grand duke.

Grace looked out the starboard window. The waning crescent moonlight flickered softly on the surface of the water in the protected marina. "I called Lillian like you asked."

"She'll know something's up."

Grace turned to Thorsen. "Can I tell her what's going on?"

His eyes were serious. "I would trust Lillian with my life. I just don't want to have to trust her with yours."

"She's one of my best friends."

"And someone connected to the palace tried to blow you up."

Grace swallowed. "Think it's him?"

"I don't want to."

"That's not what I asked."

Thorsen tapped the table. "Your grandfather is political and traditional—"

"And I have never fit inside his patriarchal box."

"No, you haven't. His loss, Gracie."

Her grandfather would never think so.

"My grandfather's supporters are saying the explosion was staged, a ploy to sway the elections." Grace's stomach churned. "Someone tried to murder me, and they're twisting it into their political game. My life is not a goddamn game, I'm not a fucking toy."

"Everything is political," he said quietly. "You know that, Gracie."

"Well, it shouldn't be." She paused. "Maybe I shouldn't go, I mean, the election is so close."

"You're not on the ballot, Gracie, they're not voting for you. You're heir to the throne, it would be irresponsible to knowingly stay in harm's way. Until we have this threat neutralized, you've got to keep your head down."

Thorsen pulled a large file out of the duffel bag at his feet. "Read these."

Grace moved to put the file into her backpack, but he stopped her. "I meant now."

His impatience was telling.

He was worried.

She opened the file, and forty minutes later, she knew more about the Tanner Family than she did about her own.

"This is eerily detailed." And tragic.

"Lillian ordered an INCEPT check when she started spending more time with Colt and his family. That's a very deep dive. We've amended it to include the more recent events."

Grace looked up. "Can I get one?"

"Let's get to the bottom of whoever is trying to murder you first. Then we can see about finding your dad."

"I have a dad," Grace corrected.

"Sorry, I meant your biological father."

Her chest tightened. "I know you did. I should be the one apologizing. Everything is just—" She didn't finish. Grace might be spinning fairy tales but wondered if the sense of disconnect she had always felt with her family would go away if she knew who her biological father was.

A tall order, indeed.

She looked down at the file. "Is this legit?"

Thorsen nodded.

"Lillian's father-in-law is suspected of setting up his oldest son to be ambushed while an agent for Canada, he tried to murder and burn down his new wife, his daughter, and her fiancé, and then frame his daughter's fiancé for the whole thing, and was also connected to the man who shot his police detective son?"

"Correct."

"And he's been missing ever since?"

"Yes, there is a Canada-wide warrant out for his arrest, though I'm not sure why Interpol hasn't been looped in. Bruce Tanner is known to have international criminal associates."

Grace gave an involuntary shiver. She had felt disloyal, thinking her grandfather could possibly want to harm her, yet Bruce Tanner had ruthlessly terrorized his own family.

"Why has Lillian's sister-in-law's eco-inn been cleared, then?" Grace asked.

"I suspect the dad is dead. Bruce Tanner is not the type to go to ground. The eco-inn is secure. Lillian's grandmother wouldn't let her stay otherwise."

Dame Maighread Kensington was a force to be reckoned with. The matriarch was careful and overprotective of her granddaughters. Her involvement explained Thorsen's willingness for Grace to set foot anywhere near the family.

Thorsen was looking at her oddly.

"What?"

"You going to caress that file all night?"

Grace looked down. She had been tracing her finger over Tucker Tanner's file. The fourth kid. His story pulled at her.

Reluctantly, she added it to the stack and slid the pile back over to Thorsen.

She asked, "Who are my allies?"

He gave her an inscrutable look before answering. "You've got good instincts. If you get into any trouble, Detective Tucker Tanner's your guy. Officer Jason Chasseur is solid, too. I trust either of them more than I trust Gabe Tanner—he's a wild card. I trust Lillian's Colt and Becca Tanner, but neither of them is in law enforcement."

"You don't trust Gabe?"

"I don't think he's come to terms with his father's treachery and likely blames himself. Lillian and Gabe aren't keen on each other, but when Colt was kidnapped, they worked together fine. Gabe's sense of duty is tied up in the family and now his girlfriend, Savannah. But I doubt he'll be a problem. Gabe and Savannah live in Toronto."

"Got it, he's a maybe, under the right circumstances," Grace said.

Thorsen picked up another folder. "We like Colt Tanner. He brought Lillian back from the brink after Fernando incinerated her life."

Grace raised an eyebrow. "*Incinerated* wasn't in the report."

"I'm paraphrasing. What he did was unconscionable, and I'm protective of anyone you care about."

She dropped her gaze to the tabletop, her cheeks warm.

Thorsen shuffled papers. "When Colt's not getting your jaded best friend to fall in love with him, he's training horses, teaching bull riding, and working as a mountain guide." Thorsen looked up. "He punched a grizzly that was attempting to maul him."

Grace smiled even as a twinge of envy sparked. As happy as she was for Lillian, Grace couldn't help feeling left behind. Flawed, even. Before, she and Lillian could commiserate on their complicated relationships with men. Now, everything had changed. Being happy did that. Lillian was over the moon in love.

Neutrally, Grace said, "This family sounds interesting."

"Colt's an ally. He was kidnapped by Fernando's crew and stayed alive. He thinks quickly on his feet, and his moral compass is pointed straight. And if you have any backcountry questions, go to him."

Grace wouldn't have time for the backcountry. She would be too busy trying to find out who wanted her dead. And her biological father.

Thorsen picked up another file. "Becca Tanner, that's whose eco-inn you'll be staying at. By all accounts, she's solid. She kept her head and didn't get dead when some nasty guys made their criminal base camp in her backyard or when her father tried to torch her and her fiancé. Her fiancé, Jason Chasseur, is an RCMP officer. He's been known to bend the rules if the reason is good enough. He follows his own compass, but it points straight. He's loyal to Becca, and his mom, Rose. I trust him more than Gabe." Thorsen gave her an inscrutable look again. "That leaves us with Tucker. He's unofficially tracking his father down. From his file, I'm guessing, like Gabe, Tucker blames himself for not seeing the signs about their father. It might get ugly if the father really is dead."

"What do you mean?"

Thorsen pulled out the last file. "You can't ask a ghost *why*." He hesitated. "Or seek vengeance, not that I'm assuming anyone would."

"Oh."

Thorsen held up an image from the next file. "Bruce fathered a son with one of his mistresses. Tanner Stone has never returned contact with his half-siblings," he pulled out another image of an older woman, "and Meredith, the second wife, is at an undisclosed location. She's terrified of her new husband."

Grace frowned. "Sounds like a rather grim Christmas for the Tanners."

Thorsen agreed.

Grace leaned closer. "Do you have a better photo of Tanner Stone? That one is pretty grainy."

"I'm sure I can get one. Why?"

"Tanner Stone looks familiar." She sat back then. "I'm not sure, it might be nothing."

Grace stared at the image, but she couldn't remember where she thought she had seen him before.

# Chapter Seventeen

"Thorsen, to what do I owe the pleasure?" Randolph looked up from the book he was reading.

He sat in one of the two wingback chairs in front of the fireplace in the master study, a tumbler of scotch within reach next to the reading lamp on the small seventeenth-century side table. It wasn't a palace, but his father's home was more than comfortable.

Thorsen pulled his gaze from scanning the room. "Princess Grace's plane blew up."

Randolph eyed him. "She wasn't on it."

"You seem sure."

"Was she?" Randolph asked.

Thorsen hesitated. "No."

"Where is she now?"

"Safe."

Randolph simply nodded before resting the book in his lap and reaching for his scotch. "Do sit down. Your looming is distracting." He took a long sip and waited for his son to settle.

Frowning, Thorsen sat in the adjacent wingback. "It's an inside job, Dad. Who wants to harm the princess?"

His father set the tumbler down, remaining silent.

Thorsen pressed, "Dad, what's going on?"

His father looked at him. "I could ask you the same thing. Perhaps I should have some time in the last eight years."

Thorsen stilled. "What's that's supposed to me?"

His father steepled his fingers. "It is one thing for you and Her Highness to have a discreet liaison. My boy, you'd hardly be the first servant to find his way into a royal bed. However, it is quite another for the grand duke to find out. He has rules."

Thorsen watched his father, neither confirming nor denying the damning words.

His father's voice was unusually gentle when he said, "Son, I know you care for her, but she is *off limits*. Dallying with her only puts her in the grand duke's cross-hairs."

Thorsen sat back as fear iced in his belly. He would never forgive himself if he had placed the princess in danger.

His father continued, "Your Gracie has made quite a political splash. Her secular, left-leaning inclinations are increasingly favored. They are also at direct odds with the grand duke's. She is a liability to him. When she gains favor, he loses ground. He wants blood. Hers." His father's voice lowered. "I'm telling you, son, leave her alone."

Thorsen had left her alone for months.

Randolph watched him. "Grandfather or not, he is a danger to her. He's fanatical about bloodlines, and if she is dallying with you, she is directly violating royal and church tradition."

"Speaking of that—"

"Yes, I heard about the grand duke's outburst."

"Princess Grace has been unable to access her birth certificate or her parents' marriage record. Why were the records sealed?"

"That is need-to-know," his father answered.

"You're not head of palace security anymore, I am. Why the fuck don't I need to know?"

His father gave him a steely look. "Because I made a promise."

Thorsen knew that look. His father wouldn't budge unless someone's life were at stake.

"Final answer?"

Randolph gave a single nod.

Thorsen shook his head. "You'd jeopardize Grace's safety for a decades-old promise?"

"This is a hornet's nest, son. Promise me you won't open it."

Thorsen would do no such thing.

His face must have said as much because his father implored, "Believe me, this is in everybody's best interests. Leave it alone."

Thorsen stood. "We're done here."

Randolph stood, too. "You don't know what you're kicking over."

"Then tell me," Thorsen snapped.

His father looked torn. "I've never given you reason not to trust me."

"You just did."

Randolph hesitated. "Very well." He lowered himself back into his wingback. "Sit down, and I'll tell you."

Thorsen dropped into his chair. When his father was done, Thorsen was stunned. "Three decades ago, the grand duke ordered you to murder the queen's American boyfriend?"

"You have to remember, he was king then, and an old school one at that, and the queen was but a princess. She had accompanied her father to Texas for an oil partners summit meeting, and while the king was making deals, she met her young cowboy." Randolph shook his head. "You should have seen those two together. I've never been accused of being a romantic, but even I could see their love was true."

"Seriously, murder? What the fuck was he thinking?"

"He wasn't. Our job is to protect the crown and country, which includes from themselves. Besides the obvious ethical implications, if it had ever gotten out, the blowback would have been swift and severe. An American citizen being murdered because a European princess fell in love with him?" Randolph threw up his hands. "Beyond foolish."

"And morally wrong," Thorsen added dryly.

"Obviously." His father shook his head. "I did what I always did. I took care of it. As far as the king knew, the kid perished in a vehicle accident. As far as the kid was concerned, the love of his life walked out without a backward glance, eager to find wealthier pastures. It wasn't kind, and heartbroken was better than dead. But the king could be paranoid, and I didn't want him to look for the kid's family or something and find out the cowboy yet lived. I arranged for the kid to receive an irresistible job offer in Canada's cattle country, and he settled there permanently. I've kept tabs on him ever since."

"And that's why Dame Kensington sent her granddaughters to Canada. She knew the area was already vetted because of your ongoing surveillance when Lillian Kensington had a double agent trying to murder her."

Randolph nodded, his eyes cautious.

Thorsen pressed. "How did Dame Kensington know?"

"That is need to know."

"Too late. I know you and Maighread are," he watched his father's eyes, "make that *were* in a relationship."

His father's eyes rounded ever so slightly, and Thorsen hurried to reassure him. "I told no one."

Relief flooded his father's eyes. "I owe you, son."

Thorsen shook his head. "We both know the danger of pressure points." He hesitated. "Grace deserves to know who her biological father is."

Randolph blew out a breath. "I know."

Pain twisted through Thorsen. "She trusted you. When were you going to tell her?"

"I don't know," Randolph said quietly. "This will blow everything up."

"And rightfully so. When he was king, the grand duke should have thought of the consequences when he ordered you to murder her father." Thorsen shook his head. "I still can't believe he would expect you to do something so brutal."

"My boy, they are different from us." His dad briefly touched Thorsen's arm. "Always remember that."

"But by then, the grand duke had spent decades with you. How could he not know you, not know your character?"

Randolph picked up his scotch. "We are *servants*. It wouldn't have crossed his mind I hadn't obeyed."

Thorsen felt the pressing weight of generations serving an oft-dubious royal family.

It wasn't a comfortable feeling.

"She trusted you. This will crush her."

Randolph nodded, sober. "I know. She's a bright light on the dark night our country has become. Her mom used to be like that."

Skeptical, Thorsen shrugged. "If you say so."

His dad looked at him sharply. "She was."

Thorsen watched as his father took a drink.

He had to tell Grace the truth. In person. This was going to crush her.

# Chapter Eighteen

The house was quiet. The electric kettle clicked off, sounding unusually harsh in the silent kitchen. Tucker made a mug of tea. While it steeped, he stacked the last pan from the fresh batch of brownies he had made and dried his hands on the kitchen towel. The meager weekend bookings for the inn hadn't spilled into the weekdays yet, and the dinner crowd always cleared out early.

Becca and Jason were upstairs, and Christopher kept to himself in his staff cabin.

Tucker was the only one around.

His gaze briefly caught on the bottle of whiskey on the counter. He hesitated before grabbing the steaming mug of herbal tea instead. Tucker needed a clear head when he checked security footage later.

His first real lead.

Now he just had to find out who the man from the photo was.

Tucker flicked off the overhead light and turned on the stove's night light before stepping into his boots by the back door. He shrugged into his jacket and headed outside into the crisp night air.

Instead of heading straight to his barn loft apartment, he stopped on the wrap-around porch. Full dark came early to the mountains in winter, and it was a clear night.

As he stood at the railing, sipping his tea, stars blinked into view. It was a trick of the light and night. As his eyes adjusted, the stars multiplied before him, and the Milky

Way glittered into view. The starlights twinkled, casting their evening magic.

Tucker rested his mug on the railing, staring. How could something be so beautiful when the world was so ugly?

He didn't deserve the accolades from the police chief. What kind of detective didn't notice his own father was a monster?

With not quite a steady hand, Tucker picked up his tea and took a long drink. He stared at the cup thinking he should have gone for the whiskey.

Long moments passed as he drank his tea and grappled with a lifetime of cruel memories. There must have been earlier signs. What had he missed?

Suddenly, a sensation whispered into his awareness.

Tucker knew he was paranoid as hell these days, but in a heartbeat, the emotions that had been tormenting him shifted to a razor-sharp focus.

He was not alone.

The ceramic mug he held wasn't his weapon of choice, but it would do. Too bad it wasn't still filled with hot tea, that would have made a nice surprise. He was still recovering from an injury, but he was faster than most and a hell of a lot grumpier.

Surreptitiously he coiled himself, ready for battle.

# Chapter Nineteen

Grace pulled out her travel backpack and quietly closed the rental vehicle's door. She had opted for a pickup truck in an effort to fit in more and had parked it on a distant side road.

She checked the map app on her mobile and started walking.

Several minutes later, Grace stood in a large ranch yard in the evening quiet. Colored Christmas lights were strung around several trees in the front yard, while white Christmas lights hung with evergreen boughs and wide ribbon scalloped the walk-around porch and lined the roofline.

The effect was lovely, even fanciful in its festive cheer.

Lillian's sister-in-law had a beautiful inn.

Silhouettes of solar panels could be seen on the inn's large roof, as well as a handful of residential-sized wind turbines, their blades a darker shade of night, as they stood guard beyond the cluster of trees ringing the yard. In the distance stood mountain peaks. Even in darkness, their pale snow-kissed crowns were visible.

Mountains always made her feel better, oddly safer. Like she could borrow some of their stoney strength, even as they towered over her. She could use a top-up. The last several days had been truly awful.

Grace shouldered her backpack and headed up the front steps, then faltered. A single, dim light could be seen through the large front windows. Lillian's friend wasn't expecting her for another couple of days. She should knock on the door, vaguely mention changing timetables or something.

But she hesitated, needing to collect herself.

Spotting a porch swing, Grace walked over, setting her bag down before she lowered herself onto the wide seat.

It rocked gently under her weight, and she smiled. It was such a small thing, but the easy sway calmed her stretched nerves as she stared at the jewels of the night sky. The rural yard afforded a precious view of forest and mountain silhouettes punctuated by starlight. The view felt otherworldly, painfully beautiful.

She burrowed deeper into her warm hooded sweatshirt, pulled up the hood, and quietly rocked. The inn's wrap-around porch offered some protection from the clear, cold night. Her jacket, still in the car, would have been more comfortable, but she didn't want to break the spell.

Grace crossed her arms. Her mom was like those stars; beautiful, radiant, and equally as impossible to reach.

Frowning, her peace broken, Grace stood and walked to the railing. The longer she looked, the more stars appeared. It was a trick of the night, daring a stargazer to look deeper. Maybe space was deep enough to catch her questions and throw them back at her, answered.

With her arms wrapped tight around herself and her hood up to spare some warmth, she paced along the porch and turned the corner around the house.

A rough hand clamped over her mouth. Her shriek had nowhere to go. Surprise paralyzed her for a fraction of a second before years of training, and a controlled rage kicked in. With predatory speed and force, Grace fired her elbow into her attacker's ribs before she shot her hand up and smashed it into his face.

The rib shot had taken him by surprise, but he recovered quicker than she would have hoped, and he ducked to avoid her second whip-shot hand.

He was fast, but Grace was faster. She snapped her heel up, connecting with his balls.

Her assailant was a fast learner. The bastard deftly rammed his thigh to intercept her second crotch shot. He spun her around with brute force, his large hands painfully holding her upper arms in place, and Grace felt fear race through her. What if she couldn't outmaneuver him?

The barest hint of sweetness tickled her nose, and she sniffed, surprised.

"Are you the brownie guy?"

The man was breathing hard, his vice-like grip still squeezing her upper arms.

Grace tipped her head back, shaking off her concealing hood.

The man immediately released her, taking several steps back and swearing.

Grace shook out her shoulders and rotated her wrists.

He immediately stepped forward, alarmed. "I hurt you."

Grace shrugged off his obvious concern. "Relax, tiger. It's habit."

"Tucker," he corrected.

"Tucker," she repeated. His name felt soft on her lips. "You *are* the brownie guy. Tuck Tanner, right?"

He steepled his hands in front of his face. "Please tell me I didn't just assault my soon-to-be sister-in-law's best friend?"

"That's me." She gave a small wave. "You forgot, princess."

"What?" He looked like he was going to be sick.

"Never mind. Call me Grace."

He stared at her incredulously. "I almost cracked a mug over your head."

"Why?"

"I thought you were a prowler."

"Do you always play worse-case-scenario?"

"Only the last few months." His hand went to his chest, and Grace remembered his file. Three bullets to the chest. If it hadn't happened in a hospital, he would have bled out.

He dropped his hand when he noticed her looking. "I thought you weren't supposed to be here for another few days."

Grace shrugged. "Plans changed." She looked closer at him. "Did I hurt you?"

He stepped back and crossed his arms in front of his chest. "I'm fine."

She stepped forward. "No, you're not. You just winced. Come on, let me see."

"Did anyone ever tell you you're pushy?"

Grace snorted. "Perk of being a princess."

"Yeah, Lillian mentioned that."

His tone brought her up short. "You don't like me."

He blew out a breath. "I don't like anyone these days."

"Why not?"

"Seriously? Did we not just cover pushy?"

"Yeah, just a heads-up, I'm not anyone's idea of a proper princess. Quiet, well-behaved ornaments can stuff it."

They stood staring at each other.

Finally, Tucker's expression softened a fraction.

It was enough.

"Let's try this again." Grace held out his hand. "Hi, I'm Grace, Lillian's friend. Sorry, I'm early."

His sigh was almost a grumble, but he met her halfway. "I'm Tucker. Nice to meet you."

His hand was larger than hers and warmer. The contact felt oddly intimate on the dark winter night.

"Enchanté," she said softly.

He looked startled. Grace felt the barest of squeezes of her hand and wondered if she had imagined it.

"Le, le plaisir … est á moi?"

She smiled at him. "The pleasure is all mine."

He pulled his hand back and rubbed his jawline. "Sorry, French class was a long time ago."

"I thought Canada was bilingual?"

"On paper, yeah."

"Got it."

"Why are you here early?"

She looked out across the ranch lawn. Clouds were rolling in, playing peek-a-boo with the starlight, and a few snowflakes had started to fall. They caught what little light there was, creating a soft glow oddly punctuated by the fragmented starlight.

She held out her hand across the porch railing, catching snowflakes. "Is it always this pretty here?"

Tucker was still looking at her. "I hadn't noticed."

Snowflakes melted on her outstretched bare hand. "I couldn't wait to start my Canadian holiday."

He raised an eyebrow.

When she didn't say more, he asked, "Why did you call me the brownie guy?"

She pulled her hand back. "You ask a lot of questions. Lillian express shipped me homemade brownies last month. I'm guessing you're *that* Tucker? The urban one of the family."

"I can ride a damn horse," he said defensively. "And I'm actually a police officer. Not that anyone cares."

"I know you're an officer. Detective, isn't it?"

"Lillian told you?"

"Something like that." Grace was not mentioning she'd read an entire file on him and his family. "What are you doing out here?"

"Helping my sister out."

Grace's eyes widened. "She needs a detective?"

"A chef, actually."

"I see." She didn't, but the details seemed irrelevant at the moment. "Did I hurt you?"

"You've got a hell of a back elbow." He rubbed the side of his torso. "I'm surprised you didn't crack one of my ribs."

"I once cracked one of Thorsen's."

He dropped his hand. "Who's Thorsen?"

She didn't want to think of Thorsen right now.

"My hand-to-hand combat trainer and the head of royal security."

He held her gaze longer than polite. Could he tell?

But Tucker just turned and looked out across the yard. "Where is your detail? Shouldn't they have come running when I attacked you?"

"They would have been here if I needed them." They weren't, but she wasn't telling him that.

Tucker still eyed the dark yard.

"Let me check your ribs." Grace placed her hand on the side of his torso. "Does this hurt?"

When Tucker's whole body stilled, she snapped her head up. "Does it hurt?"

He slowly shook his head.

"What about this?" She gently pressed again, applying more pressure.

When his breath hitched, she stopped.

He lifted his hand, covering hers, and another unexpected spark shot through her body.

Grace stared at him. Her body felt like it was cracking awake, and she was grateful for the darkness.

"He taught you well."

Grace blinked. "Who?"

"The royal guard guy."

Grace pulled her hand back. She had desired Thorsen and cared deeply for him, but he had never generated anything like the electrical storm that was currently shooting through her body.

"Did I say something wrong?"

She crossed her arms. "Of course not."

"What's wrong?" Tucker asked. "I already feel like ass for assaulting you. Could I fuck this up any more?"

Grace smiled. The guy was refreshing. "I didn't realize you were here. I would have announced myself if I had known." Or quite possibly run back to her rental truck, not ready or unwilling to face anyone.

"I just … needed to collect myself before I knocked on your sister's door. Becca, right?"

He nodded. "Why did you need to collect yourself?"

"You don't miss a beat, do you?"

"Sometimes, I do." His voice dipped. This guy had layers, and for a brief moment, she felt like she did, too, like she could be worth getting to know for herself, crown not included.

"Tucker—" Her secure mobile pinged, interrupting her.

When she saw the message, she made a face.

Tucker asked, "What's wrong?"

She glanced up. "An Australian special agent has been spotted nearby."

"So?"

Grace didn't want to stumble across any agent, international or otherwise. "He was working."

Tucker glanced down and suddenly grabbed her phone. "Who is this?" His voice was harsh when he repeated, "*Who is this?*"

Grace swallowed a sharp rebuke at his brazenness. He was clearly shaken. "I don't know. Some Australian operative. Why?"

Tucker held up the phone. "This guy was at my dad's wedding."

"Why is that weird?"

"A man was murdered at that wedding. No one was ever charged, and no one knows who this guy is or why he was there."

She tried to sound shocked, like she hadn't poured over his particular file, over and over. "Someone was murdered at your dad's wedding?"

Tucker's eyes were bleak when he looked up from the phone. "Yes. And my dad tried to murder my sister, her fiancé, and our stepmom a couple of months ago. He's missing. I'm tracking the monster down." Tucker shook her mobile at her. "This guy's somehow connected." Tucker looked at the image again, frowning. He held the phone out to her. "Does this guy look over six feet tall to you?"

Grace shrugged. "Maybe? Why?"

"He could be the same guy who picked up my dad's impounded car." Tucker blew out a breath. "Or I'm seeing ghosts everywhere."

Grace looked closer at the photo. Where had she seen that man before?

# Chapter Twenty

Tucker reluctantly handed Lillian's princess friend, Grace, back her phone.

"I'm sorry about your dad," she said softly.

"Yeah. Me, too." Remembering his manners, he added, "Sorry I snapped at you." Embarrassed, he looked down. "I've been doing that a lot lately."

"Want to talk about it? You don't know me, I can be an anonymous shoulder."

"To cry on?" Tucker cracked a smile. "Guys don't do shoulders. Not for crying anyway."

Her face fell. "Right. Sorry."

Tucker eyed the beautiful woman in front of him. "You apologize a lot."

"You sound like Lillian."

Tucker smiled. "Thank you, I think."

"It's a compliment." Her eyebrows pulled together. "You respect her."

Tucker exhaled a heavy sigh. "I didn't want to, not at first. She blew into our lives like a fucking tornado. She shook things up, faced our skeletons head on, grabbed them by the throat, really, then dared us to do the same."

Grace's expression softened. "That's Lillian. She's the bravest person I know. Your brother, bless his heart, cracked the tough shell Lillian had wrapped herself tight in."

"The feeling is mutual. I've never seen Colt so happy."

A companionable silence fell between them. Soft snow was accumulating on the porch railing, and Grace traced her fingers through it. Hesitant, she asked, "Can I trust you?"

That question, in that tone, set off alarm bells. Point-blank, Tucker said, "That depends. Do you wish me or my family harm?"

Her head shot up. "Of course not."

"Then you can trust me." He waited.

"I have to trust someone, and Lillian's not here." Her voice had thickened with emotion, possibly fear. Instinctively, Tucker stepped forward but stopped, not wanting to scare her further.

Softly, he asked, "What's going on?"

"How do you do that? You just went from suspicious to accommodating. What changed?"

"You're scared, right?"

Grace took a step back, looking around. "What do you know?"

"Nothing, I'm asking. I should have noticed immediately."

She gave him a disbelieving look. "It's dark out."

"So?"

"So I can barely see your blatant facial expressions, let alone the subtle ones."

"It's my job to know. I should have known," Tucker insisted.

Grace hesitated. "You'll help me?"

"Do you need help?" Tucker asked.

She crossed her arms again. "The fewer people who know I'm here, the better. Is there anywhere I can stay that is not in the main building?"

"Like the staff bunk cabin? Becca would shoot me."

Grace started wringing her hands. "What if you asked Lillian to ask her not to?"

"What kind of trouble are you in?"

She held his gaze. Finally, she said, "I pissed off someone powerful, someone close to me. There's a big election coming up, and there have been two attempts on my life. If I did this right, no one knows I'm here. Still okay with helping?"

*Aw, hell.*

Tucker rubbed his jaw. "My apartment is in the barn loft."

"I'll take it!"

"Wait a sec, I live there, too. If I move into one of the staff cabins, Becca and the staff will be suspicious."

Grace shrugged. "I don't take up a lot of room. I'll sleep on the couch." She eyed him. "Or the floor. I can make the floor work, too."

"You're not sleeping on the floor." What asshole would make a woman sleep on the floor?

She pressed her hands together, smiling. "A gentleman. So, *there are* a few left."

The way Grace was smiling at him suddenly made his dick take notice.

*Do not be charming. Do not sleep with them.*

Tucker frowned. "I'm going to regret this, aren't I?"

"I'll be no trouble at all. You'll barely know I'm here."

Tucker wouldn't bet anything important on it. The woman in front of him was elemental, impossible to ignore. "Where are your bags?"

She spun around and darted down the porch and around the front corner. Within moments, she had returned, a single backpack slung over her shoulder.

"You didn't have to run. I won't go back on my word."

"Good," she said, her quickened breath billowing in the chilly night. "I'll hold you to that."

Tucker was pretty sure he'd let her hold any part of him she wanted.

He reached for her bag, and with the barest hesitation, she let him take it.

"This is it?"

She nodded.

"You pack light."

"You mean for a princess?" Grace asked, an edge to her voice.

"Something like that." Tucker turned. "Follow me."

He headed in the opposite way around the wraparound porch.

"Woah, is that a garden?" Grace asked.

He glanced where she was looking. He could just make out one of Becca's oversized gardens. Several inches of snow blanketed his sister's raised garden beds and pathways. "Such as it is."

Tucker noticed a flicker of light and abruptly stopped.

Grace bumped into his back and immediately clutched his shoulders, catching herself. She whispered, "Sorry. Why did we stop?"

Tucker turned his head, putting his index finger to his lips, before pointing at the kitchen window where his sister's fiancé stood in the kitchen at the sink. Jason was naked from the waist up.

Grace leaned forward, her lips a hairsbreadth from his neck, and Tucker leaned ever so slightly back and held his breath.

Grace breathed into his ear, "Your sister has impeccable taste."

It took a second for her words to register, effectively dousing him, and he muttered, "*Jesus.*"

"What?" Grace whispered back. "Seriously, do all Canadian men look like that? Because *daaamn.*"

Tucker was still picking up the pieces of his ego when she said, "Don't look at me like that. You've got a mirror, and Colt was the *Archambeau* model, for god sakes." She pointed to the window as Jason walked out of the kitchen, shutting off the light behind him. "No one can argue *that* isn't magnificent." She whistled low. "You go, Becca."

Tucker turned. "What's *Archambeau*?"

Grace's hands flew to her mouth. "Shit, I wasn't supposed to mention that."

Tucker waited, but Grace stayed silent.

*You've got a mirror.*

He gave her one of his best smiles, the kind he had been told melted women. Grace backed up, waving her finger in front of him. "No, no. That's not going to work."

A thrill shot through him. He pulled out his phone, thumbing in *A-r-c-h-a-m-b-e-a-u.*

"What are you doing?" Grace went to snatch the phone from him.

He dodged, turning his shoulder to her. Her backpack acted as a barrier, helping him keep his phone in his possession. Tucker stared at the screen. "What the fuck?"

Colt, his professional bull riding older brother, was a model for a major high-end European cologne. Tucker stared at Grace. "How did I not know about this?"

Defensively, she said, "Colt wanted to keep it quiet. I recognized him as soon as she sent a picture of the two of them. He's kinda huge in Europe."

Tucker looked down at the pages of images of his brother.

"Please don't tell Lillian or Colt. I wasn't supposed to say anything. It slipped out."

Tucker couldn't help but tease. "Did it have anything to do with Jason's naked torso? Because I hear it's magnificent and probably hard to concentrate around—"

"Oh, stop it. Anyone who's into dudes would be flustered after seeing *that*." She tugged on the front of his shirt. "Why, what'd you have under there?" Their eyes met for several blistering seconds before Grace snatched her hand away. "That was inappropriate. I'm sorry."

Tucker tugged down his sweater before hitching her bag higher on his shoulder. "Come on. It's late, let's get you settled."

Their boots crunched on the snow as Grace followed him across the deck and back ranch yard. The snow-filled clouds had already scuttled past, and now the sky glittered again with stars, and Tucker glanced west. The dark outline of mountain peaks was subtle but visible.

He led them to the set of covered stairs on the south side of the large barn, unlocking the door at the top. "Here we are."

Grace hustled in, rubbing her hands together. "Oh, thank god, it's so warm in here."

Tucker could have kicked himself. "Why didn't you say something earlier?"

"And be considered a diva? No thanks." She was still rubbing her hands together. "I get enough fluffy princess assumptions."

Tucker's ribs and balls could attest to just how *not* fluffy this woman was. "Lady, you're about as far removed from fluffy as one can get. Guerrilla? Sure. Fluffy? No way."

Grace looked down, but not before Tucker saw her bashful smile. "That's the nicest thing anyone has ever said to me." She sounded delighted.

Tucker wasn't sure what to say to that, so he asked, "Are you hungry or anything?"

Grace shook her head.

He handed over the backpack. "The bathroom's there. Towels are in the closet behind the door. I'll just change the sheets quick."

She took her bag. "Thanks, Tuck ... for everything."

He nodded. When she excused herself and headed into the bathroom, he made quick work of changing the bedsheets, thrilled he had a clean set ready. He grabbed an extra blanket and tossed it on the couch. He heard the shower turn on. In minutes, it was off.

Christ, he took longer showers.

A few minutes later, she came out of the bathroom. She was in what looked like warm, base layer bottoms and top. Her hair was wet but combed. Quickly, she climbed into his bed.

Tucker tried to erase the image as he took his turn in the bathroom.

He dimmed the bathroom light and left the door open a sliver before making his way to the couch.

In the near total darkness, he heard Grace whisper, "Goodnight, Tuck."

"Goodnight, Grace," he whispered back and stretched out on the couch.

If Grace was aware of him, it certainly wasn't bothering her sleep. In no time, Tucker could hear the soft, steady rhythmic breathing of her sleep.

An hour later, Tucker was still awake, trying to forget the unforgettable woman sleeping mere feet away.

He rolled onto his side and curled a pillow over his ear.

It was going to be a long night.

# Chapter Twenty-One

Grace blinked awake. It was pitch black.

She heard the sound again. It was what had awakened her.

Frantic, mumbled words.

Her eyes adjusted enough for her to make out the small loft apartment. Grace propped herself up, automatically ducking when she heard the anguished cry. Pressed flat, she listened, trying to orient herself and pinpoint the threat.

Tucker was thrashing on the couch.

"*No ... no!*"

He thrashed again, then stilled.

He was in the throes of a nightmare.

When he cried out again, she couldn't stop herself. Grace slipped out of bed and tiptoed to where he lay on the couch. She spoke softly, telling him who she was before she crouched low, finding his hand. She held it and spoke softly to him, nonsensical, calming things.

He stopped thrashing about, though he was still dreaming, making incoherent sounds.

Her knees started protesting at the weird crouch, and she let her butt fall to the floor and wrapped her free arm around her knees. She never let go of his hand.

He murmured something low, and when he nuzzled her hand to his cheek, she froze.

Slowly, in the barely-there light, Grace moved her free hand up and gently brushed his temple.

Tucker exhaled a puff of air before relaxing completely. He was still asleep, though no longer gripped in a nightmare.

For long minutes, Grace held his hand, not wanting to move from where it was nestled under his cheek.

The last several days washed over her, and she finally let quiet tears roll, unhindered, down her face. She held Tuck's hand and let the fear, worry, and devastating hurt gently slip down her cheeks without judgment or containment.

Tucker stirred, then, his eyes flew open. He blinked, focusing on her so close to him. "Grace? Are you okay?"

She quickly wiped at her eyes with her free hand. "You were having a nightmare."

He caught one of her tears with his thumb. "Are you?"

She shook her head before nodding, then ducked into the crook of her elbow.

He gently pressed a kiss into her palm. It was a soft moment, and she allowed herself the pleasure of letting her fingers trace his lips.

"Grace?"

She shook her head, pressing her finger against his lips, not wanting to break the spell but knowing it was too late. He watched as she stood, and briefly, Grace hesitated. Finally, she pressed her lips to his forehead and whispered, "Goodnight, Tuck."

Their hands remained entwined until the distance between them stretched too far, and he whispered back, "Goodnight, Grace."

She slipped back into bed, pulling the covers high, and wished she was still holding his hand.

# Chapter Twenty-Two

Tucker hadn't known what to expect with royalty, but it wasn't immediate fascination and a rock-hard boner. Or the jarringly tender moments in the middle of the night. They had blown past attraction and jumped straight into a weird intimacy. Tucker didn't like it. Grace was complicated. She had held his hand and faced his nightmares, all while grappling with her own. Anything with her would be messy, and his life was already fucked.

Damn. He totally wanted her.

Strong women like her didn't tend to need or want him.

The oven timer pinged, and he pulled out the batch of fresh muffins as his sister, Becca, shuffled into the kitchen.

"Why are you up so early?" She was dressed in jeans and a flannel and headed straight for the coffee carafe, pouring herself a cup. She took a long sip and rubbed her eyes.

"It's not that early," Tucker teased, placing the muffins on a rack to cool.

She sniffed. "It smells incredible in here."

He smiled, pleased, and pushed the basket of fresh scones toward her. "Here, start with these. If you want, I can whip you up some French toast, too, or bacon and eggs."

Becca peeked into the tea towel-lined basket and snagged a fresh scone. "Who are you, and what did you do with my brother?" She sat on a stool at the large kitchen island and took a bite. "Seriously, why are you a cop when you can make magic like this?"

Tucker knew his sister didn't mean the comment as a direct hit but felt it all the same. He added the still-warm muffins to the basket of scones and mumbled, "Glad you like them."

"I *love* them." She made happy chewing noises before her face turned serious. She waited for him to look at her. "Thanks for filling in. I hope this wasn't too much of an ask."

"I think this is good for everyone," he answered quietly. He pushed the butter dish and knife closer to her. "Those taste even better with butter."

She eyed him a moment longer before picking up the knife and dutifully spreading some on her pastry. "Do you mind doing another supply run?"

"Sure."

"You'd have to take the long way. The highway is still closed. They're still clearing up that huge wreck, and a bigger storm system is expected to come in tonight and dump snow over the next three days."

"It's no problem, and you don t have to treat me with kid gloves." It was excellent, he could avoid the princess warrior curled up in his bed for several additional hours.

He picked up the basket of baked goods.

Becca's cell phone pinged.

He dropped the basket. Muffins and scones rolled across the counter.

"You were saying?" Becca asked, concern clear on her face as she helped corral the wayward pastries.

"I'm fine. Who was it?"

Becca looked at her phone before breaking into a smile. "We have two more reservations."

Relief filled him. The last several months had conditioned an annoying fear response to notifications.

He put the last breakaway scone back into the basket before wiping up the crumbs. "You'll be able to pay my outrageous salary."

"Ha ha, very funny." Becca paused. "Want a day or two off? We don't have any midweek bookings, and Roman has been giving kitchen lessons to Christopher and Radhi. As soon as I can afford it, I'm asking that woman if she'll be my general manager."

"Your new housekeeper? You're the owner, why wouldn't you manage it?"

Becca snorted. "Because Radhi's a hundred times better and faster at the day-to-day operations stuff than I am. I could focus on trail rides, the restaurant's greenhouse, and developing seasonal events. You know, the stuff I actually like doing."

Tucker hadn't really thought that much about what it took to successfully run a business, let alone how to enjoy doing it, and admitted, "I thought you were crazy, taking on such a big gamble building this place, but I was wrong. I'm proud of you. It'll work out—it is working out."

She glowed under his compliment. "Thanks, but everyone helped."

"Yeah, for someone who hates asking for help, you figured out how to delegate pretty quickly."

"Quit whining," Becca teased. "To afford Radhi and the other upgrades I want to do, I need to grow our client list."

Tucker busied himself, pouring a cup of coffee, feeling a twinge of guilt. A positive review from a public figure, like a royal princess, could put his sister's place on the map.

"Enough about me. Any news finding Dad ... Bruce? What are we supposed to call him?"

"*Jack ass* works. But no, nothing concrete yet. I've got a few leads to follow." Like the Australian operative snooping around.

"Don't forget about dinner. Our new guests arrive late afternoon. Looks like there are no food restrictions, but there are little kids."

Crap. Tucker had forgotten.

Becca added, "Christopher said he'll handle breakfast for them tomorrow morning. You can sleep in."

An image of Grace asleep in his bed flooded Tucker's head. "Sure, thanks."

His sister stood, saluting him with her coffee cup as she crossed the kitchen and headed toward her office off the back hallway. She called over her shoulder, "Make something yummy. Whatever you want."

Right. There was no menu. He had to figure out what he was going to prepare.

Tucker had first thought his sister was nuts when she had dismissed the idea of having a menu. She had lived in Germany for a few years and had taken a road trip to an agri-tourism accommodation in Italy. In the hills above the Mediterranean, she had driven her rented SUV on what she described as a goat track up the side of the arid hills and found an oasis of simple comfort and exquisite cuisine. Besides simple, comfortable accommodations, the agri-tourism venue boasted enchanting outdoor seating only, and you ate what the chef made. Apparently, the dinner had been the best meal of her life. She had chalked it up to culinary talent, as much as the only decision she was required to make was *will you be here for dinner*?

When Becca had opened her inn, she had given Roman, her chef, the instructions to make scrumptious food people would love eating. Guests were required to fill out any food allergies or sensitivities in advance, and Roman cooked just for them.

Tucker had thought she was nuts and would alienate her North American clients.

Nope. After an initial surprise, most appreciated the decadence of having someone else choose what was for dinner.

After a bit of consideration, Tucker prepped a beef roast using his sister's favorite slow-cook barbecue marinade. Squash bisque, roasted root vegetables for the adults, and homemade fries for the kids, would round out the dish. He checked their supply of fresh greens for salads and made a note to prepare his raw food apple pie.

Sarah Kades

He caught himself smiling. Staying here was good medicine. Being isolated, while so angry, had been a recipe for disaster.

He popped his head into his sister's office. She was on the phone.

He waved the list she had given and made a thumbing motion—the universal *text if you need anything else* sign.

Becca nodded, smiling, and Tucker headed back to the kitchen. He took his jacket off the door wreath Becca insisted wasn't a coat hook, and he insisted it was, and shrugged into it. He toed into his boots before looping his arm through the small basket of scones, muffins, and accouterments he had prepared, tucking a tea towel over everything. After filling two travel mugs with coffee, he headed out the back door.

His breath made large plumes as the slanting, winter morning light caught each exhale. His boots crunched on frost as he walked across the oversized back deck before heading across the yard to the small loft apartment above the newly raised barn.

He let himself in.

Then everything went black.

# Chapter Twenty-Three

Grace awoke with a start. She blinked, orienting herself. Long wooden beams stretched overhead. She propped herself up. A pale light was starting to punch through the frostwork on the outside pane of window glass.

Canada.

She had made it. Alive.

A quick look revealed the couch was empty.

Tucker.

Grace flopped back down on the bed.

That guy would be eaten alive in international espionage or politics. He was too trusting, too kind. It made her want to stay close and keep him safe, especially after those nightmares. Whatever haunted him, it wasn't pretty. Lillian's brother-in-law was a hot mess, and Grace was foolishly enchanted. Living in a fishbowl, particularly one so influenced by relentless tradition and painful church dogma, there was no wiggle room for such frivolousness. Her life was a gauntlet of command performances and unreasonable perfection, lest others call her out for not being traditional or royal enough.

Tucker was real, Grace was simply royal, and contrary to what Counsel Olsen said, Grace did know her place and filed her burgeoning attraction where it belonged, an impossible crush.

She was late checking in. Grace reached for her secure mobile and realized she had forgotten to plug it in last night. She looked at the wall socket, and her stomach clenched. She had forgotten the shiny new North American electrical adaptor on her dresser. In the palace. Why didn't she take out a billboard? *I'm in North America, come find me.*

She needed that adaptor hidden. But first, she had to charge her phone. Grace looked around but saw no charger conveniently left out. Not on the kitchen counter nor in the bathroom.

Her gaze caught on Tucker's nightstand, and she crossed the room. Hesitating, she pulled open the nightstand drawer. There was a mobile charger that would fit. And a huge box of condoms.

Grace grabbed the charger and quickly closed the drawer.

She plugged in her phone and saw three messages from Thorsen. The first was a routine check-up. The second was a news story depicting violent riots. The left blamed the right for her disappearance and called for swift justice. The right were now calling her disappearance a publicity stunt before the election mere days away. The third message, he tersely asked why she hadn't checked in yet. He could have been peeved or worried, he sounded the same either way.

Grace messaged him back.

Immediately, he responded. *Roger, that.*

She rolled her eyes at his succinct message and pulled up the image of the Australian operative. He looked taller than Tucker, though with a similar build.

Then she remembered where she had seen his likeness.

Grace heard footfalls and stark images from the news article exploded through her mind.

She stilled. It probably was Tuck, but she wasn't going to bet her life on it. She grabbed the dark gray pillowcase, dumping the pillow onto the bed, before hurdling the couch and pressing herself against the wall next to the door. Her heart was hammering, and she breathed, poised, ready.

The door opened, and she snapped the pillowcase on the intruder's head.

A surprised, aggravated noise met her antics. The figure gave a drawn-out sigh before saying a muffled, "I brought coffee."

Grace looked down, still clutching the ends of the pillowcase in a vice grip that she had wrapped around the intruder's neck. The man held two travel mugs, and looped through his arm was a tea towel-covered basket.

"Tuck?"

"The one and only. Mind unhanding me?" His reply was muffled and sounded only a little cranky.

The guy had the patience of a saint.

Grace swept the pillowcase up and over his head. She'd be embarrassed if she hadn't been so scared. "Sorry."

Tucker stood before her, blinking. His hair stood on end, and he opened and closed his jaw a few times. "Ow. Do you greet every man carrying breakfast like that?"

"Men don't bring me breakfast."

They stared at each other.

Tuck worked his jaw again. "My turn to start over. Good morning, I brought coffee and your choice of scones or muffins." He held out the basket to her.

Grace accepted it and peeked under the tea towel. Her head shot up. "You made fresh scones and muffins this morning? The sun's not even up yet."

"It's winter in the Canadian foothills, the sun takes its sweet ass time. I was hungry and thought you might be, too." Tucker handed her the other travel mug. He toed out of his boots and tossed his coat on the hook by the door. "Besides, don't you have jet lag or something?"

"I'm fine." She cradled the basket close to her chest. In her world, genuine thoughtfulness was rare. "Thank you."

She was off balance. He was helping her, not the crown. Back home, no one differentiated between her person and the crown. Save her, save the crown, hurt her, her the crown.

"It's not that big of a deal." He busied himself, taking a drink from his travel mug.

"I'm sorry I attacked you, I kind of went on autopilot."

Tucker's head came up abruptly. "You're safe here. You're safe with me."

Life had peppered him with bullet holes and catastrophic family betrayal, yet he was offering her a safe haven.

Painful, unchecked emotions flooded her, but she simply held up the basket, asking, "Breakfast?"

"Sure. The white chocolate scone has my name on it."
He walked the few steps to the small kitchen table and
took a seat, setting his phone by the basket.

Grace sat across from him, appreciating his diplomacy
and avoiding how obviously red her eyes must be with
unshed tears. His sister must have taught him well. Unless he was married.

Grace's gaze flew to his ring finger. It was bare. Still,
lots of people were married and didn't wear rings.

She busied herself with the basket, finding a warm
white chocolate treat on top. She pulled it out. "This
scone?"

He was watching her, waiting to see what she'd do.

She handed it to him with one of the cloth napkins she
had found in the basket.

He was still staring at her.

"You thought I was going to eat it, didn't you?"

"Some women would have."

"You hang out with the wrong women." Grace selected a different one for herself.

"May I?"

He was looking at her scone. She slid the cloth napkin
with her scone toward him, curious.

He split her scone in two and spread butter on each
half. "I haven't found a clotted cream I'm happy with
over here, but this butter's legit." He passed the scone
back to her. She took a bite. An unladylike sound of pleasure drummed in the back of her throat.

"*Ohmygod*, marry me now." She opened her eyes in time to see the alarm in his. "Woah, kidding, totally kidding. I am the last person to bug anyone to get married. You should see your face right now."

He dropped his gaze to the table.

Grace eyed him. "What did Lillian tell you about me?"

Tucker swallowed the bite he had taken. "That you're normal."

Grace laughed. "I am many things, but normal isn't one of them."

A smile teased the corners of his mouth. "I tried to tell her that. Why *are* you here?"

He must be good at interviewing suspects, getting them comfortable as he slipped questions in.

She diverted. "These are really good scones."

"I'm glad." Tucker took another bite. "Why are you avoiding my sister?"

"I'm avoiding everyone," Grace countered after she had swallowed her bite.

"You're not avoiding me."

"Correct. I invaded your space. I am definitely not avoiding you." Embarrassed, she realized her voice sounded like a breathless whisper.

Tucker was staring at her lips.

Grace's on-off-again relationship with Thorsen had done little to prepare her for the molten man sitting in front of her.

Tucker shot up out of his seat. "I need to run to town for my sister."

"Can I come?"

He moved behind his chair, putting a physical barrier between them. "I can pick up anything you need."

Grace was pretty sure she wanted what was standing right in front of her. She stood. He parried. For every move she made, he kept a substantial distance between them, no small feet in the small space. The blatant rejection stung.

Grace held up her hands. "You can stop skittering away, I'm not trying to assault you." *Do you have any gear besides kick-ass?* "Mind if I use your shower?"

Tucker stopped retreating. "Of course."

Grace grabbed her backpack and headed for the only door in the small apartment.

"How did you get here?" Tucker called after her.

She stopped and turned.

"I didn't see a vehicle," Tucker said. "Did you take a cab or ride share?"

"I left my rental truck on one of the side gravel roads and walked the rest."

"At night in an unknown location?"

Grace shrugged, holding her backpack to her chest. "It's a grid road, isn't it? Kind of hard to get lost if you know how a grid works."

Another one of those ghosts of a smile touched his lips. "Right."

"Thanks for letting me stay here," Grace said, unsure what else to say.

Tucker crossed to the small kitchen counter. He pulled out a sticky pad and scribbled something on it.

"That's my cell if you need anything."

"Thanks," Grace blurted. "I forgot the right adaptor for my charger, and I borrowed yours from your nightstand. I had to check in."

"Okay." He headed toward the outside door.

"I didn't mean to snoop."

"Got it. Thanks for telling me." He put on his coat and pulled on a pair of boots.

Grace let out the breath she had been holding. "I'm making this a bigger deal than it is, aren't I?"

"You are." He opened the door. "I'll see you tonight."

Tucker locked the deadbolt after him.

Feeling like an idiot, Grace crossed to the kitchen counter and entered his mobile number into her cell, hoping she'd never have to use it. She was grateful for his help, but the guy clearly didn't like her. As soon as it was safe, she'd get out of his hair.

Her family had taught her well. Grace knew you couldn't make someone like you back, no matter how much you wished otherwise.

# Chapter Twenty-Four

Tucker gripped the steering wheel of his electric truck and tried to let the all-wheel drive and antilock brakes do their job. The sketchy driving conditions forced him to focus on something besides the naked goddess in his shower.

He should have waited an hour, given the winter sun a chance to thaw some of the ice on the road, but Tucker hadn't trusted himself to stay in the tiny loft apartment with Grace and not make a fool out of himself.

Lillian's friend fought like a warrior, was smart as fuck, and was annoyingly sexy with zero makeup on and her hair rumpled from sleep. Not fair. Not that he had a chance. Grace was a princess, he was an ornery officer with anger issues and some serious family baggage.

Tucker pulled into the ranch supply parking lot and scrolled through Becca's list.

A new text came in, and for the first time in months, a burst of hope flared.

Maybe it was Grace.

It was his sister. She had added a cow.

Tucker dropped his forehead to the steering wheel. "Seriously, Becca?" His downtown city condo might be lonely, but no one had ever requested he pick up a butchered cow.

A message flashed on his phone. *Low power mode.*

That was weird. It had been fully charged a few hours ago.

He pocketed the phone and headed to his first errand.

# Chapter Twenty-Five

Grace stood under the spray of warm water. The shower was pint-sized, though it felt rather decadent with a rain fixture and good pressure, even more so knowing it was powered by solar and wind energy.

The cocoon of warmth did little to assuage the sting of Tucker's rejection. Grace had assumed, erroneously, that he had felt something last night, too. Something as unexpected as it was beautiful. This morning he had physically dodged away from her and shut down hard the option of her tagging along as he ran errands. When would she learn?

Twisting off the shower, Grace got ready. Then she paced the apartment before eating another scone.

Twenty minutes had passed.

More than a little stir-crazy, Grace walked to the window, mindful to stay out of sight lines as she peeked out the window. The barn apartment faced the back of the inn, and the only exit, the door she had entered, included the external stairs. Not exactly an ideal setup for a quick escape, should she need one.

The sound of her mobile pinging made her jump.

She fumbled for it, answering quickly, "Claire!"

"Hi, doll, what bullshit is dropping now? I got a weird message from your beefcake, Thorsen."

"He's not my beefcake," Grace reminded her best friend. Again.

"I can't believe you gave up tapping that." Claire whistled. "I would walk over coals for something that hot. *Damn.*"

"*Claire!*"

"What? We're honest with each other, that goes for fantasies, too."

"It really doesn't have to," Grace said, laughing. At that moment, she wished she could hug her best friend.

"Where are you? Your mom called."

Grace's stomach dropped. "What did you say?"

"Nothing, she left a message—"

"What did Thorsen say?" Grace pressed.

"I am almost certain Thorsen asked me to hack your birth certificate and your parent's marriage docs."

Grace gripped the phone tighter. "He asked you that?" Thorsen looping in Claire meant he didn't trust official channels, including his staff.

"What's going on?"

Hesitating only a moment, Grace concisely filled Claire in.

"I always knew your grandpa was bat shit crazy."

Grace felt obligated to defend him. "We don't know it's him."

"Are you seriously going to bet your life on that?" Softer, Claire added, "Say the word, I'll get you your records."

"You don't have to." Grace's stomach twisted.

"I know."

Grace hesitated, trying to remember the precise wording of the obscure laws protecting royalty from anything that impacted succession. With Grace's request and approval, Claire would not be in legal hot water.

"Okay, go for it."

"Excellent, hang on."

Grace heard keys clicking, and she pressed her hand to her rolling stomach, acutely aware her life could change in moments. "Sorry for dragging you into all this."

"My pleasure, doll, and quit fretting. This shouldn't take long."

Grace heard more keys clicking and tried to breathe. "I knew I should have listened when you tried to teach me this stuff over the years." If she had, Grace would have been able to hack her own records.

Claire clucked, still typing. "Didn't anyone ever tell you royalty isn't supposed to apologize so profusely? You sound like those Canadian commercials."

"R-right," Grace stammered, trying to shrug off Claire's double bullseye. Growing up royal, Grace had, of course, been properly indoctrinated, she just sucked at it. Whereas her younger sisters were masters at tradition and expectation.

"I'm almost in ... got it. Huh. That's weird."

A thousand worst-case scenarios flooded Grace's mind. "What is?"

"There's no father listed."

Grace stumbled to the bed and sat down. "What does that mean?"

"It means the digitally sealed records were fucked with, too. Don't worry, I have another idea. I'm going to get you an early Christmas present."

Adrenaline spiked through Grace. "Claire, don't—"

"Are you officially withdrawing your request for your untampered birth certificate and your parents' marriage docs?"

Grace's heart pounded. Her dad wasn't her dad, and her mom had married a dead guy. How much worse could it get? She swallowed. "No, I'm not. You have my permission."

"Excellent! Merry Christmas. Talk soon!"

"Hello? Claire?"

Her best friend had hung up.

Grace dropped her head into her hands. This hang time, the trying to sort out her life when the very foundation of her family had been obliterated, was painful. Enough. Abruptly, she stood and swiped at her eyes. She wasn't the first to find out a shocking family secret and wouldn't be the last. Her gaze caught on the wall to the right of the bathroom door, where there were three dark boards and batten wood panels.

She cocked her head. The board and batten were fussy to install and easily considered stuffy. Why didn't that look right?

Grace glanced around the small apartment. With the exposed beams and colorful touches everywhere, Grace would call the style boho rustic, certainly not fussy.

She walked over and felt the barest drafts. With an exploratory thrill, Grace carefully ran her hand along the various edges, looking for anything different.

*Click.*

Her finger released a spring-loaded latch.

Excitement flared, and Grace held her breath as she gently pressed against the lower board. It easily swung into the wall.

With a gasp of delight, she peeked into the dark hole. A ladder was fitted against the wall, and she could smell horse flesh and sweet hay.

A cowgirl's sacred spring.

Grace bounded across the room to her backpack. She pulled on a heavy sweater and wrapped an oversized scarf around her neck before lacing up her cold weather hiking boots. She slipped on a pair of gloves before sliding into the low opening and making her way as quietly as she could down the ladder.

A horse whinnied, and she froze, her gloved hands clutching the ladder.

When no human shouted at her, Grace started moving again.

She stepped off the ladder and onto a concrete floor. Large sacks made tidy stacks, and a few oversized boxes were opened while various cartons and sundries rounded out the space.

She was in a storage room.

A horse whinnied again.

Grace dusted off her gloves and peeked her head out of the room. She was at the junction of two long aisles, like a T. What looked to be an office was the next room, and an open double stall at the end held saddles and tack.

Three stalls held what Grace guessed were American Quarter Horses.

She walked up to the first stall where a large gray gelding stood and leaned against the metal gate.

Softly, she said, "Well, hello. Aren't you handsome."

She read his nameplate. *Stürmisch.*

She admired the large gray before walking to the next stall. Another huge horse stood, though this one was red, not gray. Her name plate read *Pixie.* She pressed her muzzle against the bars, and Grace gently rubbed the horse's soft, warm nose.

Grace felt like someone had suddenly let the air out of her shoulders, as much of the tension in them released. She groaned in relief before she could help herself. This *was* a sacred space.

She stroked Pixie again. "You are a magic maker. Thank you for that."

Grace walked to the next stall, where a medium-sized buckskin gelding stood eyeing her. He reminded Grace of Tucker. She traced her finger over the nameplate. *Ranger.* He cast her a final look before sticking his nose into the bucket in the trough at the back of the stall.

"Figures."

"Come again?"

Grace nearly jumped out of her skin. She spun toward the voice with her weight balanced on the balls of her feet, assessing escape options.

An older man stood several feet away, holding his hands up in a placid manner. "Sorry, I didn't mean to startle you."

The closest exit was about four yards away, should she need to run. Cautiously, she answered, "Hi."

When she didn't offer anything further, the man, still smiling, asked, "I'm sorry, who are you?"

Improvising, she said, "I'm one of Tucker's friends."

The older man looked relieved and held out his hand. "Clint Steele, nice to meet you."

His eyes were kind.

Grace shook his hand, surprised, when she supplied, "Grace, and likewise."

He motioned with his hand. "I'm just helping Becca with some barn chores."

"That's nice of you."

His eyes twinkled. "Not really, I lost a bet."

Grace laughed at his candor. "Want some help?"

"Are you sure? I'm sure you have better things to do."

She shrugged, smiling. "Not really."

It was the truth. For the first time in perhaps her entire life, she was completely without an appointment. It was as disorienting as it was intriguing. She also was more than a little intrigued at her fanciful image of a cowgirl's sacred spring and wanted to experience it such as she could.

He eyed her again before acquiescing. "All right, then, sure."

Clint showed her how to top up the water and how many oats the horses got. She insisted on mucking out the stalls when he would have done it, though wisely borrowed a pair of Becca's rubber boots when Clint suggested it. The work was earthy, common ... and completely beautiful. She had never considered the natural connection working a ranch or farm required, she had never had the chance.

Grace dusted her hands against each other, proud of herself. "All done."

Clint looked up from the spare wheelbarrow he was fixing, his eyes still shining. "When Becca finds out I had help, she'll cry foul and will be absolutely right."

"I won't tell if you don't."

Clint laughed. "How did you and Tucker meet?"

Grace froze. It was brief, but she suspected Clint had noticed.

She smiled widely. "Mistaken identity that worked out. Tucker is—" She stopped, then simply shrugged. "Tucker's great."

Clint was looking at her closely. "That he is."

He dropped the screwdriver he was holding into the toolbox and stood. "That should do it."

Clint flipped the wheelbarrow rightside up and walked it to the far corner of one of the long aisles. "Thanks again for your help. Let me know if there is anything I can do to say thanks."

The man had no idea the treat it had been to be treated like a normal person.

Then a thought popped into her head. "Any chance Becca would let us borrow a couple of horses? I haven't ridden in ages."

"Sure. She's got a whole herd that needs regular riding."

"Come again?"

"It's an eco-inn dude ranch. Plenty of mounts for guests."

"Right. That makes sense."

"They're out in the pasture. Get Tuck to round one up for you, otherwise, I can pop over tomorrow again. I have to run now."

Grace smiled, looking forward to a ride. "I'll ask him, thanks."

"Stay clear of that south face. We've had record snowfall already, and the avalanche risk there is already a four."

Grace must have looked confused because Clint added, "Tuck knows where the south face is. If you guys go out, make sure you tell him to stay clear."

Grace nodded. "I will."

Clint smiled, nodded his hat to her, and walked toward the door.

"Clint?"

He stopped. "Yeah?"

"Tucker and I … that is, Becca doesn't know. She might disapprove of me."

Grace hated lying to the kind older cowboy, but the fewer people who knew she was here, the better.

"Understood, though I'm sure Becca will love you. I'll let you and Tucker tell her in your own time."

Relief, and guilt, filled her.

"Thank you. We appreciate that."

These were nice people she was asking to lie for her.

If she believed in hell, like the church had tried for decades to drill into her, Grace would totally be going.

# Chapter Twenty-Six

Kat's knees buckled. She dropped onto her office settee and reread the report.

Her daughter hadn't been on the plane. Grace wasn't dead.

Tears of relief streamed down the queen's face.

A soft knock sounded, and her husband walked into her office.

Kat quickly blotted at her eyes with an embroidered handkerchief, darting a look at him.

He joined her on the settee. After a moment, he entwined his hands in hers. The gesture was as foreign as it was welcome.

"She wasn't on the plane," the queen said.

Jacques nodded, his own eyes damp.

"Did she tell you where she was going?" Kat asked.

Jacques shook his head. "After your father's outburst, I'd be surprised if she spoke to any of us for a while."

"What have I done? I thought if she didn't know the truth, she couldn't be hurt." Kat's heart squeezed painfully, and it felt like she was losing Grace's father all over again.

Jacques picked up her hand and gently squeezed it, and Kat looked at the man she had been assigned to marry.

Theirs hadn't been a love match, but Jacques had always been a devoted father and respectful husband. Not all of her contemporaries had been so lucky.

"What happened all those years ago?" Quieter, he added, "You never told me."

Kat traced a vein on the top of his hand. "I fell in love with someone considered unsuitable."

"I figured as much."

His words cut, though his eyes were kind, and she wanted to explain. "It was my first time in America. My father had an oil securities meeting, and I took the opportunity to check out schools. The world was a different place then, pre-nine-eleven. I only had a security detail for official events and could explore as much as I wanted. There was a rodeo." Kat shrugged. "I had never seen one. He was a young cowboy, a simple ranch hand, handsome and kind. And unsuitable."

"What happened?"

"I stayed the rest of the summer and began looking at universities in Texas. When my father found out about us, I was forcibly taken back to Jordemorden. Grace's father died a week later in a truck accident." Kat shook her head. "I never had a chance to explain to him what had happened. He didn't know I was pregnant or that I had a title. I never told him who I was."

"Grace is half American."

Kat nodded. "She is."

He smiled. "Well, that explains a few things."

"She has such a beautiful spirit." Kat looked down. "I can't bear to watch the grand duke squash her beautiful joy and passion, but I'm afraid if she keeps fighting him, she's going to get hurt. His followers are everywhere and getting bolder in their violence. Everything is just so polarized right now."

Jacques squeezed her hand.

Long moments later, he asked, "Did you love him?"

"Very much." She looked up. "Have you ever been in love?"

Jacques's eyes took on a pained look, and Kat straightened. "You've met someone." She had been so wrapped up in her own hurt that she hadn't bothered to ask why her husband had been more animated lately or smiling more.

"Now is not the time—"

Kat grabbed both of his hands. "No. Love is too precious."

Jacques sat back, clearing his throat. "This is hardly becoming."

"What are you waiting for? Do you love her?"

He gave her a look.

"Him?" It had never dawned on Kat that her husband might prefer a man's company.

"Her," Jacques corrected.

Kat smiled. "Does she love you back?"

"I don't know, nor does it matter."

"Of course, it matters! You have been a good father and a kind husband, but we both deserve more. I gave my heart away a long time ago. If you've found someone to share yours with, you must!"

"Kat, this is all rather—"

"Real? I care for you a great deal, and I always thought we had done the right thing. After everything that's happened, now I'm not so sure." When Grace's biological father died, something in her had died, too. She wouldn't wish that on anyone, especially not her husband. "I would not see you forsake love. It might not come back."

"Kat, darling, I won't leave you. That has never been an option, and certainly not now."

Kat cupped her husband's face in her palm. "Like I said, you're a good man. Please, I beg you, follow your heart. There is too much pain in this house. Not that you need it, but you have my blessing. And Grace, she's smart, she'll stay safe. Thorsen will keep her safe."

"He's here."

Kat sat up straighter. Thorsen was always Grace's security detail. "He can't be here. She's not!"

"I saw him not an hour ago."

If Thorsen was here, that meant he felt confident where Grace was. There were few places on the planet Thorsen would trust sending Grace without him.

Kat patted her husband's knee. "I'm going to find Grace. I have an idea where she might be."

\*\*\*

The door had been left ajar. Ingrid Olsen stood listening in righteous satisfaction. It was obviously by the grace of God that she had followed Jacques, and a good thing, too. It was clear the queen and her bastard daughter were here to tempt good, devout men with their wicked ways. Serpents they were, corrupting the God-fearing women of the country to do the same.

Ingrid wouldn't be tempted. She was virtuous, an obedient servant, steadfast in her fight against the wicked.

A new plan was formed. Cut off the serpent's head, that's how the righteous stayed in God's good grace. The queen and her daughter were unrepentant, shameful sinners, and Ingrid would cast out them out like the serpents they were. Jordemorden would be Eden again.

Ingrid silently retreated.

It was just like the grand duke always told her. She had to be vigilant, always ready for their just and holy wars.

# Chapter Twenty-Seven

The sun was setting as Tucker took the covered stairs to the barn loft apartment, a fresh travel mug of coffee in one hand, a picnic basket in the other, and tucked under his arm, was a six-pack of beer. There were no fresh tracks, so unless Grace was a trapeze artist, she would be inside.

A thrill shot through him. Until he remembered the look on her face when he had damn near tripped to get away from her this morning. Nor had she called. In his experience, when you gave a woman your number, she texted or called, usually too much.

Grace had done neither.

Tucker looked down at the food and drink in his hands, hesitating.

Suddenly, the door swung open.

"Hi." Grace stood before him. Her cheeks were rosy, and she looked a little out of breath. Her eyes brightened. "Ooh, is that coffee?"

He stepped into the apartment and shut the door. He held out the travel mug to her. "Peace offering?"

She smiled, accepting the coffee. "That was thoughtful of you."

Tucker kicked out of his boots and hung up his jacket. "This morning got weird."

The brightness in her eyes disappeared, but she asked, "Can I help with that?"

"Thanks." Tucker handed her the basket.

Sniffing, she asked, "Is this Canadian barbecue?"

"Here, we just call it barbecue, but yes." He crossed the small space and set his phone on the counter. "I didn't expect to be gone so long. Did you find anything to eat today?"

Grace had followed him and set the picnic basket on the bistro table. "You're down a box of mac and cheese and out of energy bars."

"Princesses know how to cook?" He teased, squatting to put the beer in the fridge.

"I know how to read and took it from there." Grace pointed to the basket of aromatic food. "Are you eating this now, or where would you like me to put it?"

Her voice was painfully polite. He stood and slowly turned. "You don't want to eat with me?"

She looked surprised. "I didn't realize I was invited."

"Why wouldn't you be?"

She shrugged. "As you said, it got weird this morning."

"You are. Come on, let's eat. Beer?"

Grace placed her coffee to the side. "Yes, please."

Tucker opened two bottles of beer and asked, "Glass?"

"Ooh, fancy."

"See, I can't tell if you're kidding or not."

A small smile finally appeared. "You will."

Tucker poured the craft ales into two glasses. He handed her one before pulling out plates and utensils. He unpacked the barbecued beef on a bun and popped a homemade fry into his mouth. They were warm but not hot to the touch.

"Want me to warm these up a bit?"

"Nah. Let's just eat." She snagged one. "Wow, these are really good. Did you make this?"

"Yeah. Becca had a young family staying, and I thought beef on a bun and homemade fries would be more fun for the kids." He looked up. "You don't mind, do you? I can go get the squash bisque."

"It looks perfect." Grace popped a morsel of barbecued beef into her mouth. "*Ohmygod.* You're a really good chef."

"Police officer," he corrected automatically.

"If you say so. Seriously, wow." She plucked another bite.

At her praise, pride-filled him instead of the usual feeling of insecurity.

They settled at the small table, knees touching. When she didn't move away, Tucker tried to ignore his semi-aroused state.

Thankfully, his phone flashed on the counter, and he reached over to pick it up.

*Low power mode.*

"Seriously, again?" He stood, happy his untucked flannel hid the front of his pants and retrieved his charger. He plugged it into an outlet in the kitchen. "I had to top up the charge in the truck, too."

Grace finished chewing. "Did you check if it was bugged?"

Tucker stilled. "No."

Grace wiped her hands on a napkin. "Give it."

Tucker handed her his cell, surprised he liked her direct, take-charge competence.

She thumbed through several screens for several seconds before looking up. "Got a paperclip?"

"Maybe."

Tucker found one holding several sheets of paper from his sister on the bookshelf. "Here."

He watched as Grace made quick work of his field-durable case before she straightened the wire and popped open the back of his phone. Gently, she pulled out a thin disk, no thicker than a sheet of paper and smaller than the head of a pencil eraser.

"Your battery should work fine now." She handed him his phone and the wee bug.

He stared at her.

She raised her hands. "Don't look at me, I didn't put it there. That's government-grade technology, not private sector. Who would want to bug you?"

# Chapter Twenty-Eight

Grace watched Tucker. He was looking a bit spooked.

Slowly, he said, "My service doesn't use stuff like this."

"I said government, I did not mean municipal."

He held out the bug in his hand. "What the hell am I supposed to do with this?"

She glanced down at the offending device. "It's not recording or transmitting now if that's what you're worried about. It's useless without a power supply and signal."

He didn't look convinced.

"Put it in the freezer. It'll be in one piece when you turn it in—if you want to turn it in." She held up her hands. "No judgment either way. Mind if I take a photo of it first, though?"

Tucker held out his hand, and she snapped a couple of shots before sending them to Thorsen with a brief message. "My contact might be able to identify what groups use that model."

Tucker stood and put the bug in the freezer. When he returned to the table, he asked, "Who the hell would want to bug my phone? I'm not even on active duty right now."

Grace cleared her throat. "Lillian mentioned your father …"

"And you still came." He took a long pull of beer. "You have faith in your detail."

"Lillian's security detail was from my country."

"I was going to ask you about that. Where's yours?"

"It's complicated." Grace stood up and walked over to get her backpack.

Tucker was watching her. "I know, complicated."

Grace rifled through her backpack before pulling out a small device. "Do you mind if I check if there's more?"

He leaned forward. "Yeah. Thanks."

Grace walked around the room, sweeping for any additional surveillance mechanisms. Nothing pinged.

She sat back down, tucking the device back into her backpack. "All clear."

"Mind doing that to my condo in town?"

"Sure." Grace picked up her sandwich and took a bite. "This is really good."

"The bug doesn't phase you?"

"Bullets and bombs scare me. Surveillance—" Grace shrugged. "It can go different ways."

Tucker picked up a fry before dropping it back onto his plate. "My father is the only one I can think of who would want to bug me. But he's been missing for months."

"About that, maybe I can help."

"Why?"

"You're hiding me on my word alone, it's the least I can do."

"Not entirely. As soon as you tipped your hood back, I recognized you from one of Lillian's framed photos."

Maybe the officer wasn't as naïve as Grace suspected.

Still, he hadn't accepted her help.

Nor touched his sandwich.

She pointed. "Why aren't you eating?"

Tucker picked up his sandwich and took a big bite.

Contrary.

Maybe he'd last longer than she assumed.

Grace ate a fry and looked around. The apartment had zero holiday decorations. "What do you do for fun here for Christmas?"

Tucker took a pull from his beer. "I meant to ask about that. I mean, it's almost Christmas, why are you here, alone?"

"Why do you assume I'm Christian?"

He shrugged. "I'm not. I celebrate a culturally secular Christmas."

"You have an answer for everything."

"I don't have an answer for you."

Grace looked at him. "I'm a long story."

"I got time."

She eyed him over the rim of her beer, then set it down. "My grandfather is trying to marry me off to one of his religious right followers. That crowd likes women to be silent, submissive, and contained, more like brood mares, to create more legions of followers. My mom supports his plan for my course-correction, as it were. My politics are too hippie-dippie for a proper heir."

"That's still a thing, arranged royal marriages?"

"Unfortunately for me, yes."

"Ew."

"Tell me about it."

"I get called hippie dippie here." He held up his hands. "Not that anyone is trying to marry me off or require me for stud services."

Grace laughed until her smile drooped. She fought hot tears that threatened to erupt.

Tucker crossed his arms on the table and leaned forward. "What is it?"

She put her elbows on the table—Tucker wouldn't chastise her for it—and rested her chin in her palms. "I just found out my dad isn't my biological father."

He waited. When she didn't elaborate, he said, "Shit, you're serious?"

She heard her grandfather's damning words, like the series of calculated blows they were intended to be.

*As uncouth as your father.*

*You're barely an heir.*

"Yes. My grandfather and I, we're politically incompatible, which makes me useless in his eyes. Apparently, I am without feelings, too, as he rather delightedly blurted out my sketchy paternity."

Tucker sat back. "That's cold."

"I thought so. He's not known as a kind man, but the way he did it was unnecessarily cruel."

Tucker's voice was rich with sincerity when he said, "I'm so sorry. That sounds awful."

"It gets worse. I found out my mom married my biological father *post modem*."

Tucker's eyes widened in surprise. "That can't be a thing."

"For a fee, our state church has solutions for any number of so-called indiscretions."

"I'm so sorry, Grace. That's … really heavy. And super weird."

Grace started picking at the label on one of the beer bottles on the table. "I keep replaying the last few weeks, trying to pinpoint what I did or said to upset him so much that he would decide to be so cruel."

"Stop."

Grace looked up.

Tucker was shaking his head. "Don't go there. How he told you is on him, not you. If policing has taught me anything, it's that we can't take responsibility for another's actions. You could have been the perfect puppet, and he still would have done what he wanted. Nut jobs like your grandfather—" Tucker's eyes widened. "Sorry, that was really insensitive."

Quiet the contrary, Grace wanted to hug him at his frankness. No one talked to her like that, not even Thorsen. She smiled and whispered, "Safe space."

He really *looked* at her, and Grace felt a current spark between them.

"Safe space," he repeated softly.

After several moments, she said, "You were saying?"

He blinked. "Right. Your grandfather. His actions have zero to do with you."

"What do you mean?" Grace was the reason the grand duke acted out, wasn't she?

"I mean this in a good way, but you're irrelevant here. It's his hate on. You got blasted, but you didn't cause it. That's on him."

"No, but—"

"But what? You may be a princess and all, but you don't have control of another. Not like that."

"You're saying it's not my fault?" she whispered.

"Of course, it's not. In what universe is it okay to blame kids for the circumstances of their birth?"

Grace felt something wiggle free in her gut. "It's not."

"Then why were you blaming yourself? Your grandfather's outburst about your parentage is his discomfort, not yours or anything you did. It's on him."

"But I constantly upset him. Surely I deserve some of the blame?"

"Your politics make him uncomfortable. Again, that's on him and his experience to navigate. Don't dim your light because it makes others uncomfortable. Fuck that. That's a fast track to crazy town." He took a sip of beer.

Grace sat back.

"You okay?"

Back home, Grace had felt catastrophic responsibility. Like if she just pushed harder and worked faster, she could help more people and ease the burdens many people suffered. It had felt like trying to stop the incoming tide with a sand castle, in a word, impossible.

And exhausting.

"I've never considered that perspective." What if the crushing responsibility she felt was because she was trying to control the impossible? No wonder she felt constantly crushed, what she was striving for wasn't possible.

Tucker shifted in his seat. "Is that a good thing?"

"Yeah, I think it is." She smiled. "Kind of like you and your dad."

Tucker leaned back. "There is no me and my dad."

***

"You just told me I wasn't responsible for my grandfather's actions," Grace reasoned.

"You're not."

"Well, you're not responsible for your father's actions, either. Am I missing something? Aren't you trying to track down your father because you don't want him to hurt anyone else, and you feel responsible?"

Tucker's anger spiked. "They're not the same thing. I'm a police officer, it's my job."

Grace's eyes flashed. "And I'm a goddamn princess. What the fuck do you think my job is? Trying on tiaras and having tea parties? Fuck you. You work for a city, I help run a country."

"That's not what I meant," Tucker snapped. But it was. He had dismissed her position.

"Really? Then explain how it's okay for you to be responsible for your father's actions, and it's not okay for me to take responsibility for my grandfather's. Enlighten me, Tuck, I'm all ears."

Tucker couldn't. She was right.

He was angry at his father but despised himself for not realizing the violence Bruce was capable of and stopping him. His family had almost died because of his lack of awareness.

He rose then.

"Where are you going?" Grace asked.

Tucker felt like he couldn't breathe.

"Out. Don't follow me."

# Chapter Twenty-Nine

Tucker gripped the railing at the top of the covered stairs. He couldn't see the stars, only feel the bite of the wind.

*You're not responsible for your father's actions.*

Grace's words damned the last several months of his life, dared him to bust out of the fortress of self-loathing he had buried himself in.

What the hell did she know?

Tucker stilled. Princess Grace continued to suffer under treacherous family members, and what had he done? In his anger, he had grasped at rebukes and petty meanness.

He heard a click behind him and turned.

Grace stood in the doorway, holding the door. "I'm sorry, I didn't mean to cross a line."

Her soft admission sliced him. "You didn't do anything wrong, I did, and I'm sorry."

"Want to come back inside? It's freezing out there."

He nodded and followed her inside. Tucker closed the door, unsure what to do or how to explain. "I'm fucked up."

Grace snapped her head up at his words. "Don't say that."

He shrugged. "It's true. I just bit your head off for telling me my own advice. That's effed up."

Grace picked up his beer and held it out to him.

He rubbed his jaw before taking it. "Thanks."

She sat cross-legged on the couch, cradling her beer. "No one in my family considers it necessary to tell me who my biological father is, that's fucked up. And when I tried to access my birth certificate, it was sealed. Same with my mom's first marriage license."

Tucker sat down next to her, shocked. "Is there any way you can find out?"

"I'm having my DNA run against those commercial genealogy databases. I'm also fairly certain a friend of mine is breaking into our national archives to get me a copy of the untampered one." Grace held up a hand. "Before you go all copper on me, as a royal heir, I am allowed full discretion of records that pertain to me. Whoever tampered with my birth certificate and my parents' wedding certificate and license is subject to some serious jail time and hefty fines. Tampering with documents concerning succession is a big no-no."

Tucker hadn't considered that. "I guess it would be more complicated than simply hiding an indiscretion."

"Succession makes people crazy." Grace's hand shook when she took another sip of her beer. "And someone tried to kill me. Twice."

Tucker stilled. "What happened?"

"Someone replaced the combat training prop gun with a real one. I wanted to chalk that up to an accident, but then a few days later, the plane I was supposed to be on blew up."

Tucker stared at Grace. "Who wants you dead?"

She dropped her head. "I'm pretty sure it's my grandfather, the grand duke. Though, I guess it could be one of his followers."

"Is it a succession thing? You mentioned that made people crazy."

Grace scrunched her brow, "I don't believe so. My grandfather was *compelled* to abdicate as king. He did not take the loss of power, such as a constitutional monarchy affords, well, and the country has become alarmingly polarized since. He blames me. There's an election in a few days that early polling declares will be historic. Everyone is on a hair trigger, and because of the risk, no one in my family knows where I am. I entered Canada under an assumed name." She looked up quickly. "Please don't say anything. I have diplomatic discretion, but the paperwork is a nightmare, and I really don't want to leave an explicit trail to whoever wants me dead."

"That's why you didn't want Becca to know?"

Grace nodded. "That's the only reason I asked you not to tell your sister. I don't ask lightly, loyalty is a big deal to me. I know we both know Lillian and all, but you're essentially a stranger, and you're helping me more than my own family." She held his gaze. "It means a lot."

Tucker shifted, uncomfortable with her praise. "We should move your truck. There aren't many people out here, but folks will start to wonder."

Grace got up and retrieved a set of keys from her backpack. She handed them to him. "Here."

Tucker took the keys. "I'll move it in the morning. Clint will let me park it at his place."

"Clint Steele?" Grace asked, suddenly animated. "I met him."

"Clint was in here?"

"No, in the barn."

"What were you doing in the barn?"

"Finding a secret passageway."

Not in a million years.

Tucker's eyebrows raised. "My sister has a secret passageway from this apartment to the barn?"

Grace nodded. "Cool, huh? And not all that surprising, considering. I've got one in my study at home and personal chambers."

The words fell heavy between them, illuminating just how different their worlds were.

Uncomfortable, Tucker asked, "Where is it?"

Grace pointed, and he turned to look. "One of those lower wall panels is spring loaded. A ladder leads to the storage room downstairs. You never wondered where that random ladder in the storeroom went?"

"No." Tucker hadn't even noticed the ladder.

"Really? That would have been the first thing I checked out. Clint's nice, by the way."

Tucker frowned. Did she sound bubbly?

Grace looked like she was glowing when she said, "I didn't really catch who he is."

Still frowning, Tucker explained, "He's like a surrogate uncle. He kept us kids normal when our parents were anything but. Usually, they were fighting. Clint and my brother, Lillian's Colt, now train horses together. He's on the next ranch and always around, or we're at his place."

"I like him."

Aw hell. Tucker had not seen that coming.

# Chapter Thirty

"Are you okay?" Grace asked.

Tucker sat back, crossing his arms. "Me? Yeah, why?"

"Your energy dropped. Was it because you didn't know about the secret passage?"

"I said I was fine."

"So you did." Grace hesitated. "I meant what I said. I needed someone to trust when I didn't think I could trust anyone again. Even family. I'm pretty sure I trust you." Since the explosive confrontation with her grandfather, the only person Grace had trusted was Thorsen. Until Tucker.

He looked up, surprised. "Pretty sure?"

"Yup." It was all she was willing to admit. She yawned, emotionally wrung out and feeling way more fragile than she would have liked. "Sorry, I think the jet lag has caught up with me."

Tucker cleared the table. "Let me just get these put away so the light won't bug you."

Grace helped him. She was clumsy at first, not having a lot of practice clearing a kitchen in the palace, but within minutes, the food was cleared and the dishes stacked in the pint-sized dishwasher.

The pot she had burned the macaroni and cheese in was soaking in the sink. Embarrassed, she held it up. "I wasn't sure how to fix this."

He grinned. "Now that takes talent." He reached under the sink and retrieved a scouring pad. "This should do the trick."

"It's my mess, I can do it."

He waved her off. "I got it. You can use the bathroom while I finish here." When she hesitated, he pressed, "Go."

"I'll just be a sec." She excused herself and closed the bathroom door behind her.

Her reflection stared back at her.

She wore no makeup to dilute the stress lines or budding crow's feet. She traced the line of her nose, over the ridges of her lips, before ending at her chin. She always thought she looked like her mother, but now she wasn't so sure.

Missing her mom, Grace quickly brushed her teeth and washed her face. She changed into her hiking base layer for pajamas. When she was finished, she opened the bathroom door, stopping abruptly.

The apartment was so small that Tucker stood only a few feet away.

He smiled at her, and Grace felt like her skin was inside out.

The family secret.

The looming, explosive election.

The attempts on her life.

The hot mess in front of her.

With a hand that shook, she clicked off the bathroom light.

His face fell. "What's wrong?"

"Nothing." Tears pooled behind her eyes.

"That didn't work when I said it either."

Frantic, Grace waved her hands in front of her face in a useless attempt to stop the avalanche of tears desperate to get out.

Tucker was across the small space in a heartbeat. He wrapped his arms around her, and she buried her face in his shoulder. Heavy sobs wracked her body, and he held her as she ugly cried into his shoulder.

They stood, wrapped in each other's arms, as the storm Grace had been holding in finally broke.

After long minutes, she pulled back, wiping her face. "Sorry. I'm so sorry."

"Why?" Tucker asked, his voice soft. "It's just me."

Grace mopped at her face with her hands, mortified.

He held up an index finger. "Hang on."

He came back from the bathroom with a box of tissues.

Grace pulled out several, catching more tears and blowing her nose. "I'm not usually like this."

Tucker shrugged. "Like what?"

Grace wadded up a clean tissue and threw it at him.

He grinned, sidestepping. "See? You're already back to your feisty self." He hiked his thumb behind his shoulder. "You okay? I was just going to go wash up."

She nodded, and Tucker retreated into the bathroom.

Grace wasn't okay. She went through a dozen more tissues, blowing her nose and mopping up the tears that were still falling. She was a mess.

When he came out, his gaze took in her still-red eyes and the mountain of spent tissues in the waste bin.

Grace wanted to disappear.

He waited until she looked at him to say, "This might be completely inappropriate, and feel free to tell me to stuff it, but I can sleep next to you if you want. And I mean sleep."

"Clothed?" Grace whispered, desperate to say yes, but wanting to be clear.

He nodded. "Yes. I can sleep on the couch or next to you in bed, it is completely up to you. Honestly, I can't believe how you're still standing after the last few days you've had." He hesitated. "Sometimes it's better not to be alone."

Grace was afraid if she tried to speak, she'd dissolve again and instead held out her hand to him.

Tucker took her offered hand. "Yeah?"

She nodded.

"Hop in, I'll get the light."

Grace slid under the covers, watching as Tucker turned out the lights. In the darkness, she felt him slip into bed next to her. Unsure what to do, she turned onto her side. There were the barest pauses before he snuggled closer, wrapped his arm around her, and asked, "Is this okay?"

She burrowed closer to him in answer, wrapping her arm around his. Finally, she whispered, "Thanks, Tucker."

His voice tickled her ear when he said, "Anytime."

She felt him relax next to her, and she closed her eyes, allowing herself the comfort of another.

# Chapter Thirty-One

*"Thorsen,"* the grand duke bellowed. "I've been looking for you."

Thorsen stopped. He had spied the dangerous former king and Counselor Ingrid Olsen in the long palace hallway immediately. He turned, keeping his face impassive as he approached, hoping the grand duke nor Counselor Olsen noticed the tactical uniform and gear still strapped to him.

He had accompanied Grace's South African friend, Claire, on her successful mission to liberate Grace's unaltered birth certificate and her biological parents' marriage certificate and license. What they had found was sure to tip over the hornet's nest his father had been so worried about. Thorsen had no regrets. Claire had reminded him, in pushy and no uncertain terms, that some things were worth fighting for, and if he wasn't on board to help Grace, he could take a flying leap.

"Yes, sir?"

The grand duke paced the wide hall several steps, hands clutched at his back, before stopping. "Your father served the crown. Your grandfather served. You are loyal to the crown. It's in your blood."

An icy feeling crept up the back of Thorsen's neck as Counselor Olsen, standing next to the grand duke, eyed Thorsen disdainfully, looking every bit the disconnected, pompous politician with her severe business suit, padded bun, and perpetual sneer.

He glanced at her before asking, "You doubt my loyalty, sir?"

The grand duke gave him a calculating look. "You know where our wayward Princess Grace is."

Thorsen was not given the opportunity to either confirm nor deny. The grand duke demanded, "You will marry the wayward girl."

Counselor Olsen gave a cruel snort.

Thorsen felt like the floor had disappeared under him, and he was in free fall, worse than any emergency skydive. "Sir?"

"You are not worthy to marry royalty, we all know that, of course. But neither is she. You will marry her. I need your loyalty, I need you to control her." The grand duke illustrated his point with a pumped fist. "She is causing immense trouble for me. Do you understand?"

"Of course, sir." Thorsen didn't, not at all.

"You will do your duty and marry that ticking timebomb."

Any emotion that might have slipped out had long ago been buried under years on the job. His turmoil was his own. "Sir, are you sure—"

"*You will marry her,*" the grand duke bellowed before he stopped himself and patted his hair, breathing hard.

Anger burned. Grace was not some disposable pawn. Neither was he.

The grand duke's agenda had become a vendetta.

*Our job is to protect the crown and country. It's a fine line, but that includes from themselves.*

Thorsen forced himself to incline his head. "Right, sir."

The grand duke looked at him shrewdly. "So we're clear, that is an order."

"Of course, sir."

\*\*\*

Ingrid Olsen waited until Thorsen saw her cold stare before she overtly let her gaze travel down his body and slowly back up. The man gave no indication he noticed her demeaning appraisal, and she sniffed. He was nothing more than an over-muscled heathen.

Ingrid didn't trust him. The black guard had not sworn allegiance to the church, as was his ridiculous right after the Brookefield Clause, nor did he attend daily, let alone weekly, services.

As she let her gaze linger over his well-proportioned body, she noticed he was in uniform. "Why are you wearing that gear?"

"Tactical drills, why?"

"Don't get smart with me, young man."

"*Enough*," the grand duke yelled. "You've been given your orders. Dismissed."

Ingrid watched him leave all the way down the long hall.

The head of royal security was going to be a problem.

He was too loyal to the princess.

# Chapter Thirty-Two

Lillian awoke and instinctively reached for Colt, but his side of the bed was empty.

She heard faint sounds coming from the kitchen and smiled. She slipped out of bed and pulled on her housecoat before padding down the hall.

Colt was stacking a bowl in the dishwasher.

She smiled and leaned against the doorway, never tiring of the beautiful sight of her beloved. "Morning, honey."

He looked up, and his face lit into a smile. "Morning. Sorry, I didn't mean to wake you. Everything okay?"

Lillian nodded, automatically rubbing her baby bump.

He closed the distance between them, and she wrapped her arms around him.

He kissed her back.

Colt sighed, holding her close. "I need to get going, but you're so … warm." He nuzzled his head into her neck.

She closed her eyes, enjoying the feel of his beard on her skin. "Are you sure you have to go? We could go back to bed and be *warm* together."

He pulled back, groaning. "I can't think when you say stuff like that."

Lillian smiled. "Good." She gave him a quick kiss on the lips. "Go, train horses. I'll be here when you get back. We're still on for dinner at Becca's tonight, right?"

Colt's arms were still around her. "Yes, I remember." He nipped her earlobe with his lips. "I'll try and be back early."

"You do that." Lillian squirmed. "That really tickles."

"Good." He made a smacking noise in her ear before kissing her. "I should be home late afternoon. There's no cell coverage there, but I left their landline number on the fridge."

After another long, lingering kiss, the door closed behind him. Lillian smiled to herself and padded back to their room. She slipped into bed, still tired and with no pressing freelance work deadlines.

She hadn't expected to be pregnant in her forties. It was as beautiful as it was exhausting, having her body hijacked by the creation of a wee one. The puking part had seriously sucked, and she had never been so tired in her life, but both had gotten significantly better after the first trimester.

She smiled to herself and adjusted the pillows. She tried turning on her other side. Several minutes later, she flopped back again. Still, sleep eluded her.

Finally, Lillian got up and got dressed, adding her favorite red cardigan. She cradled her tummy as she returned to the kitchen and made herself a cup of herbal tea. It had been days since she checked world news and pulled open her laptop. It was all part of creating her new life.

For so long, she had lived the news as a war corespondent and MI6 courier. Now, she was spacing her exposure, keeping any lingering triggers at bay.

She pulled up one of her trusted news sources and gasped. "No, no, no." Lillian quickly rescanned the article before playing the video. It was a grainy image of a plane exploding outside Jordemorden's intelligence center.

The country's heir and one of Lillian's best friends, Princess Grace, was alleged to have been on the flight.

Lillian ran back to the bedroom. She fumbled in the nightstand drawer, finding her secure mobile. Frantic, she opened it. Tears of relief spilled down her cheeks. Grace had messaged her *after* the plane exploded.

Lillian tried ringing Grace.

Nothing.

She tried messaging her friend, waiting a good five minutes.

No response.

Old terrors surfaced, and Lillian started doing her breathing exercises. She couldn't control what was happening to her friend, but she could get more information. If anyone knew where Grace was, the head of royal security would.

Thorsen answered on the second ring.

"Where is she?"

"Ms. Kensington, I believe it's good morning where you are."

"Shut up, where is she? Tell me Grace is safe." Terror like she hadn't felt since Colt was kidnapped swamped Lillian. *Breathe in, one, two, three, four, hold, two, three, four, out, two, three, four.*

"To confirm, you haven't seen her?"

"No!" Lillian had never wanted to strangle someone she liked so bad. Thorsen's calm, pragmatic demeanor was irritating as fuck. "Swear to god, Thorsen, if you don't tell me she's safe, I will find a way to ... I don't know what, just tell me my best friend's safe."

"She was safe as of check-in two days ago."

"Two days ago?" Lillian knew just how precarious a forty-eight-hour window could be. "What the hell happened?"

There was a pause. "The less anyone knows, the better."

Lillian wanted to scream. That could mean any number of things—all bad. But if Thorsen wasn't talking, Lillian knew it was in Grace's best interests. "You need anything, I will move heaven and earth, got that?"

"Yes, ma'am."

Lillian closed her eyes and gripped the phone. "Sorry I blew up at you."

"I understand."

"No, I shouldn't have been such a wanker. I know you'd do anything to keep her safe."

"Anything."

His response, maybe it was the tone or vehemence, set off alarm bells.

"Keep me posted, I mean, if you can."

"I will. And Lillian?"

"Yes?"

"She's lucky to have you as a friend."

"Keep her safe," Lillian mumbled as guilt assailed her and she hung up. She had been so consumed with staying alive and her own imploding life the last two years that she hadn't realized Grace was going through her own storm, too.

"Grace, where are you?" Lillian whispered, wringing her hands. Thorsen had been calm. Too calm for the circumstances, as the list of already cleared places he would have considered sending Grace to with no notice was short.

*Unless.*

"It can't be." It had been Jordemorden special agents, hired by her high-ranking British grandmother, that had been Lillian's security detail when she had first fled to Canada. They had secured Becca's eco-inn, and since Lillian had moved to southern Alberta indefinitely, her grandmother had made sure the family inn was routinely checked for any security threats.

Lillian ran back to her room, throwing her hair into a messy clip, and grabbed her purse and keys. All the work she had done over the last two years to bring herself back from the brink came crashing back.

*Breathe, darling, breathe.*

Lillian gave herself the space to pull herself back from the abyss.

Colt was safe.

She and the baby were safe.

She would check to make sure Grace was safe.

Less than half an hour later, Lillian pulled into Becca's drive and ran up the front stairs. She punched in the key code and let herself in. A dim light could be seen down the long hallway that led to the kitchen, and Lillian ran toward it. "Is she here?"

Becca looked up, startled, from her cup of coffee. "Lillian, what are you doing here? The sun's not even up."

"It's winter in Canada. It's always dark out," Lillian snapped.

Becca set her coffee mug down and gently asked, "Do you need one of those seasonal mood light thingies? I know the days are really short now, but we can get you one of those lights. They're supposed to help."

Lillian squeezed her eyes shut. "A plane hiccups in Britain, and the world knows in minutes. A plane goes down in Jordemorden, and it takes days to report on it."

Becca stared at her, bewildered. "I don't know what you're talking about."

Lillian wrung her hands. "Grace was supposed to have been on that plane."

"What plane?"

"The plane that exploded into fiery pieces." Lillian squeezed her eyes shut again. "Sorry, I'm not making sense."

Becca stood and gently placed her hands on Lillian's shoulders. "It's okay. Is who here?"

Lillian let out an exhale. "Grace. She messaged me after the explosion. She has to be alive."

"What explosion?"

Lillian told Becca as quickly as she could about the morning news and talking to Thorsen.

"See? She has to be alive," Lillian reasoned.

"You said Grace's plans got pushed back, though," Becca reminded her.

"She's missing!" Lillian pointed to the back door. "You said you have a staff cabin somewhere out back, she could be in there."

Lillian took off toward the back door, with Becca trailing after her.

"Lillian, I'm sure I'd know if your friend was staying here." Becca shoved her feet in her boots and raced after Lillian.

"You don't know, Grace. She's got grit and isn't afraid to use her wits. This is the only place that would have already been cleared within the requisite timeframe. She's got to be here." Lillian pulled her cardigan tighter around her and looked around the still dark yard. She pointed toward the barn. "What's that?"

Becca looked to where Lillian was pointing. One of the yard lights illuminated the outdoor stairs leading to the barn loft.

"When the new barn was built, Meredith insisted on splurging for a small apartment in the loft. Tucker's staying there while he helps out over the holidays."

Lillian beelined for the stairs. She raced up them, holding both railings as she sped up the dimly lit stairs.

When Becca reached her, she was vibrating on the landing. "Can you open the door?"

Becca gave her a look. "If Tucker throws a skillet at us for barging in on him, I'm blaming you."

But she keyed in the code and unlocked the door.

Lillian stepped in front of Becca and shot her hand out, looking for the light switch.

Becca whispered into the darkness, "Tucker? It's me. Lillian has a question."

A groan could be heard from the bed, followed by a groggy, "Becca? What's wrong?"

Lillian found the switch, and the room was flooded with light.

Both women gaped.

Tucker was in his bed.

So was Grace.

# Chapter Thirty-Three

"You're alive!" Lillian ran to the bed but caught herself before launching at her best friend.

Grace extracted herself from Tucker's arms. She was rubbing her eyes and squinting in the harsh overhead lights. "Lillian? Oh god, Lillian!"

Grace launched herself out of bed, nearly tripping, before hugging her friend.

Both women held on.

"I thought you were dead," Lillian whispered, tears were streaming down her face, and she clutched her friend.

Grace held her tight. "You must have seen the news."

Lillian nodded, and Grace pulled back, swiping at her own teary eyes. "I'm safe. I didn't get on the plane. I couldn't, it didn't feel right—Woah, that's a baby bump!"

Lillian framed her pregnant belly with her hands. "Right? And you and Tucker, nice. When did that happen?"

Grace hedged. "I needed a safe place."

"What am I?" Her voice sounded hurt.

"A friendly wants me dead, and Thorsen and I didn't trust any communication connected to the palace."

Lillian's eyes widened. "Are you all right?"

Grace nodded. "I'm fine. Just staying low."

"Of course. We'll help any way we can," Lillian insisted.

Becca kicked the end of the bed. "That doesn't explain you, naked boy."

Grace wasn't sure what the woman meant.

"It's not what you think." Tucker crawled out of bed, standing next to it. "And see? I'm not naked. Neither is Grace."

Tucker wore a T-shirt and pair of boxer briefs. Grace was covered, ankles to wrists, in a hiking base layer.

Becca was looking between the two of them. "Tucker, you promised."

He pointed. "Grace, meet my sister, Becca. Becca, meet Princess Grace."

Becca smiled thinly at Grace. "Good morning. Don't mind me, my brothers are just really annoying sometimes."

Grace tried to hide her grin.

"That hurts, little sis," Tucker quipped. "Can you guys give us a sec to get dressed?"

Becca turned to Lillian. "I heard he's offering to make us breakfast. Did you hear that, too?"

Lillian nodded emphatically. "Yes, I heard that, too."

Tucker rolled his eyes. "Fine. I'll make breakfast and more coffee, but I am not answering any more of Becca's questions until she's more caffeinated."

Becca looked pointedly at him.

"Good plan."

# Chapter Thirty-Four

"That was weird," Tucker said, closing the door after Becca and Lillian.

He was alone with Grace again.

"I really didn't mean to make trouble for you," Grace said.

"You didn't, not really." Tucker found his pants and put them on.

Grace averted her gaze. "What did you promise your sister?"

He tugged on a hooded sweatshirt. "Don't take this the wrong way, but Becca explicitly asked me not to sleep with you. Or Claire, for that matter."

She shot her head up. "What's the right way? I don't know what I'm supposed to do with that."

Tucker grabbed his watch and put it on. "You're Lillian's friend, and she's part of the family now, and Becca's trying to launch a business. If I fuck it up with either of you, I risk pissing off Lillian and sabotaging Becca's business."

"Right." Grace was completely focused on pulling clothes out of her backpack.

"Did I say something wrong?"

"Of course not." She didn't look up.

"You guys are different, that's all," he explained.

"I understand."

He didn't think she did. "Grace, what is it?"

"Nothing." She stood with her bundle of clothes and headed to the bathroom. "I'll just be a moment."

She closed the door behind her.

Tucker stared, hands on hips. Wow. He *had* fucked that up, no sex required.

Feeling like an idiot, though unsure why exactly, he paced the small apartment while Grace got ready in the bathroom.

He took his turn when she was done. "Ready?"

She nodded, already standing by the door. "I'll try to smooth things over with your sister. I didn't mean to make waves."

"Becca will understand. The last several months have put a lot of stuff into perspective." Tucker paused. "The people who love us, love us. The ones who don't, don't. As long as we don't get them confused, we should be fine."

She was looking intently at him. "That's rather profound for this early in the morning."

Tucker's smile didn't quite reach his eyes. "We had a hell of a teacher."

A weird ping rang, and Grace's eyes widened. "Shit, that's my secure line."

She crossed to where her backpack was and pulled out her phone. "Crap, I missed the message from Lillian." She pressed the screen several times before holding the phone out to him. "You asked about this man last night, right?"

Tucker leaned over. The image on her phone was the man from his father's wedding and likely the man who had picked up his father's car from the impound lot. "Yeah. You said he's an Australian operative?"

"He is." Grace paused. "I'm pretty sure that's your half-brother, Tanner Stone."

# Chapter Thirty-Five

"What the hell do you know about my half-brother?" Tucker demanded.

"You're giving me attitude?" Grace fired back. "You asked who he was. I found out."

"I didn't know you would snap your fingers and rope my phantom half-brother into this."

"Should I not have told you? You might not like it, but your family is up to their necks in international incidents. I am the heir apparent of a sovereign country, which means global incidents are my business. Now, sit down, stop yelling at me, and we'll sort this clusterfuck out."

Tucker was breathing hard, his chest rising and falling. He glared at her before muttering something about *bossy*, but he sat down on the bed. His feet were planted firmly on the ground, and he stared straight ahead.

Grace sat sideways, next to him, one leg bent at the knee, the other on the floor, facing him.

She waited.

Tucker had rested his arms on the tops of his legs. He let out a long exhale. "I'm sorry. You didn't deserve that outburst. Tanner is a sensitive spot for our family."

"What happened?" she asked quietly.

"Don't you have access to that intel?"

"I'm asking you."

Tucker blew out a breath. "Tanner's Gabe's age. We just found out a few months ago with the INCEPT check Lillian had done on Colt, though Gabe found out by accident when he was twelve. Our dad terrorized him into keeping that family secret. Bruce fucked both those kids over with his selfishness." Tucker turned to her. "I have a rule, don't fuck with kids."

Grace agreed. She had the same rule.

Tucker steepled his hands. "That kid grew up named after the bastard that didn't acknowledge him."

"You haven't met him?"

Tucker shook his head. "Becca's tried reaching out to him several times. When she first found out about him, and then when Colt was kidnapped, and I was shot. He hasn't responded. Not that I can blame him. I don't know if I would, in his place."

Grace placed her hand on his arm, unsure what else to do. "Sorry, I blurted out he's an Australian operative. I thought you'd want to know, and I should have been more diplomatic."

"Would Australia be interested in Bruce? I mean, it sounds like a pretty big stretch, but why would he be here, of all places, working? Sounds rather far-fetched."

Grace had wondered the same thing. "Do you have any idea if he's a friendly or not?"

Tucker shook his head.

"Do you want me to try and find out?" Grace asked. "No promises, but Jordemorden and Australia have shared intel in the past. I can see what I can do."

"You'd do that for me?" He looked genuinely surprised.

"Why wouldn't I? At the very least, my position allows me to try. Besides, I'd want to know if it was me and if you took me in. I kind of have a soft spot for you."

He looked at her, his face serious. "You do?"

She nodded, her heart beat accelerating.

Tucker's phone pinged. He didn't move.

"Do you need to get that?"

"They'll leave a message if it's important. We should probably go deal with my sister and Lillian."

Grace smiled. "One crisis at a time."

"Uh oh, a woman who knows my mind better than I do." Tucker stood, holding out his hand to her.

She took it and stood, too.

"Can I call you princess?" Tucker teased.

"No."

"How about Gracie?"

Grace froze. "Thorsen is the only one who has ever called me that."

"Your head of security?" His voice was light, but he had noticed her pause.

"That's him."

He moved toward the door. "How about *Your Highness*, then?"

She smiled, appreciating the space he had given her. "New world sass."

He spun around. "Did you just say I have a great ass?"

Grace rolled her eyes, pushing him to the door. "*Go.*"

On paper, Tucker and Thorsen had some similarities. In person, they were night and day.

Grace liked those differences a lot.

# Chapter Thirty-Six

Sergeant Leslie looked up from his desk.

Detective Jones had his hand up to knock on the open office door. He lowered it. "Morning, sir."

"You're here early."

Jones held up the file in his hand. "The DNA results from the John Doe OD came in an hour ago. It's Bruce Tanner, sir."

"Is that firm?"

Jones read aloud from the file. "The estimated probability of selecting an unrelated individual at random, from the Canadian caucasian population with the same profile, is one in ninety-five trillion." He closed the file. "The John Doe is Bruce Tanner, sir."

Leslie blew out a breath. "Good work. Any luck finding the vehicle from the impound, and who signed for it?"

"No, sir. We've hit a dead end."

"Then find a damn detour. This has the kind of stink that only gets worse. Find out what Bruce Tanner was into and what's still burning."

"Yes, sir." Jones tapped the file he was holding against his palm, hesitating. "The RCMP received the file to make the notifications to the family. They're making them today, sir."

"Why the hell are they doing it?"

"None of the family is within city limits since Detective Tanner is staying with his sister in the foothills."

Leslie didn't like it. He felt a responsibility to the kid. Hearing your father was dead was never easy news, even if the dead man was a monster.

"I'll keep you posted, sir," Jones said. "If Bruce Tanner had another partner besides Del Fiennes, we'll find him."

"Damn straight, we will."

Detective Jones nodded and left.

Del Fiennes had died after firing three bullets into Detective Tanner's back. Christopher Fischer, who had a mess of arms and drug dealings to his credit, had killed Fiennes in the altercation.

The whole business was a goddamn rat's nest.

Bruce Tanner might be dead, but the dominoes he set up were still tipping over.

# Chapter Thirty-Seven

The wind gusted, sending fluffy hoar frost crystals scuttling off tree limbs. Grace held out her hand to catch the dancing snowflakes. She smiled, tilting her head toward the wind as she walked with Tucker to the main inn.

The sun hadn't risen yet, and in the pre-dawn light, the wintry scene was a composition of shades of white and shadows. If Grace pretended hard enough, she could almost forget paternity bombshells or election chaos.

She bent over, snagged a handful of snow, and pressed it into a ball before heaving it.

It landed square in the middle of Tuck's back.

He spun around. "Hey."

Grace waved at him, grinning.

Tuck held her gaze when he squatted low, grabbing a huge handful and shaping the snow into a robust snowball.

She shrieked and darted off the single-track path that ran from the inn to the barn. The deep snow swallowed her legs past her knees.

Tucker tossed his snowball up into the air, catching it. "Rookie mistake. You look very stuck."

"That's preposterous." Grace tried heaving a leg up. "Wow, that is a lot of snow."

Tucker started toward her, still tossing his snowball, occasionally repacking it to keep it tight. Wisely. He stayed on the well-packed path.

"Tucker, *no*." She held up her hands, certain she was going to get a face wash any second.

"No, what?" he asked innocently, coming closer.

She turned her head to the side, eyes scrunched closed. "Okay, I'm ready. I deserve it. Hit me with it."

Grace felt him stop next to her, looming over her.

When no snowball pelted her at point-blank range, she dared open her eyes.

He squatted next to her on the trail. "I can't do it."

Tuck tossed the snowball aside and held out his hand to help her up.

Grace eyed him suspiciously but accepted his hand up. "Why do I feel like I dodged a bullet, only to have a cannon pointed at me? I totally deserved a snowball."

"Hmm, good point." Tucker pivoted and pushed her back into the snow.

Sputtering as much as laughing, Grace looped her arm around his leg and tugged hard.

Tucker landed in a heap, off the path—not on her—and largely buried in snow. "You have one gear. Kick ass."

This time, Tucker echoing Thorsen's words brought kind amusement. She leaned over and slapped his leg. "So I've been told. Come on."

It was her turn to help him up. They stomped their boots on the path and shook off as much snow from their clothes and jackets as they could.

Grace pressed her icy hands together and resisted helping Tucker swipe snow off his bum. "I didn't realize I'd need gloves."

Tucker turned, wrapping his bigger hands around hers. He had just been in the snow, too, yet his hands radiated warmth.

"How are your hands still warm?" Grace asked, welcoming the heat.

The eco-inn boasted solar panels and residential-sized wind turbines she had noticed on her first night here. To her right stood what looked to be a discreet, though large, gray water tank. Bat boxes and raised garden beds rounded out the tidy yard.

Her breath plumed in the air. "This is incredible."

"Wait until you see the inside. Come on, let's go in the front."

He led the way around the house. The trail was less packed, and Grace stepped carefully. They turned the corner, and the front of the inn twinkled with Christmas lights, still on in the low light.

She smiled, looking up as they took the porch stairs. The fresh scent of the evergreen boughs decorating the space brought bittersweet memories of home. Her family had never been perfect. However, during Christmases past, everyone would set aside their differences and simply enjoy the season and each other. She doubted family Christmases would ever be the same again.

"You okay?" Tucker asked.

"Yeah." And she would be. Whether she found her biological father or made up with her family, she had to put one foot in front of the other.

Tucker stomped his boots on the mat outside the front door, knocking off more snow, and she did the same before following him in.

"Hello?" he called, closing the door behind them.

She hung her coat next to his and removed her boots as he had done.

Grace turned and gasped.

If the outside had been an illustration of harmony with the natural world, the inside was its enchanting match.

Scents of pine and spruce mixed with cinnamon wrapped around her. An abundance of evergreen boughs and wreaths, all adorned with different shades of scarlet ribbons, were artfully arranged throughout the boho-style ranch inn. Crystals and prisms mixed effortlessly with warm wools and woods while a tall, untrimmed real Christmas tree stood against the far wall.

The eco-inn certainly hadn't had to trade comfort for self-sufficiency.

Grace inhaled the fragrant room, and the tension in her shoulders released.

"It's extraordinary," she said in hushed tones, not wanting to break the spell.

"Becca has done an incredible job."

Grace could hear the pride in his simple comment.

What would it be like to have family that believed in you like that, people you could weather the storms of life with?

She had briefly spoken on the phone with her twin sisters before she left. They hadn't been particularly sensitive to Grace's paternal ambiguity. However, they were interested in how it affected succession.

Becca breezed into the front room. "Hi, guys."

Tucker eyed his sister. "Are you better?"

"If you mean am I more caffeinated and less grumpy? Yes." Becca turned to Grace. "Can we start over?"

Grace nodded enthusiastically. "Yes, please." She held out her hand, suddenly afraid the woman would reject her.

Becca smiled and shook her hand. "Welcome, it is a pleasure to have you here."

Grace released the breath she hadn't realized she had been holding. She tried not to sound as flustered as she felt. "You have a lovely inn. Thank you for having me."

She darted a quick glance at Tucker.

He turned, heading toward a back hallway. "I will be in the kitchen making breakfast." He stopped. "Grace, you're good?"

She nodded, and he left down a long hallway.

Grace gasped, her hands together. "I am sorry about my secretive arrival. I didn't have anywhere else to go."

Becca held up her hands. "I understand secrets and safety." Becca glanced down the empty hallway. "He's going through a bit of a rough patch. I hope my brother hasn't offended you."

"I was on your porch, in the dark, wondering where the hell I was going to stay when we met." She added, "He thought I was a prowler."

Becca's eyes widened. "That could have been a disaster."

Grace felt the need to defend him. "I *was* a prowler."

"Sorry about the naked comment. Tucker's like catnip for single women. He has a real job, he can cook, and according to my friends, he's super hot."

Grace nodded. "Yes, your brother could be considered attractive."

Becca laughed. "Now that I know you're here let's get you your own room and feel right at home."

Grace didn't correct her. The palace had never felt as welcoming as this place did.

Or Tucker's cozy barn apartment.

Lillian walked into the room. "What did I miss?" She hugged Grace again, squeezing. "My best friend is here and safe, *and* I'm scoring Tucker's cooking."

Becca smiled. "It's a good morning. I'm just going go grab Grace's room key."

Becca disappeared down the long hallway.

Grace looked at her best friend. "You are positively glowing. I think Canada is good for you."

Lillian beamed as her hand curved protectively over her baby bump. "I've never been this happy. Colt is ... I love that man so much. My *seanmhair* was right." Lillian's eyes widen. "Do not tell her!"

"I wouldn't dream of it." Grace reached out, pressing her hand against Lillian's on her stomach. "Your grandmother is a force, just like her granddaughter."

Lillian blinked rapidly. "I missed you."

"I missed you, too." Grace's voice was soft. "You went through hell. I'm so sorry."

Lillian shook her head. "Don't be. It led me to Colt. He brought me back to me, I would walk through fire for that man."

Headlights flashed through the front room as a car came down the long drive.

"Kind of early for company, isn't it?" Grace asked.

Lillian frowned. "That's an RCMP vehicle, but that's not Jason coming out of it." Lillian added, "Becca's fiancé is RCMP."

The officer got out of his vehicle.

His face was grim as he climbed the porch stairs and rang the doorbell.

# Chapter Thirty-Eight

Tucker heard the doorbell and sprinted from the kitchen down the back hall. He came to a jarring stop at the entrance to the living room. An RCMP officer stood, his hat tucked under his arm. On his sleeve, two chevrons pointed down. A corporal.

Tucker had never seen the man before.

He walked slowly into the room, stopping next to Becca, Grace, and Lillian.

They stood next to the officer, their expressions similarly pained.

"Detective Tanner?"

Tucker nodded and shook his hand. "Corporal."

Becca stepped sideways and reached for Tucker's other hand.

He held on just as tight.

The mountie cleared his throat. "Your father, Bruce Tanner, has been found."

Becca clapped her hand over her mouth. Tears streamed down her face. "*Ohmygod*, who did he hurt?"

The officer shifted. "He was found dead, ma'am."

Tucker's head spun. "Dead?"

"Yes, sir. The medical examiner determined cause of death was an overdose." Quieter, the officer said, "I'm sorry for your loss."

All those weeks of hunting down his father, and the bastard was dead?

Becca started weeping openly. Lillian and Grace closed rank, flanking either side of her.

Tucker shook his head. "No, that can't be."

"He was a Jon Doe. It had been several weeks before his body was discovered." The officer cleared his throat. "I don't have to tell you what that timeframe does."

Every dead body Tucker had ever seen flashed through his mind like a macabre movie trailer.

"How do you know it was him?"

"DNA analysis just came back."

"Yes, but how can you be sure?" Tucker pressed.

"There is a one in ninety-five trillion chance we're wrong."

Becca pulled out of Lillian and Grace's embrace. "Stop. Don't say another word. He was a goddamn monster."

The officer looked startled.

Becca gripped Tucker's arms. "There are eight billion people on the planet, Tuck. That's a hell of a lot less than ninety-five trillion. They're sure. The monster is dead."

Tucker swallowed.

"He's dead," Becca repeated.

Tucker nodded. "I know. I get it."

"Good." Still trembling, Becca glanced at the officer. "Are we done here?"

"Yes, ma'am."

"Good. Excuse me."

She left then, her legs taking wooden steps, walking down the long hall to the back of the inn.

Tucker turned to Grace and Lillian, pointing where Becca had disappeared. "Can you guys make sure she's okay? I'll be there in a sec."

They nodded, heading down the hallway.

Tucker nodded to the officer. "I'll walk you to your cruiser."

# Chapter Thirty-Nine

Grace heard the sound of the front door closing.

Lillian glanced behind them, down the hall. "I always thought Bruce could rot in hell, now he is."

A loud crash sounded from the direction of the kitchen.

"*Becca?*" Lillian sprinted down the hall, Grace close at her heels.

Their host was sobbing on the floor. Broken ceramic mugs and a shattered tea pot surrounded her.

"Take my hand." Lillian reached out her hand, helping Becca safely out of the jagged circle of shards.

Grace found a broom and dustpan in the oversized pantry. She started sweeping up the sharp mess, darting looks at Lillian and their host.

"Please, I can get it." Becca's voice shook. She waved her hands in front of her face. Fresh tears streamed down. "No, I can't."

Lillian wrapped her arms around Becca.

Becca stammered, "He's dead. Bruce can't hurt anyone ever again."

Lillian held Becca, stroking her hair. "We're safe. Everyone is safe. Want me to call Jason?"

Becca stared, seeing the past. "He can't hurt Jason again, or Gabe, or Meredith."

"Or you," Lillian quietly added.

Fresh tears ballooned, and Becca ducked her head. "Or me."

She pressed her hands against her eyes for several moments before gesturing at Grace. "Stop, stop, I should be doing that."

Becca tried to get up but collapsed back on the floor. "I can't believe I'm crying. A monster is dead, we should be celebrating."

A man walked in then, from a back hallway, carrying two bottles of wine. When he saw Becca, he stilled. "Becca, what's wrong? What's happened?"

"Bruce is dead."

"I swear, I didn't—"

She held up a hand. "I know, I know. He overdosed."

He placed the bottles of wine on the large island counter, eyeing Lillian and Grace, before turning his attention back to Becca. "Are you okay?"

Becca stood and scrubbed her face with her hands. "I need to call Meredith. She doesn't have to hide. We don't have to be scared." Becca took a step back from everyone. "I'm so sorry, but I have to go. I have to get out of here. When Jason storms in, worried sick about me, tell him I took Pixie out. I'm headed to the cave."

The man nodded. "Of course."

She turned to Grace. Before she could say anything, Grace shook her head. "Go to the cave. If you need anything, we're here."

Becca launched forward, pulling Grace and Lillian into a tight hug, and whispered, "Thank you."

She pulled back, wiped her eyes, and fled out the back kitchen door.

The man turned to Grace, sizing her up.

She stared right back.

He held out his hand. "Christopher."

Lillian gave the slightest nod, and Grace took it. "Grace."

It was the shortest handshake of her life.

"Let me know if you need anything. I don't want Becca disturbed."

Grace inclined her head.

He left the kitchen, leaving the wine on the counter.

"I'll send you a spreadsheet, you're going to need it. Jason is Becca's fiancé. He's a mountie—a police officer. Meredith is her new stepmom. Bruce tried to murder her, too. Pixie is her horse. The guy that brought the wine is her sommelier, Christopher. Thorsen will have a dossier on him."

Grace's gaze flew to Lillian's. "Are you serious?"

From the intel she had read, the only Christopher in the picture was an arms and drug dealer that had tried to force Becca to stop a pipeline.

Lillian nodded. "The Tanner siblings are as kind and protective as their lives are complicated and high octane. If you want a Merry Christmas, this family will give you one." Lillian clapped her on the shoulder. "But just a heads-up, they only have one speed."

"Go?" Grace guessed.

Lillian nodded. "You got it. I need to call my husband."

Grace wished it didn't sound like such a warning.

# Chapter Forty

Tucker waited until they had cleared the front porch stairs before he said to the corporal, "Sorry about my sister. Our father wasn't a kind man." Tucker could see his breath in the cold morning air as they walked to the police cruiser.

"That's putting it mildly," the officer said.

When he opened the vehicle door, Tucker saw the paperwork on the front passenger seat.

"Is that our file?"

The officer hesitated. Tucker added, "I'm still on leave, otherwise, I'd ask my colleagues."

"I heard about that. Sounded rough."

Tucker shrugged. "Three point blank."

If it had happened anywhere else besides the hospital, Tucker would have bled out. He should have bled out, even at the hospital. But he didn't. That's what kept fucking with his head.

The officer leaned into the cruiser and retrieved the file.

He handed it to Tucker. "It's not pretty."

"An OD never is."

Tucker didn't waste any time. He knew his father had died in his apartment, in the building Tucker had checked out with the real estate agent. A DNA match had been necessary to positively identify the ripe body. Tucker skipped ahead. No indiction of foul play had been discovered, and the medical examiner had ruled the death an overdose.

Tucker closed the file and handed it back to the corporal, trying to hide his disappointment. "Thanks, I appreciate it, man."

Tucker stood in the driveway as the corporal drove away. He was no closer to understanding Bruce Tanner's cruel motives or if his business associates still posed a threat to them.

The wind picked up, and Tucker shivered in his hooded sweatshirt. Still, it was long minutes before he turned to go into the house.

The jackass was dead.

There would be no justice.

Tucker climbed the porch steps wondering where the fuck his half-brother fit into all of this?

# Chapter Forty-One

Grace had just tucked the broom and dust pan away when Becca stumbled back through the kitchen door, her phone pressed tight against her ear and her eyes as big as saucers. "This is she."

Lillian was phoning Colt in the front room, and Tucker hadn't returned yet from walking the officer to his car. Grace hesitated, wanting to give Becca privacy but not wanting to flee in case the woman needed her.

Becca closed the back door and leaned awkwardly against it, knocking the festive wreath askew. "A safety deposit box? I don't understand, why aren't you calling Meredith, his wife?"

Grace didn't move.

Becca's voice raised. "You're saying my father left my land to a partner? Are you kidding me?"

She looked at Grace. "Yes, I understand. Fine. I said that's fine," she snapped. "I will be there."

Becca hung up. "This day keeps getting better and better. I'm supposed to go to the bank. There's something wrong with the deed to the land my dad and Meredith bought for me." Becca blew out a breath. "Fuck, can this day get any worse?"

Grace gripped the back of one of the stools. "Is there anything I can do to help?"

Becca made an aggravated noise. "I wanted everything to be perfect for your stay, and instead, you got pulled into our shitstorm."

Uncomfortable, Grace shook her head. "Lillian is my best friend. As far as I'm concerned, that makes us a family of sorts. What can I do while you take Pixie out?"

Becca smiled. "I like that, sisters of a sort. Thanks, but my initial freakout passed. I should get back to work."

"Or we can day drink," Grace muttered.

Becca burst out laughing. When she caught her breath, she stopped. "Wait, why can't we? It's easy enough to coordinate logistics with our heli skiing guides."

"I'll take your word for it," Grace said, hoping she hadn't misstepped.

"Does *a friendly wants me dead* mean what I think it does?"

Grace nodded.

Becca pushed off the door she had been leaning against. She crossed to a cabinet and pulled out a bottle of Irish cream, holding it up. "Spiked coffee?"

"Count me in." The last several days had been crashing down on Grace, not that alcohol would solve anything. Giving herself permission to pause would.

Becca filled the kettle, put it on boil, and prepped a French press.

Grace found the ceramic mugs and pulled down two.

Several minutes later, they were sitting at the island stools and sipping their spiked coffees when Tucker walked in. His gaze landed on the bottle of Irish cream. "Hard coffees?"

Becca lifted her mug in salute. "After everything, the bank called."

Tucker poured himself a black coffee. "And?"

"Apparently, dad left the old Chasseur place land to his business partner, Teague Alans. It was my understanding that Meredith is primary on the deed, so I don't know what the hell is going on. The bank was unable to get ahold of Meredith, and my name is on all the paperwork, as it was supposed to revert to me in five years." Becca reached sideways and pulled something out of one of the cabinet drawers. "Think this could be a safety deposit box key?"

She tossed a small key with a noticeable patina onto the island counter.

Tucker picked it up. He read the number on it out loud. "Any idea what that's for?"

"That might be the routing number of Meredith and dad's bank. Hang on." Becca thumbed a few commands into her phone. "Yeah, that's it."

"Where'd you find it?" Tucker asked.

Becca gave a small shudder. "In the ashes of my burned barn. Honestly, I had forgotten about it. I found it this morning in a drawer when I was looking for a pen."

Grace watched the brother and sister. She had read all of this in the reports. It hadn't prepared her for the reality of those living with the fallout of their father's devastating betrayal.

"You think that's Dad's?" Tucker asked.

"I don't know what to think. But if it was his, don't you think we should check? Will you go with me?"

Tucker nodded. "Of course."

"Can we have a tactical team escort?"

"He's dead, Becca," Tucker said gently.

"Yes, but Dad's last partner put three bullets in your back. I don't want to take any chances with anyone."

Grace's mobile pinged. She read the message twice, swearing.

"What is it?" Tucker asked.

"The bug from your phone is the kind used by Australian intelligence."

# Chapter Forty-Two

"Tanner's agency bugged my phone? Why?" Tucker was going to have words with his half-brother *very* soon.

Becca interrupted, "Woah. Back up. Our brother, Tanner?"

Tucker nodded. "Grace found a bug in my phone."

"Oh Christ, not again." Becca rubbed her temples.

Grace added, "I sent a photo of the surveillance piece to a friend to see if he could identify who uses it."

"What does that have to do with Tanner?" Becca asked.

Tucker spoke up. "Because of Grace's status, she was alerted there was an Australian operative working in the area. When they sent an image, it matched the image she had of Tanner Stone."

"I was briefed on your family before I came," Grace explained. "I know that protocol is invasive."

Becca shook her head. "After the year we've had, that doesn't faze me. But can I see what my brother looks like?"

"Of course." Grace thumbed through her phone. She held it out to Becca.

Becca stared at the image. "Are you sure that's Tanner?"

Grace nodded. "As far as my security people understand, yes."

Becca got up, returning with a framed picture. "That's him, too, isn't it?"

Tucker leaned over. It was the photo from Lillian. "Appears so."

Becca blew out a breath. "Our half-brother is an Australian operative and was at Dad and Meredith's wedding."

"Where someone was murdered." Not for the first time, Tucker wondered if Tanner had anything to do with that.

Becca asked, "And Tanner, or someone he works with, bugged your phone?"

"He may have also been the one to pick up Dad's car from impound."

Becca rubbed her temple. "Is there any scenario Tanner isn't in cahoots with our father?"

Grace raised her hand. "It looks like Tanner is legitimately working. I'm assuming Australia intelligence has reason to monitor Bruce Tanner or one of his partners."

"And he just happens to get assigned to monitoring his biological father?"

Grace shrugged. "Your half-brother, with his operative skill sets, might have been tracking Bruce and uncovered something untoward. What better way to get back at the father who never acknowledged you than uncover all his sins for the world to see? It wouldn't be the first time."

"I can think of a half dozen cold cases that were solved after an ex came forward and shared evidence with police only after they were jilted," Tucker added.

Becca's eyes widened. "People cover up murders until they get dumped?"

"Yes, that is actually a thing."

Becca shuddered. "That's awful. So how do we find out? I mean, before I invite Tanner for family Christmas dinner, I need to know he's not a murderous lunatic, like Dad."

Tucker asked Grace, "Can you find out what international radars Del Fiennes was on? I worked on a joint task force with the RCMP when he came up, but I don't have access to that info anymore."

Becca piped in, "Or Teague Alans. That's the name the bank mentioned on the phone. Meredith's going to be so pissed. They used her money to buy the land."

Becca's phone pinged several times.

She looked up in disbelief.

"All of my upcoming reservations just canceled."

# Chapter Forty-Three

"All of them?" Grace asked carefully.

Becca's face had gone white. "Through New Year's. All of them. We find out Dad's dead, and my livelihood disintegrates. What the hell just happened?"

Grace cleared her throat. "There's another possibility."

"What?" Becca and Tucker said in unison.

"My mom might have figured out where I am."

"I thought no one knows where you are except your security guy," Tucker reasoned.

"Technically, that's correct. But as soon as my mom realized I didn't die in the plane explosion—"

Becca gasped, her hand flying to her chest. "Your mom thought you died? That's so sad."

Grace gave a weak smile. "It's been a hell of a week. Since the head of royal security isn't with me, my mom will be suspicious, and there are few places on the planet where Thorsen would have allowed me to go without an escort. Like this inn. With Lillian spending so much time here, there are routine security sweeps conducted. This location is considered secure."

Tucker raised his eyebrows. "You said your security detail was around."

"I lied." Grace held up her hands. "In my defense, that was before I knew I could trust you."

"Well played." He gave her a long look. "I did believe you."

Becca said, "That still doesn't explain the cancellations."

"My mom's security protocol would dictate no other guests. If she's coming, her detail would have paid off your guests." Mortified, Grace waited for the fireworks.

Becca stared. "You're telling me the queen of Jordemorden is on her way?"

"Yes, I believe so." Grace wished the floor would swallow her up.

"To be clear, I'm going to have a European princess and a queen under my roof?"

Grace wrung her hands. "I'm so sorry! If it is my mom, I'll find a way to make it up to you."

Becca's smile lit up the room. "You don't understand, if it's your mom, that means it's not my dad." She brought her hand to her chest. "You have no idea how relieved that makes me."

"You're not mad?"

Tucker winked. "Maybe have your mom write a glowing review."

"If it's her, she's going to do a lot more than that to make it up to you guys."

Becca's phone pinged again. "Ohmygod, the entire inn is now booked through New Years."

"I'm sure that's my mom. She'll have an entourage, of course, she never travels alone."

Becca grinned. "As long as I can do damage control on the guests, she booted—wait, how would she even know who was staying here?"

Grace felt her cheeks grow warm.

Tucker guessed, "She has people who can look up stuff like that and diplomatic status."

"Close enough."

Becca gasped. "Your mom hacked my booking calendar? I don't know if I should be outraged or thank her. She'll be paying prime season rates for the whole inn for weeks."

Becca's phone pinged again. When she looked up, her eyes were like saucers. "The payment has already cleared."

"Good?" Grace was so embarrassed at her mom's arrogance. Becca should tack on an annoyance fee.

"You don't understand, this much will keep my employees paid and the horses fed for at least six months."

Grace asked carefully, "And that's not normal?"

"No."

Tucker laughed. It was a deep belly chuckle. "I'm going to remind Lillian she said you were normal."

Becca slapped her brother's arm. "Stop teasing her." She looked to Grace. "Any idea when your mom will be here?"

"No, and I have no idea how long she'll stay. This is so embarrassing. I am so sorry."

"Are you kidding? I'm calling this a win, I mean, as long as the guests that were booted aren't upset. If they're happy, I'm happy. And my dad is not involved." Becca looked around. "Any pointers on what I should tweak for your mom?"

"Absolutely nothing," Grace said immediately. "Your home is lovely."

Becca beamed. "Thank you, that means a lot."

Tucker tapped the island counter. "What do you want to do about the bank?"

"Ignore it."

Tucker ignored her assessment. "Want me to come? We could drive into town now before the storm is supposed to come. Otherwise, you'll just be fretting."

Becca made a face. "I hate it when you're right. But if I wait, I'll be climbing the walls, imagining the worst."

"Come on. We got this."

"Fine. Let me give Radhi and Christopher an update. I can be ready in ten. We'll see how Dad looped the bank into his last act of terror."

Grace looked around. The kitchen was tidy, and there were no guests to attend to. "Is there anything I can do to help?"'

Becca vehemently shook her head. "Goodness, no, you're our guest."

"Please, I just want to help." Grace was acutely uncomfortable with leisure. She had always felt like an ornament, around because of tradition but with little value beyond.

Becca hesitated. "Would you mind trimming the tree?"

"Yes!" Grace blurted, relieved to be of some service.

"Excellent. That will be a lot of help."

Grace beamed. "It will be my pleasure."

In no time, Becca got Grace sorted with several boxes of tree ornaments.

The smile Tucker gave Grace before he left with his sister warmed Grace better than the cheery fireplace.

Or, if she was honest, Thorsen.

Grace had talked big back in Jordemorden, but she didn't want a fling.

She wanted Tucker to keep looking at her like that.

# Chapter Forty-Four

"I like Grace," Becca said from the passenger seat of Tucker's black electric truck. "She's kind."

"She is," Tucker agreed.

Gray clouds hung low, pressing in on the cab of the truck, and a few small snowflakes had started to fall. What worried Tucker, though, was the solid mass of pewter in the rearview mirror. It was snowing hard in the mountains. Though moving slowly, the system was tracking toward them.

"You going to tell me what's really going on with the two of you?"

Tucker gripped the steering wheel tighter. "There's nothing going on between me and Lillian's friend."

Becca looked out the passenger window. "If that's nothing, I'd hate to see something."

"Trust me, it's nothing. I'm pretty sure she likes Clint," Tucker muttered.

Becca snapped her head around. "Woah, what? How does she know Clint?"

"She found your secret passageway and ran into him when he was doing your barn chores. Thanks for keeping that a secret, by the way, a total stranger had to tell me."

Becca smirked. "You were spooning that total stranger a few hours ago."

"We were completely clothed!"

"You keep mentioning that," Becca said reasonably. "Why do you think she's attracted to Clint? There's a huge age gap."

Tucker paused. "I don't know. She's more animated when she talks about him. I just get a feeling."

"I guess some women dig older dudes," Becca said, not sounding very convinced. "You've been keeping a pretty big secret there."

Tucker darted a look at his sister. "I hated not telling you, I know how important a guest like her could be to your business."

Becca waved off his concern. "I understand. She's not a walking billboard for my eco-inn. Her family sounds as dysfunctional as ours."

Tucker rubbed his jaw. "I don't know what I'd do if anything happened to you. I guess I wanted to save you from any splash zone and keep her safe."

"You do like her."

"And I'm pretty sure she digs Clint," Tucker repeated. "Why did you have a secret exit built into the barn?"

"Meredith suggested it when she fronted me the money to rebuild, so I wouldn't have to wait for the insurance company's investigation. You should have seen the look on the draftswoman's face when we asked. I think she thought it was a fun addition. How could she understand the double meaning it had for Meredith and me?" Becca blew a breath. "I was purposely withholding it from you."

Tucker looked sideways at his sister before turning his gaze back to the road. "I'm sorry I didn't realize sooner he was a monster."

"None of us did."

"I should have. I wish I could make him dead, again, for what he did to you guys."

Becca snapped her head around. "Don't say that."

"Why, it's the truth?"

"Because it's not you! You're everything Dad never was. Dad was an *awful* person. Don't let him pull you down to that dark shit. He's dead—thank god—but you didn't kill him. You're not that guy." She added forcefully, "Tucker, you're *not* that guy."

"Sometimes, I wish I was." Some detective. He hadn't been able to track a dead man down.

Becca was practically shouting at him, "No, you don't. Hearing that he's dead is just fucking with your head."

"But I should have realized sooner that he was a monster," Tucker reasoned.

"That's a million times different than wishing you were the one to kill him. I get it, sometimes we need a pity party."

"That's not—" Tucker stopped at the slicing look his sister was giving him. "Okay, maybe it is."

Becca waited for half a beat. "You think?"

"Since when did you get so smart?"

"Since always," she retorted. "Seriously, Tucker, even dead, Dad's fucking with our heads. We can't let him get to us." Becca paused. "I'm almost afraid to believe he's gone, that we're safe."

"Me, too."

"I'm glad you're coming with me to the bank."

"Anytime." He'd do anything for his sister. "Do you mind if we stop by my condo? I need more winter clothes."

"Is *winter clothes* code for all the Christmas presents you bought me?"

"Yes. The socks and underwear are all yours."

"You're so gross." Becca turned to him. "Do you think Tanner's a bad guy, like Dad? He did bug your phone."

"I honestly don't know. To hear Lillian and Grace speak, surveillance is a normal part of their world. They expect their communications to be monitored, that's why they have secure lines." Tucker shrugged. "We're not like that. If it was Tanner, I wish he'd just ask me straight up what he wants to know. He didn't need to bug my phone."

"Good point," Becca conceded.

They both were quiet for long minutes.

Then Becca said with confidence, "Grace doesn't like Clint that way."

"How do you figure?"

"Because if she were into another guy, she wouldn't look at you the way she does."

He glanced at his sister. "What way?"

Becca smiled. "I knew it, you like her."

Tucker was definitely interested in the spunky princess. Still, he would never undermine her choice, and Grace could do a lot worse than the older cowboy.

For instance, *him*.

Becca's phone rang. She put it on speaker. "Hello?"

A masculine voice asked, "Is this Becca Tanner?"

She looked at Tucker, her eyes were worried. "This is she."

"Hi Becca," there was a pause, then "it's Tanner Stone."

# Chapter Forty-Five

Grace hummed to herself as she unwrapped another handblown glass ornament. She placed the tissue paper it had been wrapped in on the growing stack on the floor next to the decoration boxes. Carefully, she selected a spot and hung the delicate decoration, delighted with how it caught the light.

She hadn't realized the effort the palace staff must go through. Their decorations were always perfect. It had taken Grace forty-five minutes to put the lights on the tree, and they didn't look anywhere near as orderly as the palace ones did each year.

"Hello?"

Grace nearly jumped out of her skin.

She spun around. The cowboy from the barn stood at the end of the hallway from the kitchen.

He held a kitten.

She blew out a breath, grateful she had managed to catch her scream before it erupted from her throat.

"It's Clint, right?"

He nodded, looking pleased. "You and Tucker must have told Becca."

"Excuse me?"

"You're on tree trimming duty. Becca doesn't let just anyone near her tree."

Grace hedged. "They had to run an errand, and I wanted to help. Cute kitten."

Clint held up the wee tabby. "I don't think this little guy is feisty enough to make it the winter. My best mouser, Hayden, had a litter late in the fall, and Becca asked if she could try this little guy inside when he was ready, see if he'd be happy as an indoor house cat."

"He's adorable." The kitten was black and gray, with blue eyes. His ears were overly large on his small body.

"Want to hold him?"

Grace couldn't remember ever holding a proper kitten. "Sure."

She met him halfway, and he gently passed her the small bundle.

She had never considered her hands large, but they felt as big as pie plates holding the kitten. "He's so small."

And soft.

"He was the runt of the litter," Clint explained.

The kitten had yawned but barely blinked when Clint had passed him to Grace. Now he seemed to realize someone new was holding him and squirmed.

Grace cooed, repositioning her hold on him. She snuggled the small creature close, and he settled, staring at her with his clear, bright eyes. He couldn't weigh much more than a couple of pounds.

Grace inhaled. "He smells good. Kind of sweet, actually," she said, surprised.

"I have another one, a lighter tabby. He might make a good indoor cat."

She looked up. "Oh, I'm not staying long."

Clint looked like he was going to say something, and Grace blurted, "Want to help me decorate the tree?"

The older cowboy looked startled. "I haven't decorated a tree in years. That sounds fun."

"Excellent." Grace looked down at the kitten in her arms. "What should I do with him?"

"He'll be fine, probably will be asleep in a few minutes. He had a big morning, what with his first truck ride and all. I brought all his gear and set it up in the back mudroom."

Grace gently set the kitten down, and it immediately took off, romping through the stack of discarded tissue paper. The little guy darted back and forth, shredding tissue paper and skidding across the floor.

"Are you sure that's okay?" Grace had never been allowed an indoor pet at the palace.

"As long as he sticks to shredding tissue paper, he's fine. Though, it's probably a good idea to keep him corralled when he's not supervised until he's a bit older."

The kitten gave a final pounce before flopping over. He stretched once before he stood and circled the tissue paper. Finally, he settled and curled himself into a small ball on top of the tissue paper. A moment later, he opened an eye before closing it on an exhale. Within seconds, he appeared asleep.

Clint unwrapped an ornament. "I remember this one," he said softly.

He held a flat, painted miniature wooden rocking horse, no bigger than a child's palm. The loop of the cord included several shades of gold.

Clint hung it carefully on the tree. "One year, I took the kids to a Christmas market just outside of town. That year they had horses in one of the barns, and Becca would have stayed in that barn all night." Clint chuckled. "I bribed her with this ornament."

"She didn't want to go home?"

Clint reached for another ornament. "Kids are smart. Parents don't always realize how much they notice. Samantha and Bruce ... never mind."

Grace was unsure if she should mention the news of Bruce's death. She opened a carton of colorful witch balls, hanging a turquoise one. "Do you have a family?" When she looked over, Grace realized her faux pas. "I'm sorry, that's none of my business."

"It's okay. No, I don't have my own children. The Tanner kids were kind enough to take an old bachelor under their wing." He chuckled again, holding up a teddy bear with a green bow. It looked like a match for Becca's rocking horse. "This is Tucker's from that day." He picked up another ornament. "And here is Gabe's nutcracker." Clint dug deeper into the box. "Now, where is Colt's skiing, Father Christmas?"

"Tucker picked out a teddy bear?"

"He wanted a nutcracker, too, but refused to match Gabe."

Grace smiled as she hung another ornament, picturing Tucker as a little boy.

Time went quickly.

All too soon, the tree was decorated.

Grace stepped back, admiring the tree.

"That is a good-looking tree. Thanks for including me." He paused. "Are you okay?"

Not even close. "My mom and I decorated the tree back home."

"It must be hard to be away from your mom over the holidays. You must miss her."

Grace stared at the decorated tree. "It's complicated."

"Can you uncomplicate it?"

Grace shook her head. "I don't think so."

Clint started filing the empty ornament cartons into the larger boxes on the floor. "Well, sometimes life has a way of working out." He stacked the boxes on top of each other and picked them up. "I'll put these away. I know where Becca keeps them in the basement."

He left carrying stacks of empty boxes.

Grace's phone rang—the secure one.

It was Thorsen.

"Be advised, your mom is en route." He paused. "So am I. We need to talk."

# Chapter Forty-Six

"Tanner?" Becca's eyes were as big as saucers. "Tucker's here. You're on speaker. He's one of our brothers."

"I know who Tucker is," Tanner said quietly.

"I'm glad you called."

Tucker hated how hopeful she sounded. He gripped the steering wheel and wondered what the chances were his little sister wouldn't get her heart broken by their half-brother.

"I should have called sooner," Tanner said. "I appreciated your messages."

"You're calling now," Becca blurted. "Did you bug Tucker's phone."

Tucker mouthed, *what the fuck?*

Becca rolled her eyes at him before asking, "Did you?"

There was a short pause. "Will you be mad if I say yes?"

"I'll be madder if you're not honest," she quipped.

Tucker smiled.

Classic Becca.

"Then yes, I bugged Tucker's phone. Can we meet somewhere?"

Becca closed her eyes. "Look, Tanner—"

"Stone. I go by Stone."

"*Stone*, I want to meet you, but I have to know you don't mean us harm. You just admitted to bugging Tucker's phone."

There was a loud clatter and a muted swear.

Becca looked at Tucker and whispered, "Did he just drop his phone?"

Tucker nodded.

The phone buzzed back to life. "I'm here." There was another pause. "I'd never hurt you guys."

"I didn't think our dad would, either," Becca reasoned.

"My dad is the man who raised me. Bruce Tanner is nothing to me." Stone's voice was all ice.

Tucker gripped the steering wheel. "Did you know Bruce is dead?"

"Hell can have him," Stone snapped.

Time to regroup. "Becca and I will call you back."

In a noticeably warmer tone, Stone said, "I'm sorry, I shouldn't have said that."

"It's fine. Talk soon." Tucker punched the end button.

They were almost at his condo.

"What was that?" Becca yelled. "What are you doing?"

"I say we loop in Grace's people. Her guys found Stone in the first place, and she offered to help. If he's a bad apple, I don't want anyone getting hurt. If he's legit, we can't just dismiss him. I mean, he is our brother."

Becca agreed. "I'm in. I mean, as long as he's not a murderous nut job."

Tucker parked.

They took the elevator up. Tucker opened the door and swore.

His condo had been tossed.

# Chapter Forty-Seven

Tanner Stone disconnected the call.

He hadn't expected to feel so much.

"You okay?" Agent Omran Forest asked. He sat at one of the desk chairs across the table from Stone.

Stone nodded.

"I told you they were good people."

"You did."

The British special forces veteran would know better than Stone. He had helped rescue Stone's half-brother, Colt Tanner, a couple of months ago from a kidnapping. A Spanish double-agent had targeted Colt's fiancée, the decorated war correspondent and MI6 courier, Lillian Kensington, going so far as to break out of prison and chase her to Canada.

"They're nothing like him," Omran said, picking up a pen.

"I know. They're worried I am, though." Stone ran a hand through his hair, swearing. "How the hell and I supposed to get them to trust me so I can keep them safe?"

Omran rolled the pen between his palms. "Bring Tucker here."

Stone looked around the room. A handful of laptops, encrypted sat phones, and a printer covered the single long table. Two otter boxes below held surveillance equipment and four modems. The closet in the far wall held their arsenal. As far as field basecamps went, it was sparse but fit for purpose.

"He'd never agree."

"Read him in. We're missing something. He might be able to help."

The Australian government suspected Bruce Tanner and his business partners, among others, of election tampering to secure lucrative coal and iron ore contracts. The Brits and EU had uncovered similar schemes, and several global agencies had come together. The international task force had found a trail of shady business dealings, attempted murders, dirty politicians, a few dirty cops, and voter fraud in four countries. So far.

Of the original four men identified in the ring Bruce Tanner was involved in, three were dead. They also were the ones the task force had evidence on.

"You heard them just now," Stone explained.

"They've been through a lot, cut them some slack."

"What about Becca? Do you think we should read her in, too?"

He felt like such a coward for not calling her back. She had reached out several times over the last several months. First, when she found out he existed, then when Colt was in the hospital after he had been kidnapped, and when Tucker had been shot up. She had kept him in the loop like he was family.

He had thanked her for her kindness with silence.

"She's solid, but she's moved on. Tucker hasn't. He's hungry and haunted." Omran spread his hands wide. "Being read into the investigation might help him move on, too."

Stone stood, pocketing his phone and the van keys.

Omran looked up at him. "Where are you going?"

"To kidnap my brother. I need to make him trust me."

Omran stood, reaching out a restraining hand. "And you think kidnapping is the way to do it? Are you out of your bloody mind?"

"It'll only be kidnapping for like twenty minutes. Then I'll show him what we got, and if he wants to leave, he'll be free to go."

"And obliterate whatever tenuous relationship you guys have now?"

Stone hoped it wouldn't come to that.

"What do you suggest?"

"Why don't you just ask him?"

Stone hesitated before shaking his head. "No, he sounded pretty pissed. I'm going to do it my way. You coming?"

# Chapter Forty-Eight

Meredith's voice rang from the desk phone's speaker. "Let me be crystal clear. You are being entirely too cavalier with that which does not belong to you, and if you choose to aid and abet a criminal with what is mine and my stepdaughter's, I will bring you to swift justice. Do you understand me?"

Becca and Tucker looked at each other. They sat in adjacent chairs in the bank manager's overdecorated office, dwarfed by the supersized desk in front of them.

The bank manager swiveled in his large office chair, smirking, and asked Meredith, "Is that a threat?"

"It's a promise. Now stop wasting my time and put Pierre on the line. I've had enough of your grandstanding."

The bank manager stopped swiveling and stared at the phone. "You can't speak to him."

"Wanna bet?" Meredith snapped.

Tucker tried to hide his smile. Meredith was a force, more than they had first given her credit for. The sheer vehemence of her spunk always took him by surprise.

A distinguished-looking man entered the office without knocking.

The man smiled kindly at Becca first. "My, dear."

The bank manager stood. "Mr. Chamberlain—"

The older gentleman made a single shooing wave with his hand. Immediately, the bank manager snapped his mouth shut and dropped into his seat, stone still.

Becca smiled at the gentleman.

Tucker nodded. "Sir."

He inclined his head to both before saying, "Meredith, dear, are you still on the line?"

"Yes, Pierre. Thank you for seeing to it that Becca and Tucker are treated with the care and respect I expect. They are family, and I don't take lightly to them being abused." She paused. "I bank with your institution because I trust you, Pierre. Can I trust you on this?"

Pierre leveled a disapproving look at the bank manager. "You have my word. I will see to them personally, Meredith." He turned to Becca and Tucker. "My apologizes your experience with our former bank manger has been less than ideal, I will endeavor to correct it post haste."

The bank manager paled.

Meredith spoke again, "Kids, I'll call tonight. Let me know if you need anything."

"Thanks, Meredith," Tucker and Becca said in unison.

Meredith spoke, "Thank you, Pierre. I will be following up."

She hung up.

Their stepmom, Meredith, was a woman comfortable wielding her wealth and privilege, particularly when someone tried to run roughshod over someone she cared about, or more recently, herself as an older woman.

Tucker had come to understand Meredith took great pains to surround herself with respectable, loyal service providers, and didn't hesitate to compensate them handsomely for their care and attention. But she expected loyalty and service.

Pierre snapped his fingers. Two security guards who had been waiting on the other side of the floor-to-ceiling glass wall walked in. "Carl, this account is no longer yours, and from what has transpired, we will be conducting a thorough investigation." He turned to Tucker and assured him, "We will, of course, be cooperating fully with law enforcement."

Tucker nodded solemnly, though he had no idea what laws Carl had supposedly broken. Tucker thought the guy was just being a dick.

"I want my lawyer," Carl said as he was led out the door by the security officers.

Becca watched them through the glass wall. "When do you think he'll realize those are security guards, not police?"

Tucker leaned forward in his chair. Detective Jones was there, and he had just whispered something briefly into the bank manager's ear. Jones hesitated, noticing Tucker watching him, before slipping out a door.

Pierre had a pained expression on his face. "I am so sorry, you two. That was unacceptable. You know, your stepmother discreetly raised the alarm regarding what turned out to be an unscrupulous investor, as well as advised me away from an opportunity whose projected yields turned out to be significantly exaggerated. I dare say, in the last few months, your stepmother has developed an uncanny sixth sense for the dodgy."

Becca gave a firm nod. "Good."

"Right," Tucker agreed, distracted. It had been an odd exchange between Detective Jones and the bank manager.

"I'll sort out the land business in question," Pierre assured. "Now, I heard there was a safety deposit key?"

Becca pulled the charred key out of her pocket. "Is this from one of your safety deposit boxes? I think it was my father's."

Pierre examined the key. "It is. I can take you down immediately."

Tucker and Becca exchanged glances as they followed Pierre out of the office and through a labyrinth of corridors, stopping once when Pierre retrieved the necessary second key.

As they walked through an impressive marble paneled corridor with hushed lighting, Tucker tried not to gape. Patrons spoke in soft voices, and Tucker cold have sworn the space smelled of money.

Pierre led them through three secure doors before finally stopping in a medium-sized room.

Walls of small doors surrounded them, and Tucker asked, "What number is it?"

Becca checked the key, but Pierre was already leading them to the far side. Tucker guessed it was the north wall.

Pierre scanned the rows of boxes quickly. "Here we go." He fitted the key he was holding into one of the locks. "I'll wait for you outside."

Becca looked at Tucker. "This is it."

She lifted her hand, key pointing toward the lock.

The lights went out, followed by a choked scream.

# Chapter Forty-Nine

Automatically Tucker moved between the door and Becca, and she clutched his arm with both hands in the inky blackness.

It was eerie, being able to hear but see nothing. Even the emergency red exit signs were dark.

A low scuffle sounded, followed by several grunts.

"Becca, Tucker, over here."

He didn't recognize the voice.

A different voice called, one with a distinct British accent, "Guys, we've got to move. *Now.*"

Tucker strained to see in the total blackness. "Omran?" It sounded like Agent Forest, one of Lillian's friends.

"In the flesh, let's *go.*"

Tucker led Becca to the sound of Omran's voice. "What are you doing here?"

"Saving your ass."

"Thank, Christ," Becca muttered.

An auxiliary light finally flickered to life, casting an otherworldly, yellowish tinge.

"Wait." Becca pulled her hand out of Tucker's and turned back. With fumbling hands, she shoved the second security deposit box key into the lock and turned.

"Becca's, it's not worth your life, come on, let's go." Tucker had almost lost Becca three months ago, he was not losing her now.

"Give me a sec." She yanked out the drawer and tucked it under her arm. "Now, let's go."

A smile ghosted across Agent Forest's face before he led them out of the room.

"I can carry that."

Becca passed the long, narrow box to Tucker. "Thanks, it's unwieldy."

In the hallway, three bodies lay sprawled and bound with zip ties on the floor.

A man stood guard. "Let's get these two out of here."

Tucker stared as recognition flared. Tanner Stone stood armed before them.

"Where's the civilian?" Agent Forest asked Stone.

"I took that Pierre guy upstairs. They roughed him up, but he'll make it."

Tucker swiveled his head to watch Stone but followed Agent Forest, single file, after Becca.

Their half-brother brought up the rear.

Their small group took an unmarked door and several sets of utility stairs before being led out a side door into a parking garage. Stone guarded their retreat as Agent Forest half-shoved them into the back seat of a black SUV. "We've got to move."

Stone got behind the wheel, and Agent Forest jumped into the front passenger seat. As they drove out of the parking garage, Tucker saw several police cruisers, lights flashing.

Detective Jones was getting out of an unmarked vehicle.

Tucker leaned forward. "Why didn't we just wait for the police?"

Agent Forest looked over his shoulder. "Someone's dirty."

Puzzle pieces snapped into place. "That's why you bugged my phone?"

Stone and Agent Forest looked at each other briefly in the front seat.

"You guys thought I was the dirty cop?"

"Did," Stone said. "Past tense."

"Did you toss my condo?" Tucker pressed.

The two agents looked at each other again. "No, that wasn't us."

Omran pulled out a device. "I'm on it. Is anything missing? Or do you know if they were looking for something?"

"How the hell should I know?"

Becca had been eyeing the exchange. "You guys know each other?"

"I'm Agent Tanner Stone. You can call me Stone."

Becca sat back in her seat. "Are you fucking with me?"

Stone glanced in the rearview mirror. "No. I'm your half-brother."

"You are Australian."

"Yes." He paused. "Sorry I didn't return your calls."

Tucker watched his sister. "You okay?"

"This is what you and Grace were talking about?"

Tucker nodded before asking Stone, "You were at Bruce's wedding, weren't you?"

"That's classified."

Omran touched his earpiece briefly. "Three suspects have been apprehended from the altercation at the bank. They are all known to police."

"What does that mean?" Becca asked.

Tucker frowned. "If we have the world's shittiest timing, it was an attempted bank robbery."

"And if we don't?"

"They were there for us."

"We got you out before they did," Stone said.

"Even dead, he's fucking with us." Becca rested her arm on the door and cradled her head in her hand.

The security deposit box sat between them.

Tucker pulled it into his lap.

Becca glanced down. "Open it. Might as well see what shit show Dad's cooked up for us from beyond the grave."

A stack of folded envelopes were crammed into the narrow drawer.

Tucker opened the first envelope. It contained several printed sheets of paper and a thumb drive.

Tucker pulled out the papers. There were tidy columns that included names, contacts, and personal information.

Becca leaned over, frowning.

She pointed to a name. "That's Meredith's friend, Ruth. Remember, she was over for Thanksgiving."

Tucker remembered the spunky senior. She had made several outrageous, suggestive overtures. Her over-the-top attention had helped boot Tucker out of his dangerously dark headspace. Almost as much as baking with Rose Chasseur, Becca's soon-to-be mother-in-law, had.

Aw, hell, two senior ladies had hefted up his mental bootstraps.

Becca gasped, pulling him out of his rumination.

"That's a blackmail list."

Tucker looked where Becca was pointing. Next to Ruth's name, it said, *Sex solicitation.*

Becca huffed and sat back, crossing her arms. "Like Dad can talk. Fucking hypocrite. Can you picture sweet old Ruth soliciting sex?"

"Maybe?" Tucker totally could. He tucked the list and thumb drive back into the envelope and pulled out the next one. It had another thumb drive and photos.

They were images of Colt and Lillian.

Tucker swore. "Why the fuck did he have pictures of Colt and Lillian?"

Agent Forest turned swiftly. "Can I see those?"

Tucker passed them over.

Omran confirmed. "Fernando Martinez's crew took those."

"Are you saying our dad was in bed with the double agent who kidnapped Colt and tried to murder Lillian?"

"Or he found those and wanted to blackmail Fernando or one of his crew."

Becca scrubbed her forehead. "Christ, this just keeps getting more and more fucked."

Stone glanced in the rearview mirror. "We'll get this sorted."

Becca gave a weak smile.

Omran handed Tucker back the photos.

Tucker slid them into their envelope and pulled out the last one. Startled, he flipped the stack of photos over. "Becca, don't look."

Too late.

Her eyes were scrunched tight. "Is that what I think it was?"

"Probably," he answered honestly. He slid them back into the envelope. "You don't need to see whatever this is, and you can't unsee it."

She nodded, eyes still closed.

Omran held out his hand, and Tucker gave him the envelope.

Several moments later, Omran returned the photos to the envelope and handed it to Tucker. "Those should close several of your cold cases."

Becca slid her hand across the seat, squeezing Tucker's hand.

He squeezed back.

Becca turned to look out the backseat window.

Tucker pulled out the blackmail list again. Something was niggling.

Becca straightened. "Where are we going?"

"We have a safe house," Tanner said.

"Hell no. I have a safe house. I've had to put up with you spy types keeping it that way. We're all going there."

Tucker looked up from scanning the list of names. "Word to the wise, she grew a backbone this past year. Don't fuck with her."

Stone looked at Omran.

Omran nodded.

Stone switched lanes.

Becca whispered to Tucker, "What did you mean?"

"Before, you always tried to be the peacekeeper. Impossible in any family, let alone our fucked one. Ballsy suits you."

Becca objected, "I'm not ballsy."

"Fellas?" Tucker asked the men in the front seat.

"It's a good thing," Agent Forest assured her.

"You stayed alive, Becca. One could say that took balls."

"Ovaries. It took a set of steel ovaries."

Tucker smiled and returned to studying the list of names. It was a who's who of western Canadian business and politics, with several eastern magnates for good measure. Tuck looked up. "Half of this list are personal friends of Meredith's."

"How do you know that?" Becca asked.

"With her permission, I've been combing the last five years of her life. I was looking for a toehold, anything to give me an idea what Dad was up to."

"I thought you didn't find anything," Becca said.

"What if he married her for her connections?" Tucker asked.

"If that were the case, he wouldn't have tried to murder her," Becca reasoned. "Unless he had already gotten what he wanted."

"Did you say that list had politicians on it?" Omran asked.

"Yeah, about half of them are, and of those, maybe two-thirds Meredith knows personally."

"What about resource companies? Any mining, hydro, or oil and gas?"

Tuck scanned the list. "About two dozen that I recognize."

Omran looked at Stone. "He is suspected of voter fraud and intimidation to support controversial mining projects in Australia. Think he was planning it here, too?"

"Why kill people, though?" Stone asked.

No one had an answer.

Becca tapped her knee. "How did you guys find us, or even know we were in danger?"

"Funny story —"

Omran interjected, "After Colt was kidnapped to get at Lillian, I put tracers on all of your vehicles, sets of keys, cell phones, and Becca, your saddle, too, after we almost lost you."

Tucker stared. Omran played by a significantly different set of rules than Tucker did.

Stone frowned. "That's kind of overkill, isn't it?"

"Do you know how dead I would be if anything happened to these guys? They're considered assets, and Lillian would never forgive me."

"Assets, really?" Tucker muttered, "Shouldn't you at least buy us dinner first?"

Omran shrugged. "You know enough to know how the game works."

Tucker asked Stone. "So, what was your plan?"

Stone shifted. "I was going to kidnap you guys until you believed I wasn't working with Bruce."

Tucker burst out laughing.

"What's so funny?" Stone asked.

Becca was looking at Tucker like he had lost his mind. "Yeah, why is that funny?"

Tuck swiped at his eyes. "Because you handcuffed Jason to get him to listen to you, too."

Becca's face turned a bright crimson. "That was different."

"Yeah, it ended in a make-out session. This one is definitely not."

# Chapter Fifty

"I don't want her here." Grace broke off, cradling the phone to her chest.

Clint had walked back into the room.

She could hear Thorsen's muffled voice and pressed the phone tighter against her.

"I'll just be one sec," she said to Clint.

The kitten had woken and was winding between Clint's ankles, rubbing against him. Clint picked the wee furball up. "Take your time."

Grace smiled at him before placing the phone back to her ear.

"She's worried sick about you," Thorsen was saying. "This has been hard on all of you."

Grace tensed at his defense of her mom.

His first loyalty was to the crown. Just once, it would be nice if he considered her feelings ahead of duty.

"I have to go." She hung up, pocketing her phone, before looking at Clint. "Do you cook?"

The older cowboy smiled. "I can hold my own."

"I thought it might be nice to have something ready when Tucker and Becca get back. Would you mind showing me how to make something simple?" She dipped her head. "I have no idea how to cook."

Grace was also worried about Tucker and Becca. The sick feeling in the pit of her stomach had been growing steadily since they left. Having Clint nearby helped.

He looked thoughtful. "Becca likes my chili, and I think Colt and Lillian were invited for dinner. We could make it vegan, easy enough."

"That would be lovely." Grace popped off the couch and led the way to the kitchen.

Clint followed. "Where did you say they were going for their errand?"

"Something in town, I think," Grace said evasively.

Clint looked at her but didn't ask more questions.

Grace stopped in the kitchen. She had no idea where to start. "Do you have a recipe you use?" She had followed the recipe for macaroni and cheese, and the stuff that hadn't burned had been edible.

"Where's the fun in that?" Clint headed to the pantry.

Grace followed.

He selected several cans of beans, tomatoes, and corn, as well as a couple of onions, a large sweet potato, and three gloves of garlic.

"Do you know how many will be here for dinner?"

Grace shrugged. "At least seven, maybe more."

Clint tripled what he had just selected.

Grace's eyes widened. "That much?"

Clint chuckled. "You haven't seen the Tanner boys eat. Becca can freeze any leftovers, easy enough. Can you check if there are bell peppers in the crisper?"

Grace hurried to look, calling out, "Does it matter what color they are?"

"Pick your favorites."

Grace smiled. She could get used to recipes like this.

Clint placed his bounty on the large island counter before getting out a couple of cutting boards and knives.

Grace placed the bell peppers alongside everything.

He started washing the bell peppers and sweat potatoes. "What do you do?"

Panic sparked within her. "My family is in politics." Kind of.

He glanced at her. "Are you, as well?"

She smiled, drying the produce. "I like to help people. I mostly help coordinate people with services or support. Sometimes I organize petitions or rallies."

He pointed to the sweet potatoes and bell peppers. "Can you dice those up, please? Does your family help you?"

Grace picked up a sweet potato. "My family doesn't approve of how I choose to help our citizens." She turned the root vegetable over in her hand. "Do I cut the outer part off first?"

Clint smiled gently. He took the vegetable and showed her how to use a paring knife to peel off the skin.

He handed them back to her.

Grace felt clumsy trying, but she got the hang of it within a few passes.

"You mentioned *our citizens*?"

Grace glanced up. "That probably sounds weird. My family—we're complicated."

"Most families are." He placed the bulbs of garlic on a cutting board before laying the flat side of a medium-sized knife over them. He used the palm of his hand and pressed the knife against the garlic gloves.

Grace heard a faint release.

He cut the tips of the cloves off. The outer skins easily slid off. She stared. The one time she had tried to peel garlic had been a disaster.

She returned to the sweet potato and bell pepper while he minced the garlic and diced the onions.

"Now what?" Grace asked, watching everything he did.

Clint opened the cans of beans and corn, rinsing them in a colander. He placed them next to the stove. "I like to prep everything first. Then I can just enjoy cooking."

Grace had never considered cooking something done for pleasure, unlike Tucker and Clint.

Clint placed an oversized pot on a burner and turned the heat to medium. He drizzled oil in the bottom of the pan and pointed. "I put enough to cover the bottom. Can you bring everything we just chopped over here?"

Grace was eager to oblige.

He retrieved several spice canisters in the cupboard adjacent to the stove, walked Grace through sautéing the different vegetables, and when he liked to add the different spices and canned legumes. Clint was a patient teacher, and Grace was enjoying herself immensely. She was proud to be helping make food for Tucker.

All too soon, the chili was ready, and Grace realized she didn't want him to go. She liked spending time with Clint. Like Tucker and Becca, he made her feel inherently welcome, like her value and worth were assumed instead of tabulated.

It was almost a reverse culture shock. Until coming here, she hadn't realized she felt transactionally loved by her family and country. Canada had doubled the number of people she could call friend: Lillian, Claire, Thorsen, and now Tucker, Becca, and Clint.

"That's a mighty big frown."

Grace blinked, plastering a smile on her face. "Thank you for teaching me. That was fun."

"Any time." He looked so sincere that Grace fought the urge to hug him.

Her secure mobile pinged. It wasn't Thorsen.

"Can you excuse me?"

Clint nodded and tidied up the kitchen.

Grace headed through the swinging door to the empty dining room. "Claire?"

"Who's your favorite friend? Don't answer that. I just sent encrypted files of photos of your original birth certificate and your biological parents' marriage certificate."

Grace stumbled into a seat. "Holy shit. How? I mean, thank you."

"You're adorable when you're flustered. Thorsen helped. I think he was worried about me getting caught. Someday, like when we have huge glasses of wine in our hands, I will tell you the story."

Grace's email notification pinged.

Claire laughed. "That should be the email I just sent. I've gotta run. Call if you need anything."

Grace's hand shook. "I can't thank you enough." Her list of friends wasn't long, but they cared deeply for her. Too bad they were all scattered around the world.

"Anytime, darling." Claire disconnected.

Grace clutched her phone, hesitating. Without checking her email, she pocketed her mobile and marched back into the kitchen.

"Everything okay?" Clint asked.

"I hope so."

It wasn't. What if Grace had just made a huge mistake? It wasn't just her life that would be turned upside down with the contents of the email, her whole family's would be, too.

Including her mom's heart.

# Chapter Fifty-One

Tucker handed his sister a mug of coffee. "Drink your coffee. You're way easier to deal with caffeinated. When did you get a cat?"

Becca accepted the steaming mug as the kitten darted past. She squealed in delight. "Clint must have dropped him off."

The kitten bounded past the propped open kitchen doorway to the formal dining room beyond.

In the dining room, Stone was looking as unsure as Christopher usually did. Both men sat apart from the others.

Omran had no such reservations and was chatting freely with Lillian and Colt. Agent Forest and Lillian had been friends for decades. Grace and Clint also looked happy in their animated conversation.

Becca leaned toward Tucker. "This is weird, right?"

Tucker pulled his gaze away from Grace and Clint. "Our father had international agents tracking him, and now they're in your dining room? Yeah, it's fucked. How is Christopher settling in?"

The man in question looked up, holding Tucker's gaze. Theirs was a complicated relationship.

Becca noticed the stare down. "I get it. Some people don't deserve a second chance. He does."

"Jason has no issues with Christopher working for you?" Before the past year, Tucker would have given him and his brother, Austin, the benefit of the doubt. It was why Tucker had been in the hospital in the first place when he lunged and took the bullets meant for Austin. Now, Tucker wasn't so sure. It was an uncomfortable casualty of their father's treachery.

Becca kept her voice low. "Jason and Christopher have found a cautious truce, and honestly, my only issue with Christopher is I worry about him. I know I didn't know him before the fire, but he's so serious. Don't get me wrong, he's a hard worker, diligent and conscientious. Radhi trusts him, which is saying a lot. As far as I'm concerned, he and his brother Austin are part of our crazy ragtag family. I just wish they understood that."

Tucker tried not to notice Grace was leaning into Clint, laughing. Distracted, he asked, "How's Austin doing?"

Christopher's younger brother, Austin, was a computer whiz-bang, though his credentials, like Christopher's, were problematic. Though never convicted, running suspected arms and drug rings was hardly a résumé builder.

"He's serious, like his older brother. I don't know what curveballs life's thrown at them, neither speak of the past, but I doubt it was pretty." Becca rubbed her arms. "That kid is brilliant. I wish I needed a tech or chemistry genius. With his history, the kid can't exactly list references. Who would hire him? And their patent is under investigative review because of the attempted thefts. That kid has so much potential. I wish I could help."

Something tickled the back of Tucker's mind. "Is he under twenty-five?"

"I think so, why?"

"There's a new *turn around* program starting. One of the defund the police pilot programs is hiring at-risk youth, and young offenders who meet their criteria, to team up with the police." Tucker rubbed his jaw. "With that kid's skillset, he would be a boon to any police force, providing he was working for the law, instead of against it."

Becca's face lit up. "Can you check?"

"How about I ask him if he wants me to check first? If he does, we can go from there. I'm happy to help." Something inside Tucker sparked to life. He had lost more than blood after his father's associate, Del Fiennes, had fired three bullets into him at close range. Helping Austin get on a path that helped the kid and the community would go a long way. His faith in humanity needed some serious propping.

"I'm sorry I gave you crap about hiring Christopher. I should have trusted you."

Becca hip-butted him. "You were just looking out for me. I know on paper, it looks insane."

Tucker snorted. "It really does. Love you, kiddo."

Becca gaped at his declaration.

Tucker shifted, uncomfortable. "Don't make it weird."

That got her cackling. "Nope, just ready to hand you a maxi pad." She paused for effect. "Get it?"

"Yes, Captain Obvious, I got it. Hey, I thought those jokes were offensive?"

"Yeah, when a dude says it," she retorted. Quieter, she said, "Happy to have you back, bro."

Jason walked in, still wearing his RCMP uniform. He kissed Becca. "Wow, full house." He took the lid off the large pot on the stove and sniffed. "Dang, Tuck, this smells incredible."

"Grace and Clint made it," Tucker grumbled.

Jason looked through the doorway to the dining room. "Lillian's friend Grace? Isn't she royalty or something?"

Tucker turned to look. "She is." Grace was still laughing with Clint and even touched his shoulder.

Jason and Becca exchanged a look.

Jason frowned, staring through the doorway. "Please tell me Omran's here for a social visit."

"Honey, there's a lot to catch you up on."

Jason stilled, and Becca reached for his arms. "We're safe. Everyone's safe. That is," Becca cleared her throat, "my dad is dead. Like a month ago, it was ruled an overdose."

Jason folded his arms around Becca, and she tucked into him. They just held each other like that. The love that passed between them in those few seconds unhinged Tuck, and he called into the dining room, "Stone, can you help me a sec?"

Their half-brother leaped up. When he was in the kitchen, Tuck handed him a stack of bowls from the cupboard and added a handful of spoons. "Can you pass these out?" He grabbed a loaf of French bread from the counter and tucked it under Stone's chin. "That, too."

His half-brother silently obliged, though his gaze stopped on Becca and Jason before heading into the dining room.

Tuck followed him with the oversized pot of chili and a ladle. Becca and Jason joined everyone in the dining room moments later.

"Let's eat, guys. Grace and Clint made the chili." Becca's smile was bright, though it didn't quite reach her eyes.

After introductions were all made, Jason looked around the table. "Lillian and Grace, you guys know each other. And Omran, you have been Lillian's family's security detail before. You and Stone are working on a task force of sorts together, I think I got that right. How did you guys all meet up today?" Jason asked before taking a bite of chili.

"We've been tracking Bruce Tanner," Stone said.

"They thought I was dirty. Wow, good job on the chili," Tucker supplied.

Heads snapped up around the long table. Everyone was staring at him, and Tucker added, "They were just doing their job. Everyone in this room I trust with my life." He shoved another spoonful of chili into his mouth.

Christopher stared at him. "Do you mean that?"

Tuck swallowed. "Yes."

"What about me?" Stone asked.

Tucker shrugged. "You could have knocked Becca and me off today instead of saving us from whoever the fuck those guys were."

Jason's spoon clattered against his bowl. Becca placed her hand on his arm. "We're safe. Stone and Omran were there and got us out safely. I was going to tell you later, privately." She made a face at Tucker.

"Tell me now." Jason's eyes were stark.

Tucker concisely recounted the events at the bank.

Jason briefly closed his eyes, and Becca tried to reassure her fiancé. "I told you, I'm fine. We are all fine."

Jason took her hand as he looked at Stone and Omran. "Thank you."

Tucker asked, "Do you guys know who they were?"

Stone answered, "From what we've been able to piece together, Bruce had three business associates. Of the four of them, three are confirmed dead. Bruce died of an overdose approximately a month ago. Del Fiennes died by a knife to the throat."

Everyone looked at Christopher except Stone. Catching on, Stone asked, "You're the knife guy?"

Christopher nodded.

The look on Stone's face was almost a smile. "That was impressive blade work. Fiennes was in the process of trying to steal a patent. I'm guessing that was you and your brother's?"

Christopher nodded again.

Stone continued, "The dead guy at your father's wedding was Sasha Petrovanov."

"Who's he?" Tucker asked.

"On paper, he was a Russian banker. Intel suggested he'd moved from arms trading to being one of the major players in election manipulation. He was accused of assassinating candidates, voter intimidation, voter fraud, and blowing up several voting stations around the world."

"Any idea who killed him?" Tucker asked.

Stone shook his head.

Omran shifted.

Tucker frowned. So, they weren't sharing everything.

Becca asked, "The bank said Dad was trying to give the land to a Teague Alans. Who's that?"

Jason's head came up. "Seriously?"

Becca said quickly, "Meredith's bank guy is on it. If he can't fix it, Meredith will. She's way savvier than we've given her credit for. You won't lose the land again."

Stone said, "Teague Alans is the last man standing. We're tracking him now."

Tucker asked, "What do you know about him?"

"Not enough."

"Where does the dirty cop fit in?"

Omran said, "Bruce's vehicle had a score of dope in it that had evidence tags on it. Could you tell if they're legit or not?"

"I should be able to," Tucker said.

"Good. We'll get you to check tomorrow."

"Any chance whoever is dirty tossed your place?" Stone asked.

Jason glanced at Tucker.

"I'll fill you in," Tucker assured him. "I'm not sure who tossed my place, and I'm not accusing anyone of anything yet. However, I have seen one of the guys from my unit, Detective Jones, a lot lately. He was at Bruce's former apartment and the bank today, whispering something to the bank manager. It could be nothing."

Stone and Omran looked at each other.

Stone frowned. "I'll do some discreet digging. If Jones is involved, I want to know if he's just hired or another associate."

# Chapter Fifty-Two

Grace slipped outside the front door of the inn, silently following Tucker. The air was cold, almost crackling in its chill, and the winter night held a hushed silence. Christmas lights twinkled in the soft breeze.

Tuck had almost made it around the corner of the wraparound porch before noticing her. "What is it? Are you okay?"

"I wanted to check on you."

"I'm fine."

She held out one of the mugs she was carrying. "I made this for you."

"What is it?"

"Tea."

He accepted it and took a sip. "That's not tea."

"Whiskey might have spilled into it."

Tucker turned his head, but not before Grace saw his grin.

He took another sip of the hot toddy.

"Want to talk about it?"

Tucker leaned against the porch railing. "About what?"

Grace shrugged. Tucker had visibly fled after the conversation. "Anything you want to talk about."

"No."

Grace took a sip from her mug. "Can you tell me more about Clint?"

Tucker slammed his tea down on the porch railing.

"What's wrong?" Grace asked.

"He's old enough to be your father," Tucker muttered, shoving his hands in his pockets. He stomped farther around the porch.

Grace trailed after him, nearly skipping. "I know, right! That's the best part."

Tucker spun around and held up both hands. "Stop following me. You should just go talk to him yourself. You were talking to him all damn night."

"I wanted to ask you."

"Fine. Clint's a great guy."

"Good. I trust you, your opinion means a lot to me." Grace stepped closer, crowding Tucker. "You mean a lot to me."

"Grace, I can't—"

His lips always looked so soft. If she leaned forward, would he meet her halfway? "Can't what?"

Tuck placed his hand on the front of her hip and pushed her away from him. His voice sounded almost desperate when he said, "Please, no. I can't."

The cold porch railing pressed against her backside. She closed her hand over his where it was still on her hip, and she could have sworn she felt the barest squeeze of his hand.

Grace pressed closer. "Why not?"

Tuck swiftly pulled his hand away and took several steps back. "Seriously? You were just asking after another man."

Confused, Grace asked, "You mean Clint?"

"Yeah, Clint. He's like family. I'm not fooling around with someone who wants to play ball with him, too. It's just not done."

It took a second for her to process what he was saying. She blanched before bursting out laughing. "That's what you thought?"

"To be clear, you're saying you're not interested in Clint romantically?"

"No." Grace added, "I mean, he's a nice guy and all."

In half a second, Tucker closed the distance between them and swept his arms around her. "What about me?"

Heat sparked. Grace grabbed his face between her hands. "How about I show you?"

She pressed her lips against his, claiming his mouth, trying to show him with her lips what she felt for him.

He kissed her back. For precious moments, nothing existed except the two of them. Their bodies pressed tight, mouths, hands, and hips frantic with need.

Distantly, Grace heard the drone of an engine.

When the sound got louder, Grace reluctantly pulled back. "What is that?"

She looked skyward as a helicopter approached.

Tuck grabbed her hand and pulled her toward the front door of the inn. His voice was thick with concern when he said, "I don't know who that is, but after the week we've had, I'm not going to chance anything. Let's get inside."

Grace tugged at his hand. "Tuck, wait."

"Yes, to be continued." He dropped his voice lower. "Believe me, I know." He eyed the still approaching heli. "I need to get you inside, I need you safe—"

"That's what I'm trying to tell you," she interrupted.

"I'm not kidding, Grace, helicopters flying at night are rarely a good thing. Please, just let me get you inside."

"Tuck, stop. I think my mom's in that helicopter. Queen Katherine."

Tuck stopped tugging on her hand. "Your mom?"

Grace laced her fingers through his. "My life is about to blow up. I'm asking, begging actually, I need a friend right now, I need *you* right now." Grace's voice cracked, and she shook her head. "I can't face her alone."

He looked down at their entwined hands. He leaned over and kissed her. "I'm all yours."

Grace cradled his cheek with her hand, kissing him back.

Way too soon, the helicopter was landing. Christmas lights swung wildly from the tree branches from the rotors' wind wash, and snow swirled in a blinding frenzy. Grace closed her eyes and tucked her head into Tucker's shoulder.

Through her lashes, she counted three people emerging from the aircraft. Two of them were quick to unload luggage before following the third toward the inn.

Once clear, the aircraft took off into the night.

Grace swore, squeezing Tucker's hand.

It wasn't just her mom walking toward them.

Thorsen, and the new agent, Charles, were there, too.

# Chapter Fifty-Three

Grace's eyes widened. Her mom was actually running to her. They had walked down the porch steps, waiting for the trio. Tucker released Grace's hand and stepped to the side as her mom wrapped her arms around her. "Darling, you're safe."

Grace had to brace herself to keep their balance. "Mum, you're hugging me."

The queen pulled back. Tears streaked through her makeup. "I thought you were dead," she whispered.

Grace pulled her mom close, hugging her tight. "I'm safe. I'm okay."

After long moments, she pulled back. "Why are you here, Mum?"

The queen brought her hands up, cradling Grace's face between her hands. "I thought I lost you."

The queen had never shown a fraction of the warmth she was showing now.

It was disorienting.

Grace stood still, unsure what to do.

The queen smiled and kissed her forehead. "Well, I could use a cup of tea. Shall we go in?" The queen seemed to notice they weren't alone. "Who is this?"

Grace slipped her hand into Tucker's. "This is Tucker."

The queen's lips parted in surprise.

Charles looked uncomfortable.

Thorsen simply stared where Tucker held her hand.

Grace continued, "Tucker, this is my mum, Katherine. And Thorsen and Charles, they're agents."

Tucker held out his hand to the queen. "Nice to meet you."

The queen hesitated.

Grace asked pointedly, "Is there a problem, Mom?"

"Of course not." The queen shook Tucker's hand. "Charmed."

Tucker gave her a brief smile before shaking Charles's hand. He held his hand out to Thorsen. "Pleasure to finally meet you. I believe thank you is in order."

"How's that?" Thorsen asked.

"Grace pummeled me the first time we met." Tucker's smile widened. "If you're going to have one gear, kick-ass is where it's at, am I right?"

Grace darted a look at Thorsen. He did look happy.

"Did I say something wrong?" Tucker was looking between Grace and Thorsen.

"Of course not." Grace echoed her mom's earlier words. "Come on, Mum, I'll show you in."

Everyone started toward the inn.

The queen leaned close. "You pummeled him?"

"Long story, Mum. You know how I like to train."

The queen cleared her throat. "I'm glad you remember Charles."

"We met before I left." Grace looked back at the new recruit walking up the steps behind them. "Chuck, how's the foot?"

"Still has a hole in it, Your Highness."

Her mom turned her head sharply. "What does he mean by that, darling?"

"Never mind."

"Good. I wanted you two to spend more time together."

"Why?" Grace asked, suspicious.

Stopping on the porch, the queen huffed out a breath. "It is cold here, isn't it?"

"Mum. What are you on about?"

"The grand duke wishes to see you married. Charles comes from the right sort of family."

Incredulous, Grace turned toward her mother. "Are you fucking kidding me right now?"

"Grace, language," the queen chastised.

"Now I know why you were so happy I wasn't dead. It was so you could marry me off." Grace shot Charles a look. "No offense, Chuck, but we're not happening."

Charles wisely kept his mouth shut. Thorsen and Tucker did, too.

"That's not fair," the queen said.

"But not untrue," Grace retorted.

Her mom glanced around the ranch yard. The darkness concealed more than it revealed, still, Grace's stomach flared again. The queen didn't spend much time with people who were not royal or politicians.

"Mum, these are my friends. Don't be rude."

"I'm never rude."

Grace arched an eyebrow. "Really?"

"I have an eighty-seven percent approval rating," the queen argued.

"Not with these people. Last week, they had no idea who you were."

Grace noticed several heads peeking through the front room windows and sighed. Helicopters were not discreet ways to travel.

"I'm serious, be nice," Grace whispered, her hand on the front doorknob.

"Darling, relax, I'm not going to do anything to embarrass you. I'll be on my best behavior."

"I'm holding you to that." Grace led the small group into the inn.

In the foyer, Grace and Tucker hung jackets and filed suitcases to the side.

Grace knew she was going to regret this. "Be nice," she reminded her mom.

The queen plastered a smile and stepped boldly forward, leading the small group into the front room.

She stopped suddenly, and Grace ran into her mum's back.

Embarrassed, she side-stepped, whispering, "That's your idea of best behavior?"

But the queen was paying her no attention. Her whole body was trembling, and she looked like she had seen a ghost.

"Clint? Is that you?"

# Chapter Fifty-Four

In disbelief, Clint stared at the small group that had just entered the front room. "Kat?"

The room was dead silent.

Tucker watched as Grace's mom and Clint drank each other in.

Clint stood from his seat on the couch then, rounding the coffee table.

She met him halfway.

Grace motioned with her hand when Thorsen and Charles would have interjected.

In three strides, the reunited couple were wrapped in each others' arms. No words were spoken, they just clung to each other.

Grace watched them with tears, but she was smiling. Tucker slipped his hand into hers, and she held on tight.

Becca made a soft clicking sound before silently circling her forefinger and pointing to the kitchen hallway.

Christopher moved first. Colt, Lillian, Stone, Omran, Jason, and Becca silently followed.

"She's safe with him. Let's give them some privacy," Grace said.

Thorsen eyed the couple. Clint and Grace's mom hadn't moved. They spoke softly to each other, cocooned in their world.

Tucker did as Grace bid, following Charles down the hall.

He would have to be blind to not notice the undercurrents between the head of royal security and Grace.

Becca shut the kitchen door once Grace and Thorsen had filed inside. "Holy shit, your mom knows Clint?"

"Looks like it."

Christopher had opened a bottle of wine. He waited until Grace noticed before offering her a glass.

"Read my mind, thank you." Grace accepted the glass, her hands shaking. She took a large swallow. "Come on, guys, don't let me drink alone."

Becca accepted the glass Christopher handed her. "What should we drink to?"

"Pretty sure that's my dad in there."

# Chapter Fifty-Five

"I thought you were dead." Kat clung to Clint's shirt. Fresh tears streamed down her face, and she didn't care if she was being proper and presentable or not. "Please, don't let go. Not yet."

"I'm not going anywhere, Kat." He coiled his arms tighter around her.

She lowered her head to his shoulder.

His voice had aged, and gone was the lanky cowboy. He still had a wiry strength, but Clint had grown into a man.

She felt him shift, swiping his hand across his eyes.

Katherine had never stopped dreaming of Clint. When her life closed in too tight, feeling unbearable and choking, she would imagine what their lives could have been like had he not died.

"Why did you think I was dead?"

Kat pulled away, pressing the palms of her hands against her eyes. "My father told me you were."

His voice bleak, he said, "You just disappeared, without a word. I thought you felt the same way I did. I had no way of contacting you, I couldn't ask why or what had happened. You just left." His eyes were filled with the pain of decades in the dark.

"I know," she whispered.

"You were secretive about your background, but I respected that. I trusted you would tell me when you were ready. I didn't care who you were, I just cared about you. And you left."

"I didn't want to!" Kat reached for his hands, holding them fiercely. "I was a stupid, obedient girl who should have trusted her instincts."

"What do you mean?"

"You didn't *feel* dead." Kat practically cried the words. "My heart thought surely I would know if you were really gone." Kat dropped her head, filled with shame. "Instead, I listened to my father. I listened to those I had always been taught to obey and who I naïvely assumed had my best interests at heart. We missed a lifetime together because of my foolish obedience. Clint, can you ever forgive me?"

Tears were in his eyes as he cupped his hand around the back of her head and gently kissed her forehead. "We were just kids back then. There is nothing to forgive."

He wrapped his arms around her, and she borrowed some of his strength.

She needed it for what she was about to tell him.

"We have a daughter."

# Chapter Fifty-Six

Grace let Lillian pull her in for a fierce hug.

"Do you want me to stay?" Lillian asked, her eyes searching Grace's.

They had been friends long before Lillian had been duped by a double agent and falsely accused of treason against the British crown. The ordeal had bonded their friendship into something much deeper. This would, too.

"No, I'll be okay." She looked at the closed kitchen door. "I'm not sure how this will shake out. Can I call you tomorrow?"

"Of course. You need anything, we're here for you."

"I know. That means a lot." She cleared the lump in her throat. "Go on. I'll see you," she winked, "and your handsome cowboy tomorrow."

Colt turned a bright shade of red.

Lillian burst out laughing. "I told you guys she was normal. Come on, honey."

Lillian and Colt left. Becca, Jason, and Omran excused themselves, and Christopher had slipped out already. Tucker and Stone spoke quietly, and Charles perched on one of the island stools.

Thorsen walked up to Grace. "We need to talk."

Grace's gaze sought Tucker's. He was watching them. "Later."

Thorsen reached for Grace's hand. "It's important."

She felt, more than saw, Tucker tense.

Grace placed her hand over Thorsen's. "Will it keep?"

He hesitated. "Affirmative."

"Then let it keep. I've had a hell of a day." She shook his hand off and walked over to Tucker. She tried to keep her voice bright. "Can I steal Tuck away?"

Stone nodded and filed out the same side hallway door Christopher had earlier.

"Your head of security is still staring at you."

"That's his job." Grace leaned in. "Becca's got a room ready for me here," she pointed toward the front room, "but I can't deal with that right now. May I stay with you again tonight?"

Tucker had leaned in when Grace did, and she knew Thorsen was still watching them.

"You're always welcome. I told you that."

"I was hoping you'd say that. Can we go now? I'm not ready to face my mom and Clint just yet." Her stomach was knotted with excitement and fear for the Pandora's box she'd opened.

Tucker nodded. "We can go now."

Grace squeezed his forearm. "Thanks, I'll wait for you outside while you say bye to your family." She darted for the door, jamming her feet into a pair of Tucker's boots and swiping one of his jackets off its hook. She slipped out the backdoor in record time.

The winter night air had a bracing effect, and she inhaled deeply.

"Where are you going?"

Grace spun around.

Thorsen stood close. His face could have been carved out of granite, save for plumes of his breath in the cold night.

She answered honestly, "I'm staying in the apartment above the barn."

"With Detective Tucker Tanner?"

Grace crossed her arms. "Don't look at me like that. He gave me shelter when I needed it."

"I bet he did." Thorsen zipped up his fleece base layer against the cold.

Grace stared. It was the first time Thorsen had ever sounded even remotely jealous. She shook her head. "You don't get to comment on stuff like that. Not anymore."

He let out a long breath, it hung in the air between them.

"I don't suppose I do." He jammed his hands in his pockets. "I'm sorry, Gracie."

Her stomach started churning. "For what?"

He stepped closer. "For everything. I fucked up, and I'm sorry."

She shrugged helplessly, shaking her head. "Don't—I can't, Thorsen, not anymore."

"I know," he said quietly. "I'll walk you to Tucker's."

"You don't need to do that. It's the protocol I tell someone where I'm going. I told you."

"I'm walking you, Gracie."

The door opened. Tucker stepped outside. It was clear he had not been expecting to see Thorsen.

"You need a place to crash, too?" He asked, deadpan.

"No, he doesn't," Grace answered in a rush.

She could have been less emphatic.

Thorsen's frown deepened. "I'm just walking you guys over. This past week has been unusual, Gracie usually has a substantial detail."

*Gracie.* She used to love his nickname for her, but now it grated.

Tucker glanced at her.

She willed him to be patient with her and understand that she was worth the baggage she came with.

"As long as Grace is cool with it, be my guest." Tucker motioned for Thorsen to go ahead of them. The path from the eco-inn to the barn apartment stairs was a single file track through the snow.

Grace followed Thorsen. Tucker brought up the rear.

Thorsen walked up the steps first. He waited to the side as Tucker keyed in the code before entering the apartment first. He cleared the small space quickly before waiting at the door for Grace.

She appreciated that Tucker gave them space, such as it was in the studio apartment, while at the same time wishing he would be unsettled. She would if their roles had been reversed.

"Grace? Did you hear what I just said?"

She stared at Thorsen blankly.

"I said I need to speak with you soon. It's important."

"You said it'll keep." Grace rubbed her forehead. She needed to process the current life-shattering revelation before Thorsen dropped the next one on her. "I'll see you in the morning."

He was standing so close. In the past, his nearness would have sent her into a spiral of giddy passion.

Now, she simply missed the friends they had been and likely never could be again.

"Do you trust him?" Thorsen asked.

Grace looked at Tucker. He was in the apartment's wee kitchen, mixing something in a large bowl.

She smiled. "I do. Completely."

"Well, that's good, at least," Thorsen said, still frowning.

He leaned forward, hesitating before he pressed a kiss to her temple.

She didn't move.

He had been an important chapter of her life, but that part of her story was over. She had wondrous new chapters to live, if she dared.

"Call if you need me."

"I will," she promised.

Thorsen hesitated. "It's only been a few days, but you've changed."

"About time." Grace forced a smile.

Thorsen looked over her shoulder. "Tucker?"

Tuck looked up.

"Take good care of her."

Grace didn't know if she, or Tucker, was more surprised at Thorsen's words.

Thorsen gave Grace a final, inscrutable look.

Then he was gone.

# Chapter Fifty-Seven

"Where's the queen?" Thorsen asked. He had walked into an empty kitchen, and dining room, before making his way to the front room, where Charles, Omran, and Stone sat.

His new agent looked worried. "She left with Clint. She ordered me to stay. Is that even allowed?"

Before Thorsen could chastise the new agent, his secure mobile pinged.

Thorsen swore when he read the message.

"Sir?" Charles had stood.

Thorsen glanced at Omran and Stone, still sitting on the couch. "An unconfirmed security threat. Looks like the French-flagged this one." He looked up. "It's an automatic orange. Do you know if Christopher's little brother visited him? They routinely trigger threat assessments."

Charles's eyebrow raised. "At an international level?"

"Yes," Thorsen answered, distracted. "Until we confirm it's those two, we need the princess and queen to say put. Ask Becca if Austin was here recently."

Charles left with his order.

Thorsen dialed Grace's number, when what he wanted to do was charge back up to the apartment.

After several rings, it went to voicemail.

He frowned, not wanting to imagine what she was too busy doing to answer her phone.

She deserved a lifetime of happiness. The French memo would be sorted, he could at least give her tonight.

He messaged her, instructing her to stay put until the memo was clarified.

Thorsen tried calling the queen.

Again, voicemail.

His message was a simple one. Stay put.

# Chapter Fifty-Eight

"Here we are." Clint unlocked the front door to his house, acutely aware of Kat standing behind him. She was like Lillian. She held herself with wealth and privilege, from how she carried herself to the cut of her clothes and the agents guarding her. She had informed Agent Lawson she would accompany Clint alone to his residence.

She hadn't said much else on the short drive from Becca's inn to his ranch.

*We have a daughter.*

Clint reined in the questions flooding his mind as Kat followed him into his old ranch house.

It was more cabin than not, and Clint noticed every worn, aged surface of his home in detail.

Kat looked around, interested, though he figured it was for his benefit. He was a tidy man, his house was clean, but it wasn't pretty.

Large, old timber beams loosely outlined the open living space of the kitchen and living room. The walls were drywalled, and the moss-green paint was relatively recent if five years could be called relative. The floors were made from planks hewn from reclaimed wood long before it had become fashionable. The river stone fireplace was old enough to be made from actual stones, not the synthetic molds preferred by builders today.

She turned to him and smiled. "Your home is lovely."

His home was comfortable and enough for him. Functional and practical, it was the home of a bachelor who spent more time on the land and in the barn than at home bothering with decorating details or trends. It wasn't lovely.

Clint had never paid much attention, but he was looking at his place the way she must see it, old and worn around the edges. It looked like him.

"Sorry, I wasn't expecting guests." He scooped the pile of mail from the kitchen table and filed it on top of the refrigerator. He made a beeline for the living room, folded the throw blanket the long way, and draped it across the back of the couch.

He hoped solidly built and clean counted for something because that was about it for him and the house.

"Clint—"

"Want some coffee or tea? I think I have a package of cookies somewhere." He paced back to the kitchen, but she touched his arm. It felt like branding.

He stared at where her hands were still touching his forearm. "Make yourself at home. I'll make some coffee."

"I don't want tea or coffee."

It was painful having her here. All the memories and love and promises came rushing back.

And the betrayal.

Finally, he met her gaze. "Kat, what do you want from me?"

She sat down, and he knew she expected him to follow.

He remained standing. "I want to meet our daughter. She needs to know I didn't know about her, I would have moved heaven and earth to be in her life—" He broke off.

Too many emotions were swirling too close to the surface.

Kat hedged, "It's complicated—"

"Then uncomplicate it," he snapped. The initial joy of seeing her was crumbling under the tension that had been building between them since her declaration. *We have a daughter.*

Clint looked at her, the woman he had given his whole heart to decades ago before she had stomped all over it.

But a stranger was in front of him. All trace of the young woman he had fallen in love with was gone, and in its place was an elegant shell. Pretty enough to look at, but not much substance. None that he could see, anyway.

"Who are you? I don't know you anymore." He shook his head. "I don't think I ever did, did I?"

Kat folded her hands in her lap. "I'm Queen Katherine of Jordemorden."

"So?"

Startled, she asked, "What do you mean, 'so'?"

"How is that relevant to you walking away? You never said a word, you were just gone. Now, three decades later, you turn up and drop the bombshell we have a daughter. So, you're a queen. What's your game?"

A stricken look crossed her face. "There's no game. I never told you who I was because you liked me for me. I was afraid you would stop."

Pain lanced through him. "Love."

"What?"

"I loved you for you," Clint corrected, angry at himself that he still cared and had never stopped loving her.

She was so close.

And so devious.

It was tearing him up.

Quiet tears slipped down Kat's face. "Her name is Grace. I—I named her after your mother."

An impossible hope flared. "Tucker's sweetheart?"

The queen's eyes widened. "That can't be. She is to be betrothed to another."

"Does she know that?" Clint asked dryly. It was plain as day the two kids were smitten with each other.

"Of course. She knows her duty. She's next in line for the throne."

Clint crossed his arms, smiling. Kat hadn't seen it, but she would. The kids were in love. Grace spoke of Tucker like Becca spoke of Jason and Lillian of Colt. "Who's my daughter supposed to be betrothed to?"

Kat inclined her head. "Someone suitable, of course."

Anger flashed. "You think Tucker is unsuitable?"

Kat explained, "We have traditions. Sooner rather than later, those may become law. Regardless, it would be unseemly for Grace to marry someone common."

"Common?" Clint's voice rose. "That kid is loyal to a fault. He took three bullets meant for another, we damn near lost him. The measure of a man is in his character, not some trivial archaic bullshit—*oh my god.*" Clint stumbled backward. "That's why you left me. You thought I wasn't good enough for you."

Kat jumped up, following him. "Stop it right there. I left without a word because my father told me you had died in a truck accident."

"That's absurd."

"Is it?" Kat demanded. "I was young and stupid and didn't realize I shouldn't trust him."

"Why would he say something like that?"

She pumped her clenched fists. "Because he thought you unsuitable, and I thought you dead. I was alone, pregnant, and drowning in grief. I married who he told me to. Raised our daughter, as assigned, with a *suitable* man. And not a single day has gone by where I haven't grieved you, so do not sit there and past judgment on me."

All the pain and heartache scorching through him froze when he saw the raw pain bleeding from her.

Hesitant, he took a step forward. He cupped Kat's face in his hands, and she taloned her hands around his forearms.

"I missed you so much," she whispered, crying openly.

New pain burst inside Clint. "Please, don't cry. I didn't know."

"I didn't either. I would have come back to you."

"I would have done right by you and Grace."

She turned her head and kissed his hand.

Clint blinked back tears. "I missed you, too, every damn day."

Kat shook her head. "I don't want Grace to turn out like me, spending my life in a palace with a husband I don't love—bloody hell." Kat's eyes were round, and her face had paled.

"Kat, honey, you're scaring me. What is it?"

She stepped back from him, wrapping her arms around herself. "You're not dead. That means Jacques isn't my legal husband. Ohmygod, the twins are bastards. What have I done?" She looked up at him. "What did my father do?"

Clint tried to follow. "How's that? We were never married."

Kat's whispered, "We were, *matrimonium postmortem.*"

"What the hell is that?"

"There is a caveat in my country's law that recognizes our church law. The church can bless a marriage even if one of the parties is deceased. I was pregnant with Grace, I was told you were deceased. I was required to marry so she wouldn't be born a bastard. It had to be done."

"Are you insane? What did you call it?"

"*Matrimonium postmortem,*" Kat answered quietly.

"Yeah, that. We're not married."

Clint lived his life by a code of conduct, which certainly did not include manipulating individuals, or what he considered sacred vows.

He pointed to the door. "I think you should go."

# Chapter Fifty-Nine

He had called her Gracie.

Tucker tried to stir and not stab the batter in the large mixing bowl.

Tucker had sized Thorsen up the moment he laid eyes on him. The man was likely a few years older than Tucker, and they had a similar build, though Thorsen was taller and had that undeniably European look about him. He carried himself with confidence and competence.

Tucker didn't like him.

He looked up when Grace came back in and closed the door. She walked over and sat on one of the bistro chairs. "Are you making brownies again?"

"Yup." Tucker used a spatula to transfer the batter into a square pan.

"Why?"

"Baking helps me think."

"About?" Grace asked.

Tucker looked at her before returning his attention to what he was doing. "Roads not traveled," he said quietly.

When he held out the spatula to her, she accepted it. Her tongue darted out to lick the sweet batter, and he tried not to groan.

He popped the pan into the small oven and set the timer. He quickly tossed the dirty dishes in the sink before wiping down the counter. He washed his hands and darted a look at Grace.

She was lost in thought.

Tucker dried off his hands on a kitchen towel. "Want to talk about it?"

He wasn't sure if she'd want to talk about Thorsen or Clint.

She leaned, tossing the spatula from her seat into the sink with the rest of the dirty dishes. "He was an important part of my life for a long time."

Thorsen it was.

Tucker rested his hands on the counter, steeling himself. "What happened? He obviously still cares for you."

Grace looked up at him from the bistro chair on the other side of the counter. "I don't know how to explain it without sounding like a spoiled princess."

He laughed. "Try me."

She gave him a weak smile. "I want someone loyal to me. Thorsen's loyal to country, crown, and then me. In that order. I've already played second, or should I say fourth fiddle to crown, country, and church my whole life."

"You've mentioned the church a lot," Tucker said. Canada was considerably more secular than it's well-known southern neighbor, and Tucker had never been able to get past the church's continuing legacy of unconscionable transgressions to find any sort of peace within its structure.

Grace shrugged. "It's always been like that in my country, though that's shifting. Where once the church was seen as a means of organization and support, beyond any soul salvation if you believe in such things, now it is seen as a yolk of oppression. More and more citizens are peeking behind that curtain, and they *really* don't like what they see. They feel duped." Grace dropped her head. "So do I. It's one of the biggest things my grandfather and I disagree on."

"I can't say I know what you're going through. My only point of reference is what I see in the news. Some are super religious here. Most aren't."

Grace shook her head. "Blind obedience is a dangerous thing. The attempts on my life have been leaked. There has been media speculation because I'm an openly secular heir apparent. I believe in climate change and that we need swift climate action. I'm an ally to our immigrant and LGBTQ+ communities. I believe in gender equality, and I'm pro-choice. My grandfather thinks I'm the devil incarnate."

Tucker had a new appreciation for Thorsen, he'd kept Grace alive.

Grace swiped at her eyes. "I need someone as loyal to me as I am to them. Without that balance, there's an imbalance of power which sets the relationship up for failure. It's also what makes me a horrible heir." Grace looked down. "I'm selfish. I'm putting my needs ahead of my duties."

"Are you insane?" Tucker blurted.

Grace's looked at him crossly. "No. I'm telling you what my experience is."

Tucker checked himself. "Sorry, what I should have said was knowing you need someone as loyal to you is smart. Those imbalances are what fucks everything up.

That's what policing has taught me, anyway. Power imbalances create power struggles. Resentment is guaranteed, if not outright violence." He couldn't imagine Grace in a marriage of duty and tried to assuage her. "Look at Colt and Lillian or Becca and Jason. They are deeply committed, and completely loyal. Why shouldn't you have something like that?"

"It's different for me," Grace pressed.

"Why?"

"Crown, country, and church, that's why I exist."

Tucker laughed again. "No, that's not why you exist."

She was staring at him like he had grown another head. "You don't understand, everything I do is supposed to be in support of the crown, country, or church." Grace visibly shuddered when she spoke the last one. "I can roll with crown and country most of the time."

"Sure, you have responsibilities few on the planet have, but that doesn't exempt you from basic human emotions, wants, or needs. Cut yourself some slack."

"Royalty isn't allowed slack." She was vibrating. He couldn't tell if it was with anger or hurt.

"In this apartment, you are."

She was right. How could he understand her experience? Everyone viewed their life and the world around them from their vantage point. Grace's might as well have been in a different galaxy, for how different their worlds were. It wasn't an easy lesson, meeting people where they were, not where he wished they would be.

He hung up the kitchen towel. "Look, I'm sorry. I should shut the fuck up. I have no idea what it's like being you."

She watched him. "Thank you for not making me feel like a selfish sinner for wanting something more. I already have so much more than others."

"Regardless of bank account, we all want personal sovereignty. And those who don't, there usually is a history of abuse of some sort."

Grace hesitated. "What's your job like?"

Tucker clapped his hands against the counter. "I'm a chef, at least for the rest of this month anyway."

"Do you always use humor to deflect?"

He looked up sharply. Her face was open and earnest. She couldn't have known the powder keg she was attempting to open.

Then a bigger bomb went off in his head.

"You think I'm funny, not angry?"

"You've been grumpy a few times, but I'd say your default is humor."

The timer pinged, and Tucker spun toward the oven, fleeing the intimate turn the conversation had taken. He pulled the brownies out and set the pan on a cooling rack.

With his back still to Grace, he asked, "Want to talk about Clint?"

When she didn't answer, Tucker turned.

She looked lost in thought.

"I don't think I'm ready to unpack that tonight."

Fair enough.

"Want popcorn?"

"Now?"

"Yeah, we can watch movies and avoid thinking about everything."

Grace jumped up. "That sounds perfect."

Tucker smiled, happy to have found something that brightened her mood after such a heavy day.

"What about you?"

"What about me?" he asked.

"You had a crazy day, too."

"What?"

Grace's eyes widened. "This morning, you found out your father died of an overdose."

"Right." That was only today.

Grace was still staring at him. "And you and your sister were attacked at the bank, and your long-lost brother and a British special forces agent rescued you guys. Ringing any bells?"

Tucker pulled out a large pot and its lid. "That was today, wasn't it?"

He had filed both events in his head under The Past.

She was looking at him oddly.

"What?"

"Nothing. Just trying to figure you out," she said.

"I'm about as simple as they come," he said, pulling down the jar of popcorn kernels and a bottle of canola oil.

She actually snorted. "Pull my other leg."

When he would have protested, she asked, "Can you teach me how to make popcorn?" She held up her hands. "Please, no princess jokes."

Tucker bit back his retort. "Sure. Regular or kettle corn?"

"What's the difference?" Grace asked.

"Sugar."

She cocked her head to the side. "Is that the regular one?"

He shook his head.

"Then kettle, please."

"Coming right up." Tucker poured oil into the bottom of the pan before adding a spoonful of white sugar. He swirled the pot as the oil heated and the sugar dissolved.

"Can I do that?" Grace asked.

Tucker moved to the side. Grace took the pot's handles and swirled it over the burner like he showed her.

"That's it." Tucker poured enough popcorn kernels to cover the bottom of the pan and fitted the lid.

"You don't measure anything."

"I like to cook by feel."

She had been steadily swirling, but at his words, her hands jolted. "Maybe you should help me," Grace said carefully.

Did her voice sound husky?

Tucker's heart started pounding. He stepped closer.

"I can do that."

When he would have reached across her, she asked, "Maybe you should stand behind me."

Tucker swallowed but moved to stand behind Grace. He slipped his arms on either side of her, his chest pressed against her back, as he covered her hands with his. "This okay?"

Her sigh nearly undid him. "Hmm, mmm."

She leaned ever so gently into him, and he felt his cock stir.

Grace was so close.

Tucker turned his head.

Her eyes were closed.

His mouth was a whisper from her neck when he said, "Probably should keep your eyes open for this part."

Grace's eyes flew open.

"Easy, there." Tucker smiled, swirling the pot with her cradled in his arms.

He would never look at popcorn the same way.

A kernel popped. Followed by another. Soon the drum of popping kernels filled his ears.

The building crescendo of popping corn was way too on point.

In a few seconds, he could let go and regain control of his runaway libido.

He wanted to go down on her, make her scream in uninhibited pleasure. Give her release after release until all that weird church bullshit was orgasmed out of her.

Heathen healing.

Then Grace slid the pot to the side and snapped off the burner. She spun in his arms and grabbed his face in her hands, pressing her lips to his.

Tucker wrapped his arms around Grace and kissed her back.

Their mouths parried.

Wildly, they pinballed into kitchen counters and the bistro set, knocking over one of the chairs.

Grace broke off and whispered, "Please?"

Tucker shifted, lifting her. Grace wrapped her legs around his waist and drank from his lips again. Without breaking the kiss, he carried her to the bed. They fell in a tumble of limbs and discarded clothing.

She scrambled under the covers, pulling them over him.

He shimmied lower.

"What are you doing?"

Tucker poked his head out from the covers. "Going down on you ... I mean, if that's okay?"

The smile she gave him sent him back under the covers.

Slowly, he trailed his hand down her body before settling his shoulders between her thighs. With patience and attention, he took his time pleasuring her.

Grace writhed and shook, at times grabbing his head as he worked his lips and tongue to please her. When he brought her to completion, Tucker almost came. Her passion was intoxicating.

"Your turn." Grace rolled. She straddled him low on his hips, his hardness bobbed naked in front of her.

"Nightstand," he rasped. It was hard to think straight with her naked over him.

Grace reached into his nightstand and pulled out a condom. When he had sheathed himself, she slowly slid over him.

Tucker almost exploded.

"Hang on, honey ... you feel so good."

She smiled down at him before she moved, seductively slow.

Grace set a languid pace, and Tucker held her as she rode him. Suddenly, her face changed, and Tucker realized she was coming again. He held on, riding her high until he couldn't any longer. In that instant, he tightened before exploding.

They stayed like that, locked in each other's arms, while their runaway breathing slowed.

Finally, she opened her eyes.

Tucker turned his head, kissing her forearm.

"You exist for you. Don't let anyone ever tell you differently."

# Chapter Sixty

Kat's hands were trembling as she collected her purse.

Clint hated that it was like this between them but was unsure what could heal the distance.

Her mobile beeped, and she withdrew it.

"Is everything all right?" Clint asked, concerned. Kat had visibly paled.

She looked up from the device. "It's my head of security. There is an unconfirmed threat. He's ordered me to stay put until he can clarify the risk. He wouldn't have made the order if it wasn't considered credible." She hesitated. "May I stay?"

"Here?" He looked around. "This is hardly a fortress." He couldn't bear it if anything happened to Kat.

She nodded. "It's safer." Quieter, she added, "No one knows about you."

It didn't sit well, being considered disposable.

"I know this is all a lot to take in, and for what it's worth, I'm sorry."

Clint's mind was trying to connect the dots. "When Lillian first arrived, her security detail was from Jordemorden."

Kat nodded. "I think I remember hearing something about that, yes."

He continued, "And your agents are some of the best trained in the world."

"Correct."

"Yet Grace came here alone and then hid at Tucker's. What's going on, Kat?"

"Grace is … spirited. She has no time for tradition or conservative ideals."

He shrugged. "I'm not seeing a problem."

Kat pressed, "Our country is a small island nation in the North Sea. Early Norse originally settled us, but a contingent of persistent French explores arrived in the sixteenth century, adding a distinct continental flavor to our Nordic roots."

"I'm sure it's great. What does that have to do with Grace?"

Kat looked put out. "*Culturally*, we were quite progressive until the church gained substantial power in the fourteenth century. The Catholic French explorers entrenched the power of the church, though there was much unrest during the Reformation of the sixteenth century. We've been dogmatically conservative since. Until this new generation, including Grace. The kids want more and demand more. Their astute questions make sense and are shifting a significant portion of our older populations into questioning what our country can and should be. Grace is the heir apparent and critically vocal about the paradigms she feels need changing. She is jeopardizing my father's power structure, which comes strictly from the church. He may not be king anymore, but he knows how to keep and wield power. She's a threat, and his fanatics are loyal to him. I'm afraid our country is at a turning point, and our daughter is the fulcrum."

Clint asked, "Where does that leave you?"

"Choking on the past and too afraid to spit it out."

It was an inelegant visual.

"You think the spirited young woman you just described, that fulcrum, is going to knuckle under and marry someone *suitable*? Can you honestly say you want her to?"

Kat looked ready to retort, her eyes flashing, but stopped. "Do you mind making a fire?"

"Now?"

"Yes." She exhaled. "Please, Clint."

The tension between them had become unbearable. He took the out. "Sure."

Clint crossed to the fireplace, his back to Kat, as he scrunched paper and set the kindling at alternating squares, log cabin style.

"You're angry. You don't approve," Kat said.

Clint kept to his task. "I know nothing of your monarchy."

"Do you still love me?"

Clint gave up no ground. "You're a queen, that changes things."

He'd lived in two countries but had never settled real roots anywhere. She was the root of her country.

They couldn't work, not that he was sure he wanted it to.

Clint struck a match and watched the small flame catch each time he touched it to paper.

Kat appealed, "The whole queen thing, it's just a job. Well, kind of a lifestyle, like being a cowboy."

"You don't know anything about me, Kat, not anymore."

The kindling had caught and hissed, making small snapping noises. He added a few small logs. Soon a cheery blaze crackled in the hearth.

He realized his mistake the moment he turned around.

Kat had dimmed the lights and settled into a corner of the couch. The dancing firelight made her skin glow. Clint remembered the last time he had seen her like this. It had been pure magic then, too, and they had made pure magic for hours.

His breath caught, the memory vivid in his mind. "Kat, what are you doing?"

"What I should have done decades ago. Come back to you."

His heart squeezed. It wasn't her crown that was between them, he didn't want his heart shattered again.

Kat stood. Slowly, almost hesitantly, she walked over to him and held her hand.

Clint stared at it. She had always been impossible to ignore.

When he slipped his hand in hers, it was terrifying. It felt like he had come home.

He stood, though, following her.

Kat led him up the stairs. At the top was a single loft bedroom.

His bed loomed in the center against the back wall. Starlight shone through an oversized skylight above. Flames from the fireplace below flickered shadows across the loft wall.

She was in firelight and starlight. It felt almost mystical.

"Can we just lay down like we used to, wrapped in each others' arms?"

He nodded and pulled her close.

They stayed like that, wrapped in each other, letting the past heal.

He could hear her heartbeat.

She traced his jaw.

He didn't know how much time had passed when Kat lifted her head and pressed her lips to his.

The kiss was soft, like another hug, until it wasn't. Passion took the place of comfort, and soon her hands slipped between them, and she started unbuttoning his shirt.

"Kat?"

"Love me, Clint."

He stopped fighting himself. He wouldn't, couldn't deny her anymore.

They worked in unison, and in moments, each was bare to the other, years of misunderstanding shed with their clothes. Whatever had happened, the love he had for her was still there, in the very core of him, and he whispered, "I never stopped loving you."

"Me, either." Her voice was just as soft. "I love you, Clint. I always have, I always will."

He tightened his arms around her but knew no matter how tight he held, it wasn't enough. Their love had taught him that.

Then an equally dark thought surfaced.

Grace was a princess. She had grown up in wealth and privilege.

How could she want a father who had shit on his boots?

# Chapter Sixty-One

A brisk knock sounded, and Grace bolted upright in bed, blinking. It could have been midnight or six in the morning—winter nights were long and dark here.

Tucker was already out of bed, his sidearm in hand as he crouched low and made his way to the door.

A muffled voice came through the door. "Guys, it's Thorsen."

Tucker looked at Grace in the near darkness, and she nodded. "Let him in."

Grace snatched Tucker's shirt draped over the side lamp. She clicked the light on and squirmed into the shirt.

Tucker donned his robe before opening the door.

Thorsen quickly took in Tucker's lack of clothes with a frown.

He looked at Grace. "I'm sorry to interrupt. We're clear. Christopher's brother Austin stopped by, triggering an automatic threat warning. However, it's imperative we talk. There are several outstanding concerns you should be briefed on."

The tone of Thorsen's voice had Grace nervous. "Okay."

"You guys stay here. I'll go make breakfast for everyone."

Ten minutes later, Tucker had left. Grace was dressed and sitting on the couch. Thorsen was pacing.

"What's going on?" Grace asked.

He stopped. "You received the digital images of your original birth certificate and your mom and Clint's *matrimonium postmortem* marriage certificate?"

Grace nodded. "I got them."

"Remember when Lillian first came here with a contingency of Jordemorden agents for her security detail?"

"Yes." It was something Grace would never forget. Her friend had a murderous lunatic hunting her.

Thorsen continued, "Her grandmother, Dame Maighread, called my father."

"Your father's retired."

"That's how she got me instead." Thorsen sat down then, as far away from Grace as the small couch would allow. "She sent her granddaughters here because she knew my father had been keeping tabs on an American living in western Canada. A young cowboy turned rancher. She trusted his intel and vetting of the area."

Grace's stomach churned. "Thorsen, what are you saying?"

He pressed on, "When my father retired, he passed that file to me, and I continued the surveillance. No one in the palace, and I mean no one, knew."

The humiliation and betrayal threatened to swamp Grace, and she jumped up. "I trusted you! With my safety, with *my body*," she hissed. "You knew where my dad was, and you never told me."

"I found out three days ago he was your dad," Thorsen snapped. "Don't you get it? My father protected yours. He kept him alive. The grand duke ordered my father to tamper with his brakes and make it look like an accident. Your grandfather wanted him permanently out of the picture, but my father refused. Be mad at me, be mad at my father, but we kept yours alive when *your grandfather* would have him dead."

Grace dropped her head into her hands. Her grandfather had ordered a hit on a kid. Her father.

Grace's knees buckled, and she dropped back to the couch.

The grand duke had put Thorsen's dad in an impossible situation.

When she looked up, Thorsen's eyes were hard. "My father made the king's problem go away without fucking murder. Clint didn't have your mom or you, but he was alive."

Grace squeezed her hands together. "I'm sorry. You're right. He's alive because of your dad and you."

Thorsen shifted, uncomfortable. "The grand duke has given me new orders."

"Christ, what now?" She braced herself.

"To marry you."

Grace laughed. "That's impossible."

"I'm serious. He's ordered me to marry you."

"We're not considered an appropriate match to him or the church."

"The night I returned from the National Archives with Claire, he was with Ingrid Olsen. They pulled me aside, and he gave the orders."

Fear iced Grace's veins, then. "To what end? What's in it for him?"

"That's what worries me. I haven't been able to figure that out."

# Chapter Sixty-Two

Tucker stood at the stove, finishing up frying another batch of bacon, and eyed the back hallway door that led to Becca's office.

Yesterday, Stone and Omran took over Becca's office as their field office. Thorsen had briefed them on the evolving situation and along with Thorsen and Charles, were in the office now.

Tucker had not been invited.

His clearance level did not touch their international ranking.

The kitchen's back door started creaking open, and Tucker's adrenaline ignited.

He grabbed a cast iron frying pan from the counter and spun around, ready to heave it.

Grace peeked her head around the door. "Hi," she whispered. Her face dropped when she saw the pan. "Woah, it's just me."

Tucker set the pan on the counter, rattling dishes.

"What are you doing here? You're supposed to stay in the apartment."

"I know. I'll be quick." She pointed to the pan. "Were you going to launch that thing at me if I was a bad guy?"

"Kind of feeling under attack. You're supposed to be in the apartment," he reminded her, keeping his voice equally low. "Why are we whispering?"

She glanced around the room. "Are we alone?"

"Yes."

"Good." She stepped into the room. No longer in his shirt, she wore hiking pants and a fleece zippy.

"What do you need?"

"Will you be my pretend fiancé?"

Bacon grease splattered.

Tucker snapped off the heat and pulled the pan off the burner.

Grace held up her hands. "Don't freak out. I need a pretend fiancé."

"So pick Thorsen."

Though he was loath to admit it, Thorsen would be a more believable, suitable choice.

"I can't. He's now the grand duke's choice."

A volcano of insecurity erupted inside Tucker. "No one will believe you fell for me. You're royalty. I'm a grumpy cop with anger issues. I have zero redeeming qualities."

Her smile was as old as Eve's. "Oh? I can think of a few."

Before Tucker could comment, Thorsen walked into the kitchen. "Grace, what are you doing here? You're supposed to be in the apartment."

"I was just going." She smiled at Tucker. "Deal?"

Wary, yet unwilling to disappoint her, he agreed. "Fine."

Thorsen was distracted by his phone but looked up. "On what?"

"That's need to know, buddy," Tucker said.

Grace was looking at Thorsen suspiciously. "Why are you frowning like that?"

"Because the grand duke now wants to come for Christmas."

# Chapter Sixty-Three

"Absolutely not." The queen had lost too much deferring to the grand duke's demands over the decades. He wasn't ruining this Christmas, too.

She stood in Becca's lovely eco-inn kitchen, helping herself to a cup of coffee as soft Christmas music played. It was a delicious experience with Clint and their daughter at Christmas.

Thorsen stood at the counter. "Final answer? He'll ask."

"Final answer and I outrank him. You have your orders."

"I do, Your Highness."

"Excellent. Now that it's settled, my daughter and I are going horseback riding. Shall we, dear?"

Grace nodded.

Clint walked into the kitchen. "Tucker and I've got two of Becca's mares saddled and ready to go. Stay clear of the south face, and mind any avalanche chutes you see. We've had a lot of snow, and the temperatures have been all over the place. That snowpack won't be stable." He handed both Kat and Grace devices.

"What are these, darling?" Kat asked.

"Beacons. I've already switched them to transmitting. If you run into trouble, not that I'm expecting it, this will let us know where you are. Are you sure you don't want me to come with you?"

Thorsen agreed, "That would be the safest plan."

Kat shook her head. "Guys, we'll be fine. My daughter and I need this time alone."

\#

Several minutes later, Thorsen watched Grace and the queen ride away across the snowy pasture. The sun was bright, and the day mild. Still, he had reservations. They should have an escort.

He turned. Tucker and Clint were just finishing saddling two more horses. "Please tell me, you guys are following them, right?"

"Oh yeah," Tucker said, checking his tack before mounting. "The backcountry can be cranky with city kids, myself included. Right, Clint?"

Clint smiled, already on Stürmisch's back. "You do fine for a city slicker.

"There it is." Though Tucker was laughing. "I make a fine weekend warrior. I have the apps to prove it."

"When I was your age, we went outside to check the weather and knew how far we'd gone by how tired we were." Clint shook his head. "Apps."

Tucker looked at Thorsen. "We'll keep you posted. If you'll excuse me, I need to bring Clint into the twenty-first century."

Thorsen smiled in spite of himself.

Grace could do a lot worse than the good-natured detective.

# Chapter Sixty-Four

"Can you believe this? Freedom!" the queen said, her voice sounding more youthful than Grace had ever noticed.

The slow, easy gait of the docile mare she rode gave Grace's mom a relaxed, comfortable look.

Grace had never seen her mom like that.

She smiled, not mentioning Tucker and Clint were following at a discreet distance. She was happy to have them near. Grace hadn't spent much time in remote areas, and her mom even less.

Once, she had hiked in the Austrian Alps with a group of friends. At the time, global politics were different, and she hadn't required a constant security detail. They had taken a tram up the mountain from the small village they were staying in. At the top, panoramic views and a trail beckoned. Several hours of unplanned exploring later, the sun had long since set, and they realized they were running out of daylight. They would likely be spending the night on the mountain.

They were lucky. A compact man appeared, seemingly out of nowhere. He offered directions to a trail that led to the next town, where they could secure a ride to their accommodations. In moments, he was gone, disappearing around a bend in the trail.

The day could have ended significantly worse, and Grace had experiential respect for being prepared when venturing out into Mother Nature.

She inhaled the fragrant winter day. "Thanks for inviting me, Mom."

The day was mild, and the bright sun on the fresh snow made everything appear clean and new. They followed a trail of sorts, though, at times, snow drifts made it impossible to be certain. They had crossed a pasture, and a mixed aspen and spruce forest flanked them. The evergreen branches dipped precariously low under the weight of snow.

It wasn't an exaggeration to say it was a winger wonderland.

Her mom said, "I'm sorry I wasn't as strong as you."

"What are you talking about?"

"If I had been, I would have spent the past three decades living with the man I love. You would have grown up with your father."

Grace shook her head. "Mom, you'll drive yourself crazy turning circles of what wasn't. The past is done, and who the fuck knows what the future holds."

"Grace, language!"

"Say it, I dare you. It's just me out here. No one else will hear, and I'm not judging."

"Say what?"

"Who the fuck knows what the future holds," Grace repeated.

Her mom hesitated before tipping her head back and yelling, her voice cracking, "Who the fuck knows what the future holds."

"Feel better?" Grace grinned.

"I feel stupid."

"What?" Dismayed, Grace pulled her horse up close to her mom's.

Her mom reined in her mount. "I've wasted so much time being dutiful. Hurt the people I love in the name of duty. I haven't been loyal to the ones who matter. I'm sorry for that, Grace."

Grace bit her lip. "Tell me about my dad."

Her mom clicked her horse into walking again, and Grace did the same.

"I was young when I met your father. We were in America, in Texas, for business. I had just turned eighteen, and it wasn't long after my mother had died. I went to my first rodeo, and there he was."

"Are you serious?"

"Yes." Her mom looked nervous. "You don't approve."

"As if." Grace smiled. "Lillian met Colt at a rodeo."

"I can relate." She made a throaty sound. "Cowboys."

"I'll take your word for it," Grace said. Her type was Tucker.

The queen got a faraway look in her eye. "We would ride for hours, just the two of us. He was so vibrant, so kind. And handsome. Lordy, you should have seen him. Us, really. We were inseparable." She looked down. "Until we were separated.

"Grandfather didn't approve."

The queen looked out across the blanketed forest. "Your grandfather is—"

"A pretentious, stubborn ass?" Grace supplied.

Her mom's shoulder's sagged. "I was going to say challenging. But you're right. After mother died, it got worse. It wasn't that he particularly loved her, it was just that when she was gone, any of the softness that she knew how to bring out of him died, too."

"That sounds awful."

"It was. I was pregnant and terrified to tell him. Your grandmother was a pious woman, she would have been incredibly disappointed in me, but she would have come around. Or that's what I liked to tell myself."

Grace knew just how judgmental people could be. It was usually what fueled the programs and cases she worked on.

"He called Clint *my foreign embarrassment.* I still remember the horrible night my father found out about us. He packed me up in the middle of the night and we were gone." Her mom stared straight ahead. "I never had a chance to explain why we left or say goodbye. He had no idea I was pregnant, and by the time I found out, I thought he was dead." Her mom had a bittersweet smile. "I was scared but so excited to be pregnant with you. I loved your dad, and you were a part of him."

After several moments, her mom continued, "My father was livid. He shipped me off to live with his sister, as was done in those days. Your aunt was nice enough, but I knew I had embarrassed the family. I was not allowed back home for the duration of my pregnancy. They acted like falling in love was some kind of sin."

"What happened?" Grace asked.

"After you were born, I was allowed back, with conditions. I wasn't allowed to raise you until he deemed me worthy."

"*What?*"

"It was a different time then, Grace, and I didn't know how to stand up for myself." The queen looked down. "I still don't. Meeting your father was the most scandalous, beautiful thing I ever did. And I have never stopped paying for it. Enough is enough."

"Why didn't Clint try to find you?"

"I never told him who I was or where I was from. It was thrilling that he loved me for me, not my crown, and I wanted to hold on to that for as long as possible. I'd planned to tell him but never got the chance. He thought I had chosen to leave him."

Grace understood the allure of being wanted for you alone. "Mom, I'm so sorry."

"And I'm sorry about trying to assign Charles to you. He's a good sort of chap with the right pedigree. I had thought to see you married to someone you could at least be companions with before the grand duke assigned one of his followers."

Grace didn't mention her and Tucker's faux engagement. She would keep that ace in her sleeve until she needed it.

"I really like Clint, Mom. He's kind, and I've never seen you so happy.

Her mom laughed. "I feel like a kid again, like I've exploded back into me."

The sound of a plane engine interrupted them. It was coming in fast and low.

Grace frowned. "That doesn't look right."

From afar, it looked like the top of the mountain was splitting. Then it fell, a massive roar screaming in its wake as the shelf of snow released and tumbled toward them.

# Chapter Sixty-Five

Tucker saw the plane buzz the mountain before the slope spider-webbed.

An ungodly cracking sound followed.

Clint was already turning his mount. *"Move, move, move."*

Tucker tightened his legs, and his mount Ranger shot forward. He angled them down and out while a deafening roar chased them—the mountain was sloughing off its crown of snow.

Tucker heard his brother Colt's patient voice from the past, whispering instructions, and Tucker wondered if he was hallucinating.

Then, Ranger was no longer beneath him.

Tucker was swept up in a wave of snow. He angled his body, trying to find Clint. The man was waving wildly at him. A second later, the older cowboy's mount got sucked under, too.

The last words Tucker heard was Clint yelling, *"Swim, swim, swim."*

Then he heard nothing except the roar of surging snow and the pounding of his heart.

Tucker desperately mimicked the forward crawl, pressing his body to stay on top of the charging sea of snow.

But he was losing the battle. Snow was taking the place of sunlight.

Tucker kicked and pulled sweeping armfuls of snow, grappling for purchase in the tumbling ice crystals.

Sunlight played peekaboo with eerie darkness. His arms and legs ached, and his lungs burned, yet still, he fought to swim higher.

When everything stopped, Colt's voice came back to him.

Tucker filled his lungs deeply while punching at the snow in front of his face like Colt had taught him years ago before the snow settled.

Within seconds, the snow had cemented. It was hard as fuck.

Tucker breathed.

He almost wept tears of relief. The tight cocoon of snow he was encased in had not squeezed the air out of him. His arms were another matter. The snow could have been made of rock, it was that unyielding.

Tucker couldn't get at his pockets.

That's where his phone and beacon device was, and his beacon was set to receive, not transmit.

Being handcuffed would have afforded more pur-chase than the locked embrace of the snow and ice. There was no way he could reach his gear.

Clint was gone, swept up like Tucker had been. So had Ranger and Stürmisch.

What if Grace and her mom had been caught in it, too?

Waves of desperate agony crashed over him.

Tucker hadn't told Grace the truth.

Against some serious odds, and in record time, he had fallen completely in love with her.

And she was never going to know.

# Chapter Sixty-Six

"That sounded close." Lillian stopped her yogurt spoon mid-air.

Colt looked out their kitchen window in time to see a mid-sized plane just clear a mountain peak before heading north. It was flying dangerously low for the mountains. Flying that close to peaks was inherently dangerous and typically reserved for rescue missions.

He scanned the skyline, and the inexplicable sense of doom that had dogged him all morning flared.

Something wasn't right.

He looked down. The water in the glass he had placed on the counter was rippling.

He pulled his gaze back to the distant horizon.

Then he saw it. They always minded the south face, it had always carried more danger. But the snowpack that had been on one of the east faces was gone.

"Shit." He sprinted for the door, grabbing gear.

"Where are you going?" Lillian asked, alarmed.

"Pretty sure we just had an avalanche." Fear gripped him. Someone was in there and he had to act fast.

"What do you need me to do?"

"Call Becca, see if anyone was out by that east face. And keep your phone on."

Colt sprinted to his truck, hoping he wasn't too late.

# Chapter Sixty-Seven

Grace stared in horror. It looked like the mountain was breaking. A mountain of snow was crashing down, uprooting trees and lifting boulders in its fury to the bottom.

Both she and her mom's horses were sidestepping.

Grace sat back in her seat, making steady cooing noises. She felt when the mare eased under her and took a moment to grab the reins of her mom's now stomping mare. Grace gave several firm clicks before the mare stopped snorting. She started cooing before the horse gave a final shiver.

When she looked at the mountain, the avalanche was already over.

"Come on," Grace called to her mom.

The queen turned her horse, following, and asked, "Where are we going?"

"To make sure Tucker and Clint weren't caught in that." Grace picked up the pace.

"They're at the inn," her mom called.

"No, they're not. They've been following us the whole time."

Fear threatened to swamp her.

*Please be okay, please be okay*, Grace chanted as they backtracked as far as they could.

A field of tumbled snow, and mangled trees and boulders, stretched out before them.

She heard a whiny.

Followed by a second.

Two horses trotted close. They looked scraped up and crusted with snow.

Grace had no idea if they had been the ones Tucker and Clint had been riding.

Her mobile in her pocket started beeping. Grace scrambled with her gloves to answer it.

"Hello? Hello?" Lillian's frantic voice echoed. "Are you guys okay?"

"Mom and I are. We're trying to find Tucker and Clint. There was an avalanche."

"Colt's on his way. He just left our house."

"How did he know?"

"He's been antsy all morning."

"What do we do?" Grace asked. "I have no idea where even to start looking, *ohmygod*—" Grace squinted and saw what looked like a head bobbing on the far side of the snow field.

"Lillian, I'll call you back." Grace hung up. "Mom, can you grab those horses' reins?"

"Of course, I can." With expert horsemanship, the queen took off after the horses.

Grace rode around the field. As she got closer, she saw it was a man walking upslope. His jacket and clothes were torn in places, and it looked like he was missing a boot. He hobbled as he walked.

It was Clint.

Grace dismounted and sprinted to him.

"Grace?" He rasped out.

She wrapped her arms around him.

"We've got to find Tuck. Come on."

The grumble of engines sounded. Four snowmobiles crested a rise, two riders each and loaded with gear, angling toward them. It was Colt and Jason, Stone and Omran, Thorsen and Charles, and Christopher and Austin.

Colt hustled over to Clint. "Are you okay? Anything broken?"

Clint shook his head.

"Where'd Tuck go down?"

Clint pointed. "See that spruce gnarled at a weird angle? That's where he got sucked under. Once I thought I saw him, maybe a hundred yards farther down, and he was on this side of the run."

Colt started barking out orders. Everyone sprung into action. Using ski-pole probes and carrying collapsible shovels, they started a grid survey.

Kat returned, leading the two horses. She secured their reins before hurrying to help, too.

With laser focus, Grace paced where Colt directed.

"I've got something," Austin yelled. He found Tuck's wool cap fifty yards down from where Clint had seen him surface.

They kept searching.

Stone gave a piercing whistle, getting everyone's attention, and held up a boot.

Colt barked more orders, shifting their search in line with the debris trajectory.

Grace's focus was becoming desperate. Too many minutes had passed, and the temperature was falling fast.

She shivered, in fear and cold, when she slid her ski-pole probe down and hit a pocket of air.

Gently, she probed again. This time she hit something solid.

"Guys," she screamed.

Frantic, she dropped to her knees and started clawing with her hands.

Colt was closest to her and started shoveling like a demon. A muffled *help* sounded.

Stone and Jason reached them next. Grace scrambled out of the way as the rest of their crew shoveled under Colt's instructions.

Tears streamed down Grace's face.

He was alive.

For now.

Her mom and Clint materialized next to her, and each held one of her hands.

Jason and Christopher readied the spinal board.

They didn't need it. As soon as enough snow was displaced, Tucker was scrambling to get out.

When Colt and Stone pulled Tucker out of the cemented snow, everyone cheered.

The tears wouldn't stop.

Tucker was alive.

When his gaze found hers, she knew, without a shadow of a doubt, that she had fallen hard.

Grace was in love with him.

# Chapter Sixty-Eight

Tucker sucked in lungfuls of air.

He was stretched out on his back, staring at the bright blue sky.

When he thought he could speak without puking, he said, "Merry fucking Christmas."

Colt shook his head. "You scared the shit out of us."

"I scared the shit out of me." He exhaled. "I didn't think I was going to make it."

Colt patted his leg. "But you did. I'm expecting an epic Christmas present."

Tucker laughed. "I am. Baby diapers. I hear those are expensive."

"Glad you're safe, bro."

Tucker stared at the sky. "Me, too. I heard your voice."

Colt looked at him.

"As I was getting tossed around, I heard your voice telling me what to do."

His brother nodded but stayed quiet.

Tucker stood before it got weird.

Jason had taken the lead, while Tucker and Colt took a few minutes. He looked at them now. "Colt, how about you and I ride Kat and Grace's mounts and lead Ranger and Stürmisch home? They got tossed around, but neither looks lame. Folks will have to triple up on the snow machines, but that's doable. The sun will set in an hour, and I don't want anyone left behind."

Colt agreed.

Jason added, "Some will be riding without helmets, everyone okay with that?"

Everyone agreed staying past dark presented a greater risk, and mounted their respective snow machine or horse.

Christopher and Austin led, followed by Thorsen, Kat, Clint, Stone, Grace, Tucker, Omran, and Charles on snow machines. Jason, Colt, and the four horses between them brought up the rear.

Tucker watched the assembled party depart. Their family had faced a series of tragic events, but out of those ashes, a tight knit new family had emerged. Some were blood-related, and others were chosen. All were family.

Tucker didn't want to waste another second holding on to old anger. Getting tossed around in the avalanche had broken free something inside him — the part that had clung so tightly to the anger.

He didn't need it anymore.

"You okay?" Grace asked over the whine of the engine.

Tucker nodded, wrapping his arms tighter around her. It might be shock settling in over his system, but he was pretty sure the temperature was dropping fast. He was freezing.

"Do all Canadian urbanites know avalanche survival protocol?" Grace asked.

"Not a chance. I was one of the lucky ones."

As they approached Becca's inn, Grace tensed.

Tucker looked ahead to see what had alarmed her.

"Who's that?" Tucker asked.

She looked over her shoulder at him. She did not look happy.

"The grand-fucking-duke. I apologize in advance. My grandfather's a dick."

# Chapter Sixty-Nine

"You're not staying here." The queen had launched herself off the snow machine and stormed up to her father.

Grace had never heard that tone of voice come out of her mom or seen her so livid.

Her mom had grown a backbone. It was beautiful to see until it wasn't.

When the queen's hands shot up to shoulder height, Ingrid Olsen stepped out from behind the grand duke, pointing a gun at the queen.

Tucker stepped in front of Grace, his body a shield to protect her.

The grand duke yelled, "No one move. She's put charges around this whole place."

Grace looked around, noticing a series of lumps sitting in the snow. The whole yard looked wired. And where they had stopped the snow machines, they were surrounded.

Then she noticed her grandfather's hands were tied behind his back.

Ingrid waved the gun. "Get back. Everyone, hands up."

Thorsen called, his hands up, "Those are military-issued explosives."

"Ingrid, what in the world are you doing?" the queen asked, her hands in clear sight.

Ingrid sneered. "Clearing the country of serpents."

"You know we're in Canada, right?" Grace snapped.

*"Grace,"* Tucker whispered under his breath. "Not exactly negotiation protocol."

"So what is this, some weird church exorcism?" Grace asked.

Ingrid puffed up at that. "Yes, I do believe it is. I always knew you were a serpent, I just didn't realize the queen was, too. The church tells us what to do with serpents. And to think I came across your whole snake pit."

Grace couldn't see Thorsen, Charles, Omran, or Stone behind them but knew they would have to work their way around the explosives. Grace and Tucker stood between them and Ingrid, blocking any sniper shot.

Grace needed to stall. "What's a snake pit?"

Ingrid stared at her. "Where snakes go in winter."

"Do you mean a snake hibernacula?" Grace asked. "Because that's where snakes hang out in winter, in a hi-ber-nac-ula."

Ingrid shook her gun at Grace. "Stop it."

Tucker was still in front of her, and Grace moved to step around him. "You're right, Ingrid, science is scary."

He moved again, positioning his body between Ingrid's gun and Grace. Annoyed, she said, "Dude, let me pass."

Ingrid darted her eyes left and right, muttering, "I need to cut the heads off the snakes."

"With a gun?" Grace snapped.

With surprising speed, the grand duke hauled his arms up and clobbered Ingrid. She spun before crumpling, falling awkwardly in the deep snow. The gun dropped, disappearing from sight.

The grand duke looked astounded. "Ingrid, how could you? I never suspected you, ever. I mean, you're an old woman, you've always been loyal to me."

Grace rolled her eyes. "Grandpa, not now."

"I'll get her." Tucker circled the yard before pulling Ingrid out of the snow.

Jason and Colt were just riding up when Becca ran outside then.

"Woah, what did we miss?" Colt asked, eyeing everyone.

Becca called, "Sorry I'm late. She handcuffed me."

Jason would have charged toward his fiancée, but Becca held up a staying hand and smiled to reassure him. "Stop, honey. We need to make sure it's safe."

Thorsen was eyeing one of the charges when Becca called to him. "She used lithium polymer batteries."

Thorsen looked up.

"It's minus seventeen and still dropping," Becca said. "I'm no bomb expert, but I'm hoping that means she'd have better luck with a potato to set those charges off."

Jason was staring at his fiancée. "You are so hot right now."

"Honey, shhh." But Becca was smiling.

"How'd you get free?" Grace asked Becca. "She handcuffed you?"

Tucker interjected. "Trust me, you don't want to know the answer to that."

Becca sighed. "You walked in on Jason and me *one time*."

"That's all it took. I'm scarred for life."

"You're fine," Becca quipped. "Who here knows how to disarm bombs?"

Stone, Omran, Thorsen, Charles, Christopher, and Austin raised their hands.

"Good. You guys are on bomb duty. Call it in or disarm yourself, I don't care as long as no one gets hurt. I'm going inside and pouring hot toddies. It's freezing out here. Merry fucking Christmas."

# Chapter Seventy

The grand duke looked between the queen and Grace. "This is my fault. I brought her."

Grace cocked an eyebrow. "You've fed her fanaticism for years. This goes way beyond you bringing her here. You created a fucking monster. What did you think was going to happen?"

For once, her mom did not correct her language. The queen stood, arms crossed, her eyes glittered with anger as she shook with a wild feminine flame.

It was the first time Grace had seen her mom like this. It was stunning to behold.

"If you two hadn't run off," the grand duke said, his head shaking, "I would never had to come. Do you know how bad this looks? My own army is revolting."

"So this was all just to keep up appearances?"

"The election is tomorrow," he reminded the queen. "Or have you forgotten with all your galivanting?"

"You said you wanted to come for Christmas," the queen snapped.

"I did. I do," he hastily corrected.

"You have an army?" Grace asked. It was illegal to raise arms against the government.

The grand duke glared at her. "That's none of your business."

But it was. Grace was the heir apparent.

"Three more questions," the queen interrupted. "Why did you order Thorsen to marry Grace?"

The grand duke shrewdly looked first to Grace, then the queen.

"Stop conniving, I demand the truth, and that's an order." The queen stared her father down, not giving an inch.

The grand duke took a step back. He held up his hands. "That was a tactical error on my part. I thought it would swing voters loyal to Grace to my side. Grace is loyal to Thorsen, I knew there was no danger she'd actually marry the guy, she would never make him marry her on my orders. And come on, he's completely unsuitable."

Grace shook her head, incredulous she could still be surprised at the depths of his cruelness. Using her loyalty as a weapon against her was unconscionable.

"So you were just fucking with her?" the queen asked, outraged. "What the hell is wrong with you?"

Grace's eyes widened.

"I did what was best for the country," the grand duke retorted.

"How did you find us?" the queen demanded.

"When you called Jacques to tell him Grace was safe."

"I used secured lines."

"I had his calls forwarded to his other phone. I could track you from there."

Grace shook her head, beyond disappointed. Her grandfather did not think laws applied to him.

Point blank, the queen asked the grand duke, "Did you cause the avalanche?"

He squirmed. "Kat, you know I don't like helicopters."

She held his gaze.

"Fine. Yes. But that was a mistake. I didn't know the plane would cause an avalanche."

It was Grace's turn to snap. "You buzzed a mountain top. What did you think would happen?"

"It's all in the past. No one was hurt."

Grace launched herself at the grand duke.

"Woah, don't we have a wedding to plan?"

Grace stopped. Tucker had just walked into the room. He looked at the grand duke. "Guess I should start calling you grandpa, huh?"

The grand duke puffed out his chest while veins appeared on his neck. "What is this madness?"

Tucker grinned at Grace and held out his elbow. "Shall we?"

"I'd love to." She linked her arm through his.

He leaned low, whispering, "You really only have one gear, kick ass." He looked at the queen. "Clint's in the dining room. He wanted to wait for you guys to finish."

"Thank you, Tucker," the queen said. "But we're finished in here."

She snapped her fingers. "Thorsen?"

Thorsen stepped forward, out of the shadows. Grace hadn't even seen him.

"Yes, mum?"

"Time to clean house. I'm guessing you're going to want to interrogate him, but don't let it ruin your Christmas."

"Yes, mum."

"I'm family. I am staying for Christmas," the grand duke declared.

"No, you most certainly are not," the queen promised.

# Chapter Seventy-One

Grace and Tucker had bundled up and were walking down Becca's driveway. The sun had long ago set, and the temperature had parked at a brisk minus twenty. The night was dark, silent, and cold.

"Wow, it gets chilly here." Grace pressed closer to Tucker, her arm looped through his.

"We can go inside."

She shook her head. "Let's just look at your sister's Christmas lights and let the fresh air take away the aches of the day."

"They might freeze away, instead. Is that okay?" Tucker teased before dropping a kiss on the top of her head.

"I don't care as long as I'm here with you." She watched as the festive lights twinkled in the light breeze. "I can't believe you pulled out the fake fiancé card."

"Honey, you were going to annihilate your grandfather. I know he's a jerk, and it sounds like he more than deserves it, but you'd flatten him. Then you'd feel bad."

"I wouldn't feel *that* bad," she complained.

"You would because you're kind. And even though he doesn't deserve you or your mom's compassion, you know he's the way he is from something, right?"

Grace eyed him. "You're a good cop, aren't you?"

Tucker shrugged. "I try to see the big picture. I don't always, but I try. Otherwise, I'm just another jerk with blinders on."

They walked in silence and snuggled into each other.

Grace whispered, "Today really does feel like the darkest night of the year."

Tucker squeezed his arm, pulling her closer. "But tomorrow, the sun will shine longer than it did today. And the next day. And the next day."

Grace eyed him. "Indeed."

They walked a little farther down the driveway.

"I guess we know who is behind switching out the prop gun and the plane bombing," Grace said.

"She is a piece of work," Tucker agreed. "Jason called. She's been processed. She'll stay in custody while Canada and Jordemorden sort out their respective lists of charges."

"Canada doesn't let people wave guns around or set explosives in people's yards?"

"That's a hard no."

"There goes my New Years plans," Grace teased.

Tucker stopped. "I hope you're not upset Clint and I followed today? We both wanted to keep you guys safe. Any number of things can go wrong, as I proved. But we also wanted to respect your privacy. I hope we didn't cross a line."

Grace smiled. "I saw you guys right away and felt better having you both near. My mom was so excited, and I like this new adventurous side of hers, but let's be real, most of the times we've been on horses have been for ceremonial purposes or in environmentally controlled riding rings."

Tucker grinned. "Excellent. I'm not the only city slicker in the family."

"Ooh, that sounds like we need to play outside more." She gasped, "Look."

Shades of green lights rippled and shimmered across the night sky.

Tucker looked up, his face lit into a huge grin. "I haven't seen the northern lights in years."

"Happy Yule," Tucker whispered.

Grace looked up at him, startled.

"It is Yule, right? On winter solstice?" Tucker asked.

Grace nodded. "I didn't realize you knew."

He just shrugged, looking back at the flickering lights undulating across the sky. "Becca celebrates it, too."

Grace swallowed. "And you're okay with that?"

Tucker turned his head, looking at her like she was daft. "Yeah, why wouldn't I be?"

"In my experience, most people aren't."

Gently, he suggested, "You should hang out with more open-minded people."

"Like you?"

"Definitely like me," Tucker agreed and pulled her close.

# Chapter Seventy-Two

Grace enjoyed herself in front of the fire with a cup of coffee while Tucker put the finishing touches on breakfast. Nearly dying in an avalanche hadn't phased him as much as it had Grace. He had jumped out of bed, eager to cook for everyone.

The queen walked into the front room and sat on the couch. She looked sad. "The twins just called. Their husbands have filed for divorce."

Grace lowered her glass. "Why?"

"Because in the eyes of the church, the twins are now considered bastards."

"Because Clint wasn't dead, your *matrimonium postmortem* trumps your and Jacques's regular wedding?"

"That is what the church is saying, yes."

"Isn't there a fine or fee to take care of that?" Grace didn't agree, but it wasn't right lives were upended because of random church dictates.

"I don't think so, dear, not this time."

"I don't know how they explain that. The logic is fucked." Grace winced. She was trying to cuss less in front of her mom.

The queen didn't correct her. "There is no logic, only pain and a perverse irrationality." She rubbed her forehead. "I've blown up my kids' lives."

"Please, if the twins were with good guys who actually loved them, not their royal status, their birth circumstances wouldn't matter."

"That's not how it works when wedding royalty," the queen explained.

"It didn't work when lies, control, and weird church loopholes were used, either. Maybe this time, letting love flow where it will, it'll work out."

The queen looked at Grace. "I love how you can reframe something truly devastating to something that can shine a light."

"Light is when we shine out, dark is meant for us to reflect. It's a cycle. No one can be on all of the time." Grace shrugged. "That's what this season means to me, anyway."

Grace had never revealed to her mom anything so private. She suddenly felt exposed.

Her mom smiled, "Merry Christmas, Grace."

"Happy Yule, Mom."

The front door swung open.

"I need the loo." Lillian bustled in, calling over her shoulder. She was already making her way down the hall.

Colt smiled, shutting the front door with his elbow. His hands held a box of something. "Good morning." He nodded to Grace and her mom. "I'll just take this straight-away to Tucker."

He disappeared down the hall, passing Becca.

The queen smiled. "Your brother must be something else. I never thought Lillian would settle down. Now look at her, she's so happy."

Becca agreed. "They're good for each other. Colt was as skittish as they come, until Lillian."

Lillian reappeared, rubbing her hands with lotion. "Is breakfast almost ready? I've only had one so far."

"Tucker has been busy making a feast," Grace reassured her.

"Excellent, I'm famished." Lillian's eyes lit up when she saw a plate of brownies. She reached for one and popped a chunk into her mouth, then sighed. "Pure bliss." Her eyes rounded. "Oh, bloody hell. Becca, I forgot to tell you—"

"Hello?" The front door opened, and a striking woman let herself inside, a wheeled carry-on bag at her side.

"*Claire.*" Grace and Lillian squealed in unison. They jumped up and swarmed her, wrapping the newcomer in a ginormous hug.

Lillian spun around. "I'm so sorry, Becca. Is it okay? I hoped there was room." She darted a look at the queen, daring a cheeky smile. "Since someone booked the whole place."

"Lillian, what did you do?" Claire asked.

"Baby brain is real. I forgot to tell them you were coming, that's all."

"*Lillian,*" Claire's eyes rounded.

"There's room," Becca assured her. "Or we could always check if there's room in Tucker's apartment."

"Who's Tucker?" Claire asked.

"Ha ha," Lillian quipped. "Tucker would shoot me. He only has eyes for one woman."

She winked at Grace.

Grace smiled, she only had eyes for him.

# Chapter Seventy-Three

The dream was a lucid one.

Grace felt like she was uncoiling. *Liberated* was the best way to describe the emotions washing over her.

In her mind's eye, Grace saw the image of a woman's form. It was like the small Goddess pendant Becca wore. The Goddess smiled at Grace before turning into a large coiled serpent.

Grace stared, surprised she held no fear or trepidation. The serpent was beautiful, enchanting Grace with its loveliness and patience.

Then Grace realized, in the logic that dreams alone followed, that it was she who was the serpent.

She looked down, her body now a magnificent serpent.

Grace didn't understand.

The Goddess stood before her, smiling at Grace before disappearing.

Grace opened her eyes. Surprised and more than a little confused. The dream had spiked something primal inside, infusing her with a deep sense of peace and trust.

The serpent wasn't evil, it felt like lost pieces of herself.

Tucker snuggled closer, murmuring something, before dropping a kiss on her shoulder. His breath was the slow, steady cadence of sleep.

Grace stilled.

"Say it again," she whispered, hoping.

"I love you," he said, his voice sleepy.

Happiness spread through her. "Really?"

Tucker snuggled her tighter and made a soft hushing sound. "I didn't say anything, this is all a dream."

Grace's voice was equally soft when she teased, "Pretty sure you did."

Tucker burrowed his head in the back of her shoulder. "Nope. You must be hearing the snow falling."

She turned in his arms, wrapping her arms around him.

"I love you, too."

# Chapter Seventy-Four

Christmas dinner was a full house.

Tucker was in the kitchen preparing the Christmas Day feast when Colt appeared. "I'm filling drink orders."

Tucker handed Colt the plate of appetizers. "Can you take these out first?"

Colt selected one and popped it into his mouth. "I love these little things, what are they again?"

"Bison tartare." He watched Colt grab another two. "Dude, make sure some make it to the table."

"No promises, bro." Colt grinned, popping another into his mouth before disappearing.

The dining room door swung behind Colt, and Gabe, their older brother, appeared. He and Savannah had flown in from Toronto last night, and Savannah's parents, Dallas and Elinor, would be arriving shortly.

Tucker glanced up. "Can you pull the scallops out of the small oven?"

Gabe sniffed. "I smell bacon."

"Yeah, it's wrapped around the scallops. Pull 'em out."

"You're bossy in the kitchen."

"You won't be complaining when you eat. Tick tock."

Gabe dutifully pulled out the bacon-wrapped scallops.

Becca shot through the kitchen door, eyes wide. "You're not going to believe this. Mom just got here. She carpooled with Rose, Ruth, and *Meredith*."

Gabe turned from pulling out the scallops. "Seriously?"

Becca nodded. "The garage got a call. Gerry is helping fix a minivan. He'll be here as soon as he can."

Gabe looked between his siblings. "Mom's dating the mechanic Gerry? Did I know that?"

Tucker gave a rueful smile. "You've missed a crazy few months."

Colt walked in then with Stone, beelining for the refrigerator. "We've always been crazy."

Gabe and Stone cautiously shook hands.

They had met for the first time last night.

"*Stop*," Becca said.

Startled, everyone looked at her.

"Guys, we're all here." She spread her arms wide, beaming. "Bring it in."

Tucker, Colt, and Gabe groaned but walked over to her.

"What is she talking about?" Stone asked.

Tucker already had his arm around his sister and Colt. "Trust me, it feels weirder if you don't do it."

Stone hesitated before stepping into the circle between Gabe and Colt.

The guys closed ranks around him.

Becca closed her eyes and squeezed an arm around Gabe and one around Tucker. "We're actually all together."

Tucker felt a well of emotion start to rise.

A timer went off.

"Sorry." Tucker broke the big circle first.

He turned off the burner under the giant pot of potatoes that had been parboiling and was about to drain them when Meredith's friend Ruth came in and goosed him.

Tucker stopped, still holding the giant pot of parboiled potatoes destined for roasting.

"Ruth," Tucker said patiently. "You can't go around pinching people's bums."

"Couldn't resist, sonny boy. If your princess doesn't work out" — she waggled her eyebrows — "You know I'll be next in line."

Grace walked in. "Woah, looks like I found the party."

Becca smiled. "We were just leaving." She nodded. "Good luck with that one."

Becca slid the scallops onto a plate while Colt, Stone, and Gabe grabbed drink refills. They filed out of the kitchen, leaving Tucker, Grace, and the spunky senior, draping herself over Tucker's shoulder.

Tucker looked at Grace and mouthed *help me.*

"Ms. Ruth, did you goose Tucker again?"

"I don't see a ring on either of your fingers," Ruth reasoned. "And his bum is so cute."

"It is," Grace agreed. "But you know what we talked about."

"Men aren't playthings."

"That's right," Grace said patiently.

"Unless you pay for it," Ruth added.

Grace's eyes widened. "Ms. Ruth!"

The senior grinned. "I'm only messing with you kids. I'm sorry, Tucker. I shouldn't have made you uncomfortable." Ruth shook her head. "Have times changed, a woman pressuring a man." She cackled. "Can't say there's not a little poetic justice, the shoe being on the other foot."

With that, she sauntered out of the kitchen.

"Who is that again?" Grace asked.

"Meredith's best friend."

"And Meredith is your stepmom?"

"Yup. Pretty sure Lillian has a spreadsheet to keep track of everyone." Tucker opened the oven to check on the turkey and continued, "It'll be a full house. Christopher and Austin should be here any minute. Claire, Thorsen, Charles, and Omran are here, and Gabe's best friend Andy, and Savannah's best friend Maggie should be coming, too. Claire's already here."

Grace counted. "Twenty-six will be here for dinner?"

"That sounds about right." Tucker set the timer again and double-checked everything bubbling on the stove. If he had timed everything right, dinner would be ready in sixty minutes.

Tucker smiled at Grace. "It's time."

Grace squeezed Tucker's hand. "This has been the best Christmas ever. Thank you."

He smiled and kissed her.

They walked hand in hand into the front room. It was boisterous, filled with their family and friends.

Tucker nodded at Gabe.

Gabe stood and clapped his hands. "I need everyone to put on their boots and jackets. Becca, wrap a scarf around your eyes, we have a surprise for you outside."

Becca looked up, stricken. "Say what?"

Jason pulled her up. "Come on, honey."

In record time, the entire group was parading down the driveway.

"Where are we going?" Becca asked, her arm tucked in Jason's and a scarf wrapped around her head, covering her eyes.

"Just down the drive," he answered.

When they had walked the length of the long drive, he turned her around and gently took off the scarf.

Becca gasped before covering her mouth with her hands. "It's beautiful," she whispered before taking Jason's hand. "Ohmygod, I love it."

Large wooden trunks flanked the entrance to the drive, with a wooden crossbar spanning the top. Hanging from the crossbar in stylized wrought iron, read *Hearthstone Ranch*.

"Everyone helped," Jason said.

"Was this what all the pounding was?"

Colt nodded. "Digging frozen ground sucks."

Becca was staring at the entrance sign, smiling. "It's got a good ring to it."

"You built a home and invited all of us in. Of the family, you're kinda our hearthstone, Becca," Tucker said.

There were cheers and a couple of tears.

"Now, for part two." Lillian led the way back to the living room. Once everyone was settled, Lillian said,

"Becca is this family's hearthstone and you, dear Jason, have her heart. You're her hearthstone." She handed him a small, flat-wrapped gift. "For you."

"What is it?" Jason asked.

"Open it," Lillian said softly.

Jason gently pried apart the colorful paper. Inside were two books.

He held up one. "This is the blank fur trade era journal I found as a kid." He opened the cover of the second before looking up. "A book of poetry?"

Lillian nodded. "The restoration and antiquities people I sent the journal to were able to tease out a lot of its secrets." She smiled. "The journal was a book of poetry." She pointed to the second small book. "They made you a copy of what was inside."

Jason rubbed his jaw, clearly moved by the thoughtful gift. "I don't know how to thank you. This is incredible."

"You just did." Lillian lifted a dainty shoulder. "It's what family does."

With reverent hands, he passed it to his mom, Rose. Becca rubbed his shoulder. He covered her hand with his own and lowered his head, collecting himself in front of the large crowd.

Tucker clapped his hands, drawing everyone's attention to him.

He smiled. "Time to eat."

# Epilogue

"I watched him die," Stone said.

Tucker and Stone had walked past the swing bench and brushed off the Muskoka chairs on Becca's wraparound porch, then sat down. A Chinook had blown in. The mountain wind had brought a welcome warmth after so much cold. Melting snow dripped everywhere.

Tucker looked at his brother, but Stone saw another place, another time.

"When I got there—his apartment, he had just injected. I watched him pull the needle out. He was quick to toss it aside like I wouldn't notice."

Stone stopped before looking at Tucker. "I had a Naloxone kit with me."

The admission hung in the air between them.

"What happened?" Tucker asked, unsure he wanted to know the truth.

"I couldn't use it. I couldn't try to save his life, not after what he'd done. He shot and tried to torch our sister and the man she loves, even his own wife. He knowingly provided intel to ambush Gabe while on a CSIS mission. And you. His partner pumped three bullets into your back at point-blank range."

"The bullets were meant for another," Tucker said.

"Were they?"

Tucker stilled.

Stone continued, "Anyway, what kind of father does that?"

*Were they?*

Tucker was reeling from the implications.

Stone continued, "Omran and I found more intel. Carl, the bank manager, was on Bruce's payroll, and Bruce was broke."

"As in no cash, broke?"

Stone nodded.

Tucker was thoughtful. "Do you think that's why he married Meredith?"

"Yeah. And her connections. She's still loaded." Stone laughed. "Like filthy rich loaded, and knows *everyone*."

"And she's kind," Tucker added.

Stone looked at him.

Tucker brushed past the moment. "Any idea on the leak?"

"Omran and I've done some discreet digging. Up until two months ago, Detective Jones was heavily mortgaged and carrying substantial credit card debt. Now he's not."

"That doesn't sound like Jones."

Stone said quietly, "His son was an addict. Looks like Jones and his wife tried scores of private rehab facilities when their son got kicked out of the public ones."

Tucker frowned. Detective Jones had been the first one to visit him in the hospital.

"It'll probably take a few days to unpack where the money came from. Jones's record is spotless. My guess is Bruce threatened or blackmailed Jones into cooperating."

"Jones is a good man. A dedicated father. Bruce would have been able to find the man's pressure points."

Stone's face was granite. "The monster's dead."

Tucker nodded.

They sat like that, each lost to their thoughts.

Finally, Tucker spoke. "He never claimed you as his son. That was pretty shitty."

Stone scrubbed his face with his hands. "That's water under the bridge."

"It is?" Tucker asked, genuinely curious.

Stone shrugged. "My stepdad adored my mom and accepted me as his own. He was everything Bruce Tanner wasn't. I didn't have to grow up with the monster. Knowing now what we do, I honestly don't know how you guys did it."

Tucker sat back. "We didn't know then, I mean, none of us saw this coming. He was narcissistic and cruel, but none of us realized what he had become. Growing up, we had each other. And Clint. Our mom is fucked in her own way. Actually, I think she did the best she knew how." Tucker blew out a breath on a realization.

Both men sat, quiet, staring out across the ranch yard. The mid-day winter light was weak but growing. Every day since winter solstice, the days were getting longer again.

"What's next for you?" Tucker asked.

"Becca insists I'm here through New Years."

"She's like that."

Stone smiled. "I like it. It's been a long time since I let someone care for me."

Tucker clapped him on the back. "You are so going to eat your words. Between Becca, Grace, and Lillian, you don't stand a chance. I'm sure Savannah would mother hen you just as much, but with them living across the country, we barely see them."

Stone hesitated. "What about you, Colt, Gabe, and Jason? Are you guys okay if I stay through New Years?"

"We're good." Tucker meant it.

"Even—"

Tucker cut him off. "I don't know what I would have done if I had found him first. That's haunted me since the fire."

Stone looked out across the snowy yard. "You'll never have to. I consider that a win."

Tucker looked at his older brother, uncomfortable. "Teague Alans is still out there."

Stone smiled at Tucker. "I've got this one, little brother."

# Author's Note

The more I write, the more intrigued I am with exploring concepts and themes within a story. For this one, loyalty, duty, and obligation kept popping up, sparring with each other as the characters grappled with their paths and choices.

My writing process is character-driven; they tell me what they're doing. Sometimes it feels like they're working out their *why* as I'm writing, as eager to understand themselves as I am to understand them. That's one of the reasons I love this medium. Writing helps me unpack life. The characters always show up, patient and ready to help me explore the world around me—motivations, choices, and why people do what they do.

Why do people do what they do? There's no lack of polarity or angst in the headlines, though compassion and engaged listening are painfully absent. What would this world be like if everyone gave themselves permission to have a character arc? To pivot and change as needed? Is that what we collectively need? Permission to grow? It sounds suspiciously simple. I'm totally going to try.

The characters in *Loyal to You* have wound around my heart as they wound around each other's hearts. Repeatedly, they challenged me to face my loyalties and gently reminded me of the danger of misplaced loyalties. Smart, those feisty characters are.

This book was a joy to write as it put me through my paces. Well done, Tanner Family and friends, well done. This author is still reeling from the epic adventure you took me on. Cheers to the next one. XOXO

Sarah Kades
Calgary, Canada
October 2022

# Acknowledgements

I am always humbled by the generous love and support
I'm surrounded by. Whether I'm writing my next book or
making the decision to go back to school, I feel those who
care close ranks, circling me in their belief and support,
helping me develop that sacred space to create, explore,
breathe, and remind me to believe in myself. I am surrounded by kindness and incredible talent.

Harold Johnson, I miss you. If the Other Side reads ac-
knowledgments, know your inspiration burns ever-bright.
Dave Sweet, thanks for the cop craft and unwavering friendship. You're also the best cat-sitter on the planet. Jonas Saul,
years ago, when I was walking across the tower bridge at
*When Words Collide* at the same time you were, I decided you
would be my friend. Years later, I had no idea that you
would be there when I needed you in a series of serendipi-
tous events. The Universe winks again. Tania Therien, for
every text, coffee break, writing retreat ... *céad míle fáilte.*
Mark Leslie, your steadfast belief in my stories, characters,
and me, is a true gift. Thank you for taking a chance on this
author. To my patient family, who takes it in stride when
I'm under deadline, my head stays in a story for weeks at a
time, and the food, coffee, and clean house that magically
appears—thank you. I appreciate every act of kindness as I
navigate my way, sometimes precariously, through whatever epic adventure the characters take me on.

I wish to acknowledge the generous support of the Canada Council for the Arts for this project. Art matters. I am
honored to be included in our national arts community.

# About the Author

Sarah Kades writes eco-thrillers, and narrative nonfiction as Sarah Graham. Her writing is largely inspired by her previous careers as an archaeologist and Indigenous Knowledge study facilitator, where she routinely lived in tents, caught rides in helicopters and gaped at the awesomeness of the landscapes around her.

Sarah is a two-time Energy Futures Lab Banff Summit storyteller, a recipient of Canada Council of the Arts and Calgary Arts Development individual artist grants, and has presented at the British Society of Criminology conference on the application of using arts-based approaches.

When she's not writing you can find her biking, bumping into her next adventure, going back to school to be a professional drone pilot, or trying to figure out where in the garden to put the makeshift wood fired pizza oven.

Learn more about Sarah online at:
sarahkadesgraham.com

## DON'T MISS: GOOD KIND OF GONE

Book 5 in the *Hearthstone* series

# GOOD KIND OF GONE

Book 5 in the *Hearthstone* series

*Sometimes healing from the past is possible when we find someone we want a future with.*

Maggie Monroe never imagined she would be breaking into her dead twin brother's apartment the first time she saw Paris. Desperate to feel safe after their tumultuous childhood, Maggie has built a quiet, staid life as a librarian, completely avoiding adventure or romantic entanglements. Keeping their family's dark past a secret wasn't hard when you didn't let anyone in. Sebastian had been all she had left. Finding the truth of his murder was the only thing that mattered to her.

Tanner Stone is his family's dark secret. Though his diabolical biological father, Bruce Tanner, never claimed him, most of Stone's Canadian half-siblings have welcomed the family bastard with open arms. After more than a decade with Australia's Security Intelligence Service, Stone isn't quite sure jumping into the Tanner clan's orbit is such a good idea. He spent the first half of his life ignoring the fact the man he called dad wasn't his biological one, and the second half unraveling just how dangerous and deep Bruce Tanner's global crimes went.

As Maggie and Stone's paths intertwine, they dance around their budding attraction as each must decide who to trust. When a dangerous force threatens the global power scale and their loved ones, Maggie and Stone cautiously team up. Will they be able to put their distrust aside long enough to avert a global disaster, or will old family feuds destroy all hope, and their chance at love?

www.ingramcontent.com/pod-product-compliance
Lightning Source LLC
Chambersburg PA
CBHW030553020726
47494CB00005B/1597